AN IMPROPER SUITOR

MONICA FAIRVIEW

THORNDIKE
CHIVERS

This Large Print edition is published by Thorndike Press, Waterville, Maine, USA and by BBC Audiobooks Ltd, Bath, England.
Thorndike Press, a part of Gale, Cengage Learning.

LIBRARY OF CONGRESS CATALOGING-IN-PUBLICATION DATA

Fairview, Monica.
   An improper suitor / by Monica Fairview. — Large print ed.
     p. cm. — (Thorndike Press large print clean reads)
   Originally published: London : Robert Hale, 2008.
   ISBN-13: 978-1-4104-1232-4 (alk. paper)
   ISBN-10: 1-4104-1232-6 (alk. paper)
   1. London (England)—Fiction. 2. Large type books. I. Title.
PR6106.A38I47 2009
823'.92—dc22   2008056020

BRITISH LIBRARY CATALOGUING-IN-PUBLICATION DATA AVAILABLE

Published in 2009 in the U.S. by arrangement with Robert Hale Limited.
Published in 2009 in the U.K. by arrangement with Robert Hale Limited.

U.K. Hardcover: 978 1 408 42117 8 (Chivers Large Print)
U.K. Softcover: 978 1 408 42118 5 (Camden Large Print)

Printed in the United States of America
1 2 3 4 5 6 7 13 12 11 10 09

AN IMPROPER SUITOR

PROLOGUE

March 1818

The summons came at eleven o'clock at night.

Julia Swifton was not yet asleep, but she had blown out her candle and lay on her back, staring at the orange patch of light on the ceiling, a reflection of the changing fire as it lost its intensity and started to fade.

Sally scratched at the door and entered with a candle. She was like a ghost in her white nightdress, standing in the white glow of light. She whispered quietly into the darkness, 'I'm sorry, miss, but Lady Bullfinch is asking for you.'

Julia sprang up from the bed, gripped the shawl which was tossed over the end of her bed and, wrapping it around her, made to follow in her bare feet.

'She's not worse, is she?' she asked.

Sally paused before answering. When she spoke, her voice was puzzled. 'I didn't think so, Miss Swifton. But she was that insistent, it frightened me.' Sally had been her grandmother's maid for over twenty years. She knew her well.

Julia shivered in the cold corridor. *Please let her be all right, please let her get well.* After almost a month of lung fever, her grandmother had been on the road to recovery. The doctor had said there might still be a setback, but only this morning they had all celebrated in the kitchen — Sally, and Julia's maid Bethany, Rumbert the butler and Cook and everyone else on the staff, most of them people she'd known all her life. Julia had had wine brought up from the cellars and they'd all drunk her grandmother's health.

She can't have got worse.

But when Julia reached the bedchamber, she found her grandmother upright in her bed, propped up by the pillows. She looked well enough, though she still had dark-brown circles around her eyes, and her cheeks were hollow from her long illness.

'Don't let her talk too much, miss,' said Sally, before closing the door. 'She'll tire herself out.'

Julia nodded and approached the bed, perching herself gingerly on the edge of a chair beside her.

8

'You can come closer, child. I'm not going to bite.'

Some of Julia's alarm receded at the snappish tone. She sounded like her old self. Julia's relief brought a wide grin to her face, and she tugged her chair nearer to the bed.

'I need to talk to you. Urgently,' she said.

The smile left Julia's face. Her grandmother was not given to dramatic gestures. Her urgent tone brought back a rush of anxiety and Julia clenched her hands together. 'I'm listening,' she said.

'My health is not what it was,' she said. An understatement, considering she had been on her deathbed for a good part of a month. 'And although Dr Lincoln says I am likely to make a complete recovery, I can't pretend everything is exactly as it was before.'

Julia nodded, partly in relief, and partly in acknowledgement. 'I understand that.'

Magnificent black eyes met Julia's, sharp as a sword. 'Then I hope you will understand what I'm going to say to you.' She took a deep breath. 'Though perhaps you will not forgive me for it.' She hesitated. That itself was so unlike her that Julia's unease returned.

There was a brief silence. A twig flared up in the fireplace with a sharp snap, startling

9

Julia. It blazed briefly before fading.

When her grandmother spoke next there was no longer any hesitation in her voice. 'You know I have strong beliefs about the relationships of men with women. Several of my friends have written about the rights of women, including Mary Wollstonecraft, as you are well aware, and I would have myself, if it were not for the fact that I'm such a poor writer.' She gave a croaking laugh, to which Julia did not respond.

'What I'm about to say goes against many things that I've taught you. But as I lay in bed, thinking how close I was to death, I realized that I had been remiss in my duty. I can't continue to be negligent.' She paused. 'I have decided that it is time for you to marry.'

Julia recoiled in shock. The illness must have damaged Grandmother's mind. She had always preached that it was better to become an old maid than to marry and live a life of misery as Julia's mother had. A woman with an income had no need of a husband, she said frequently.

Safe in this belief, Julia had made no attempt at all to secure one. Now, at the age of almost twenty one, she did not think it likely that she would. Women younger than her were already considered old maids, after three Seasons in London.

Julia stood up, barely able to contain her anger. 'I did not think that you, of all people, would turn on me. How can you be such a' — cold fury left her sputtering — *'Brutus?'*

'You are hardly Julius Caesar, even if your name is Julia,' said Grandmother, a twinkle in her eye.

Julia rubbed her palms together, trying to bring her feelings under control. She had promised Sally she would not disturb her grandmother and, when all was said and done, she was still trying to recover from a dangerous illness.

Nevertheless, she could not remain silent. 'How can you sit there so calmly and order me to do something that goes against everything you've taught me my whole life? And how can you actually *laugh* about it?'

She sighed. 'I haven't abandoned my beliefs. I still believe in everything I always believed in. But on one's deathbed life looks suddenly very different. When I came close to dying, I began to worry about your future. For you to live respectably within society, it is essential for you to marry.'

Her hand swung out suddenly, and she gripped Julia's arm with fingers that were surprisingly strong. Tears sprang into her eyes. The tears moved Julia as nothing else could have done. The last time she had seen her cry was in the few weeks following the death of her daughter Olivia — Julia's mother. She had grown up in this household, yet she had never since witnessed her tears. Until now. 'And besides that, I would not for anything have missed the joy I experienced bringing up my two daughters, and then you. You should have the opportunity to explore that pleasure as well.'

Julia looked down at the fingers on her arm. Their strength was deceptive. The veins stood out under fragile skin, the bones protruding and skeletal.

'I took care of you all those years after your mother died,' she said, 'and I taught you what I thought was right. But I recognize now that your situation is too complicated. Without my presence to prevent it, old gossip will rear its ugly head. Your father is still alive, but he abandoned both you and your mother, and his departure for the Continent was mired in scandal. You do not have his protection. Society has tolerated you because of my status, even though I am thought an eccentric. But I am not so sure they will tolerate you after I am gone. I am an old woman, Julia, and I do not know how much time I've been given. You must marry, and you must marry soon.'

With a few words, Julia's world had turned topsy-turvy. She opened her mouth to protest, but Grandmother raised a hand to silence her.

'I know this comes as a shock. You may even think my brain has been touched by my illness. But believe me when I say that I have never been so clear minded as I am now. If you can't find a husband for yourself, then I will choose a husband for you.'

'You've always spoken against such practices,' Julia managed to say, her voice coming from a distance. 'You've always condemned arranged marriages.'

'I'm sorry, child, but I can think of no other possibility. Left to your own devices, you won't do anything. I won't, however, go so far as to deprive you of all choice in the matter.'

'I suppose I should thank you for that,' said Julia, bitterness making her voice harsh.

'Here is my proposal. I'll give you three months, until exactly one week before your twenty-first birthday. You can look for a suitable husband yourself until then. If you are unsuccessful I will send a notice to the *Gazette* to inform Society that you are engaged.' She paused, this time for effect. 'To Lionel Blake, the Earl of Thorwynn.'

13

Julia tore her arm away. Grandmother had gone completely mad.

The Earl of Thorwynn was one of London's most notorious rakes. Known as the Laughing Rake, he was famous for his devil-may-care attitude. She had never set eyes on him because he did not frequent the kind of places she frequented. It was said he had never set foot in a ballroom since he had returned from the Peninsular War three years ago.

Anybody less suitable for a husband she could not imagine.

But Julia knew better than anyone that it was useless to argue with her grandmother. Once she had an idea in her mind, she would defend it as staunchly as a mongrel defending a coveted bone.

'What makes you think he'll agree to such a thing?'

'I know Lady Gragspur. As you are aware, she's a very close friend of mine. I don't doubt that she'll have her way. She usually does, once she sets her mind to something.'

Not very different from Grandmother. Julia had met Lady Gragspur, of course, and she had no difficulty believing she was right.

'Do you plan to inform the rake — Lord Thorwynn — of this . . . situation?'

'I see no reason to do so, unless you fail

to produce a suitable husband.'

'But you are going to speak to his grandmother.'

'Of course. I will be sending for her tomorrow morning. And in the event that I am no longer alive at that time, I will entrust her with the task of making the announcement herself.'

The idea that she was making provisions beyond the grave increased Julia's agitation.

'Have no fear,' she said, reassuringly. As if anything she said could reassure Julia. 'No one but Lady Gragspur will come to hear of it until it's necessary.'

Julia rose from the side of the bed and paced the room. She was trapped like a bear in a cage.

She had thought herself free.

'I don't believe you, of all people, would submit me to such a nightmare.'

Grandmother smiled. Actually smiled.

'I know only too well that if I don't force your hand, you will do nothing. That is why I have given you this time. Choose your own husband: or marry a rake.'

CHAPTER 1

May 1818

The horses snorted impatiently, their breath coming out in balloons of white fog. She could feel Hamlet's excitement, the strained tension of his muscles.

The silence stretched.

Hamlet shuffled.

At long last, Grandmother raised her arm.

'Goooo forth!' she cried.

Hamlet sprinted forward. Julia abandoned herself to the thunder of hoofs as the ground began to fly beneath her. She grinned as startled faces whizzed past her. The aroma of earth and grass filled her senses. Above her, white clouds darted across a blue sky that bobbed in and out of her vision. She lost herself in the motion, allowing everything to stream past her, green blurring into brown and blue blurring into white.

She loved their early Thursday morning

races in Hyde Park, promptly at half past seven every week during the Season. Of all her grandmother's eccentricities, this was the one she treasured most. And it was clear she was not the only lady who did. The thudding on the ground behind her proved it.

The few riders at this unfashionable hour in Hyde Park moved out of their way and watched as they galloped by. Fashionable society did not approve of the Ladies' Cavalry Charge, as Grandmother jokingly called it, but that had never stopped her.

Julia spurred Hamlet on. This was as close to flying that any mortal could reach. Certainly with the whoosh of air past her ears and the sensation of hovering above her side-saddle she could imagine herself a swallow in flight, or even a sparrowhawk swooping down on its prey.

A high-pitched scream brought her down to earth.

She checked her horse. Colours resolved themselves into shapes. Hyde Park settled back into green grass, Rotten Row, South Carriage Drive, and lines of oak.

From the corner of her eye she glimpsed a lady fighting to control her mount. It reared, then suddenly broke into a fierce gallop. The rider pulled at the reins, and for a moment it looked like the horse had slowed down. But it was only objecting to her clumsy handling. It tossed its head then bolted, running as if pursued by a colony of bees.

There was no time to think. Julia veered off the path and chased after the renegade horse, urging Hamlet onwards. Delighted to show the racing skills for which he had been bred, Hamlet lengthened his stride and accepted the challenge.

So far the girl was still on the horse, hanging on precariously. Julia willed her to remain seated for a few minutes longer, until she could reach her.

They departed the avenue of trees and headed into an area that was more thickly wooded. Julia redoubled her efforts. She did not want the girl to be felled by a low hanging branch. Not far behind her, the beating of hoofs showed that she was not the only rider who had witnessed the event. She did not look back. Her gaze stayed fixed on the unfortunate girl, as though her eyes themselves could pin the girl to her saddle.

Then something large hurtled into Julia, emerging from behind a copse of trees to her right. The impact jolted her. She slid down in her saddle, dangerously close to losing her seat. An iron arm wrapped itself round her throat. A hand reached out and gripped the reins of her horse, pulling them from her.

In a daze, her mind registered that someone was abducting her. She recalled horrible tales she had heard about foolish debutantes who rode in the park without a chaperon or groom. Tales of abductions and ransoms. Only this time, she was in the tale.

She looked desperately around her, but there was no one else in sight. The trees hid her from the main path, and apart from the endangered rider some way ahead of her, there was not a single person who could help. Perhaps someone was around, out of view, but not out of earshot. She opened her mouth to scream.

The iron arm clamped down on her mouth. 'Don't be bird-witted,' said a man's voice close to her ear. The voice did not sound uncouth. His accent was refined, clearly that of a gentleman. But gentlemen of the *ton,* too, could be villains. 'If you scream,' he continued, 'we'll have everyone within earshot descending on us.'

Why exactly did he think I was going to scream? To frighten the magpies?

She sank her teeth into the flesh of his palm and bit down. Hard. She could feel her teeth cut the skin.

He yelped. 'Damnation, woman! What did

you do that for?' But to her utter surprise, he did not take his hand away. He kept it firmly in place. A grudging respect for his resilience passed through her.

'If you give me your word not to start shrieking, I'll remove my hand.' She nodded as well as she could. How did he expect her to give him her word when his palm was smothering even the tiniest squeak?

He moved his hand away and examined it. She noted with satisfaction the red marks she had made. An impulse to scream as loudly as she could rose up in her, but she restrained it. She would not act dishonourably, even if clearly he did not have an honourable bone in his body. It was possible, of course, that he was a bedlamite. The idea gave her more confidence. She was used to dealing with unreasonable people. Her grandmother was one of them, as was her aunt Viola.

'What the devil do you think you're doing, sir?' she hissed. 'Unhand me instantly.' Her words had no effect at all. She tried to pry his fingers off the reins, but he held fast. She soon gave up. Her attempt only made her seem childish. 'You're making a terrible error,' she said, attempting once again to reason with him. 'You must have mistaken me for someone else.'

He did not answer. He seemed to be running into difficulties, trying to control his own horse, Hamlet, and her all at once. A tiny traitorous part of her admired his skill. But the intelligent part recognized that if she kept thrashing about, he would sooner or later be forced to let go of something. So she wrestled with his arm, waiting for him to tire and lose his grip.

A vigorous twist brought her assailant's face to view. He was exactly the kind of villain they warned young girls about. A pronounced jaw, thunderous brows, piercing black eyes, and a nose like one of Lord Elgin's Greek statues. What made matters worse, he was gnashing his teeth; a bad indication, surely.

Then Hamlet reared. *My worthy horse.* He came to her rescue, hoping to throw off her assailant. 'Well done, Hamlet!' she said.

But instead of releasing the reins, the man tightened them, forcing Hamlet down. Hamlet succumbed with an angry whinny. The reins pressed into her right shoulder now, biting into her.

'Let go,' she said again, mustering as much arrogance as she could. 'And let go of my horse. You're injuring his mouth.'

'If you weren't so hen-witted, and just stopped struggling, I'd be able to let go,' said the villain. 'I'm only trying to protect you from injury.'

Definitely a bedlamite.

'I . . . do . . . not . . . need . . . protection,' she said, very slowly, articulating each word clearly. Meanwhile she craned her neck over the very solid arm that was wrapped around her and tried to discover what had happened to the girl with the bolted horse. The arm, however, obstructed her view.

She went limp. It was worth a try. Perhaps he would relax his hold if she acquiesced.

She had not realized that going limp would imply leaning into him. Her position on the side-saddle meant that now her whole back moulded into his chest. His breath tickled her ear. The musky scent of his shaving soap filled her nostrils.

He let go abruptly and moved sideways. 'It appears your horse has settled down.'

'Of course he's settled down,' she snapped. 'I'm sure he's a great deal more comfortable now that you aren't tugging at his mouth.'

She could see him more clearly, now that he was not breathing into her face. He raised one of those thick brows, his eyes gleaming with amusement. 'Such ingratitude in a young lady, considering I saved you from certain injury.'

'Certain injury?'

He smiled, his teeth gleaming like a tiger about to pounce on its prey.

All the pieces suddenly fell into place. 'But it wasn't my horse that had bolted,' she said, rueful now that she knew why he had grappled with her.

His smiled faded, replaced by a frown. 'I heard a scream, and someone shouted that a horse had bolted. I saw your horse leave the path and take off like the devil.'

She tried to be patient. But they had already lost precious time. 'When you chose to bring me and my horse to a halt, I was chasing after a bolting horse. Meanwhile, as you held me prisoner, the lady riding the other horse has been thrown to the ground.'

He whirled round, following the direction of her gaze. She could make out a crumpled form on the ground, under a large oak tree, next to a small ditch.

'Confound it!' he said, abandoning her as suddenly as he had caught her, and racing in the direction of the fallen woman.

Julia raced after him. She slid to her feet almost before Hamlet had stopped.

Her abductor sank to his knees next to the figure in blue. She was completely motionless. Julia knelt on the grass next to her, dew soaking into her riding habit. The

24

damp made her shiver. It seeped into her chest and settled around her heart. *Suppose she's badly hurt? Suppose she's — suppose the fall has killed her?*

He felt for the girl's pulse. The tension strung Julia's nerves and she chewed at her lower lip.

'Her pulse is strong,' he said, finally. Julia almost cried with relief.

Another rider arrived. Judging by his livery, he was the girl's groom. He jumped down and ran to her, his face crumpled in alarm. 'She isn't badly hurt, is she?'

'I've had some experience with injury on the battlefield,' said Julia's abductor. 'As far as I can tell, your mistress doesn't appear to be seriously hurt.'

'Heaven be praised,' said the groom, dropping down on to the ground next to her.

Her abductor turned the young woman over gently, subjecting her arms and legs to a quick examination. 'I don't think she has broken anything, but it will be up to a physician to ascertain that.'

'She must have hit her head,' said Julia.

Before anyone could answer, the young girl stirred, groaned, and opened two round blue eyes. She reminded Julia of a cherub she liked to stare at in church when she grew tired of the sermon. The cherub

25

blinked in confusion at the two strangers leaning over her, then exclaimed in obvious relief when she spotted her groom. She sat up tentatively, fingering her head. 'What happened, Jake?'

'You've taken a fall, Miss Neville,' said the groom. 'Stargaze bolted.' *Stargaze?* 'And this gentleman and this lady have been making sure you haven't been harmed.'

'Yes, I remember now.' She tossed back her perfect ringlets and looked peeved, not at all like the cherub, who only smiled. 'It was those *perfectly horrid* old ladies. They came galloping down the path *straight* at me.'

Injury or no injury, Julia prepared to give her a piece of her mind. *Horrid old ladies, indeed.* But their Cavalry Charge could be quite intimidating, she supposed. Especially from Miss Neville's perspective, since it had led to her accident. 'Miss Neville, perhaps I should introduce myself,' said Julia, before the situation grew embarrassing. 'I am Julia Swifton, and the old ladies you're referring to are my grandmother, Lady Bullfinch, my aunt, Lady Talbrook, and a number of their friends.'

The gentleman threw back his head and guffawed. 'Are they, by God! Well, if that doesn't top it all!' Julia noted he made no attempt to introduce himself.

Julia found herself looking into a pair of obsidian dark eyes, brimming with merriment. The eyes tugged at her, reeling her in. She found herself unable to breathe.

She peeled away her glance from his, severing the connection. Only then was she able to breathe normally.

'Well,' she said, very inadequately. She rose to her feet and dusted her hands. A quick look at the cherub's face satisfied her. It had changed from alabaster to a more mortal-like shade.

'Have you recovered from your fall, Miss Neville? Do you think you can stand up? Should I send for a physician?'

'No, no,' said Miss Neville, revealing an even row of pearly teeth as she smiled. 'I think I'm well enough to ride again.'

'You need not worry yourself, Miss Swifton,' said her abductor. 'I'll escort Miss Neville home.'

Just then the Cavalry caught up with them.

Lady Bullfinch dismounted immediately, producing a vinaigrette which she waved under Miss Neville's nose. She chafed the girl's cheeks and tut-tutted over her. 'Poor child,' she intoned. 'What a shock you've had.'

Aunt Viola remained on horseback. 'We shouldn't crowd the poor thing,' she said. 'She needs some air.'

'What happened?' said Lady Bullfinch.

'Miss Neville's horse bolted at our Cavalry Charge.'

'Nonsense!' retorted her grandmother. 'Horses simply don't bolt just because they see other horses racing by.'

'Miss Neville said we charged straight at her,' Julia replied, amused.

Lady Bullfinch was very proud of the Cavalry Charge. 'No one who knows how to ride would allow their horse to bolt like that,' she said, severely.

'Grannie,' said Julia gently, 'Perhaps she's just learning to ride.'

She snorted.

'Now, now, poor child,' said Aunt Viola, sending a look of rebuke towards Lady Bullfinch. 'Can't you see she's had a shock?' She dismounted and went over to the cherub, gripped her hands and rubbed them vigorously between her own. 'And to think it was all our fault.'

The dark-eyed gentleman intervened. 'Miss Neville doesn't seem to have sustained any injury. Perhaps, ladies, it would be best for her to return home and rest.'

Lady Bullfinch took out her quizzing glass

and peered at him. 'You're Lady Gragspur's grandson, aren't you?' she asked.

'There are three of us, Lady Bullfinch.'

'Lillian's son. I remember you when you were in leading strings. Grubby little boy you were. And from what I've heard, you've grown up to be a bit of a rakehell,' she remarked.

He laughed. 'You can't believe everything you hear,' he retorted, his eyes sparkling with humour.

'Perhaps not,' she said, still examining him with her quizzing glass. She turned to Julia.

'I should perhaps introduce you. Miss Swifton, my granddaughter.' He nodded formally. 'And this,' said Grannie turning to Julia, 'is Lionel Blake, Earl of Thorwynn.'

Julia forgot to smile. It was not that she didn't *want* to smile. Courtesy had been bred into her since she had cut her milk teeth. But the knowledge that the stranger was Lord Thorwynn crushed the sense out of her, like a medieval war hammer.

'Rest assured, ladies, that Miss Neville is in good hands,' he said, tossing them a smile that exuded charm.

'We'll call on you later, to assure ourselves that all is well,' said Lady Bullfinch, addressing Miss Neville. 'If you'll be kind enough to tell us your direction.'

Meanwhile Lord Thorwynn joined his hands to help Julia mount. He grinned up at her, one of those beguiling grins that she was sure he used to good effect on a great many women. 'I trust I am forgiven, Miss Swifton.' His tone left no doubt that he believed himself forgiven.

'Of course,' she said, woodenly. Her ability to think was returning, gradually. She settled her riding habit around her then turned her attention back to him.

He had already moved away to lean over Miss Neville. The hands Julia had stepped on enfolded the hands of the girl, who was struggling weakly to stand up. She did not appear at all like a cherub now. More like a new-born foal finding its feet.

Perhaps it was petty of her, since the poor girl had gone through a terrible shock and really did need his assistance, but Julia wished Miss Neville to Jericho.

She had not heard the last of Miss Neville, however. The Cavalry could talk of nothing else.

'I hope that poor girl doesn't suffer any after-effects from the fall,' said her grandmother.

'She's such a small slip of a girl. Lucky she didn't break any bones,' said Aunt Viola.

But behind the talk about the accident, there was something else. Lady Bullfinch was impatient for her friends to leave. When they all reached the gates of the park, she did not linger as she usually did. Outside the park their progress was slow. The city had awakened, and street vendors, hawkers, and loaded carts obstructed their movement.

'So you've met Lord Thorwynn,' said Grannie. *Ah. We're coming to it now.* 'Yes.' Before she could say anything, she rushed in, 'I hope you aren't planning to say anything in his favour, Grannie. I found his behaviour quite abominable.'

He had certainly lived up to his reputation as a rake. Attacking one lady, then escorting the other to her home. She was being unfair, of course. In both cases he had done nothing ungentlemanly. If his touch had provoked unladylike sensations in her, it was hardly his fault. *The attack has shaken me, that's all. I'm not the victim of abduction every day.* What surprised her more than anything was that, after the initial jolt of fear, she had remained calm throughout. And despite her attempts to free herself, she had not been truly frightened. Perhaps some instinct told her that he meant no harm. Nevertheless, she fretted over her re-

31

actions. She had always scorned the role of the swooning heroine. Today she had come perilously close to that.

'If I chance upon him again,' she said, resolutely, 'I'll give him the cut.'

'Of course you won't,' said her grandmother, forcefully. 'Now that you've been introduced to him, you have to acknowledge him. To cut him would imply that something untoward had occurred between you.'

Julia let out an irritated breath. 'I did not mean the direct cut, and well you know it. But if you think that I'll look more favourably at him as a possible husband after today, you're very much mistaken.'

She expected Grannie to berate her, to tell her not to be childish or some such thing.

Instead, Grannie nodded. 'I don't expect anything at all, although I must say he seems a tolerable young man. Quite attractive-looking, too. But if you are really planning to choose your own husband, you had better move a bit faster. Time has wings, and it doesn't wait for anyone.'

CHAPTER 2

There was no mistaking those elaborate flourishes. The small white letter lay on the silver tray, looking harmless. But a letter in this particular handwriting never boded well. He picked it up and tore the top with his silver letter opener. The content was perfectly familiar.

Dear Lionel
I *must* see you *urgently.* Please do not delay.

Your darling Mama

He threw the letter into the fireplace. Though not an accomplished letter writer, his mother always made herself clear. He sighed and reached for the bell-pull.

Hodgkin appeared immediately.

'Do I have any matters that require my immediate attention, Hodgkin?'

Hodgkin's expression did not change, but

he glanced towards the silver tray, empty of its letter, and then up at the ceiling. The ceiling apparently did not inspire him, since he answered, 'I'm afraid not, my lord.' His voice held a note of apology.

There was no escaping it, then.

'In that case, Hodgkin, I'd better be on my way.' Had the old retainer's mouth actually twitched? There was no knowing with Hodgkin, of course. 'If anyone asks for me, I'll be visiting my mother. And you can let Cook know I will not be returning for dinner.'

'Yes, my lord.'

'And Hodgkin' — the butler's impassive face did not change — 'have you heard any rumours I should know about?'

'No, my lord.'

'Thank you, that will be all.'

Hodgkin bowed.

Lionel stepped out of his townhouse on St James Square. It was a beautiful spring day. He could so easily be tempted to dawdle. His mother would not take kindly to it, however.

'Good afternoon, Mrs Duffel.' The house-keeper's big round face was as familiar as his mother's. 'Has my mother already worked herself into a state?'

The housekeeper, clearly torn between loyalty to her mistress and her soft spot for him, replied with a tiny smile. 'She's been expecting you this last hour, Lord Thorwynn.'

He grinned, 'In other words, since the moment she finished writing the letter.' He tossed his hat and topcoat to the footman, and waited to be announced.

'His lordship's here to see you, my lady.'

Mrs Duffel allowed him to pass, and closed the door slowly, careful of her mistress's nerves. She shot him a quick look which he could only interpret as sympathy. Damn if he needed sympathy to face his own mother.

Lady Thorwynn was lying on the sofa, surrounded by a variety of herbal concoctions for her nerves, each more evil looking than the other. She had tasted none of them. As the door closed she struggled up into a seated position, wringing her hands.

'Come to me. My poor, poor boy,' she said. 'What have you got yourself into this time?'

He had come to the conclusion some time ago that, no matter his age, his mother still saw him as a five-year-old boy with scraped knees. She pulled his head down to plant a kiss on his brow, then cupped his cheeks and peered into his eyes.

'Let's see how you get out of this one,' she said, releasing him and sinking back on to her sofa. 'Sit, sit.'

Confound it. I'm not a dog.

He sat and prepared himself for the lecture that he knew was coming. He searched through his recent past, the last two months, at any rate. His latest mistress, the luscious (though very greedy) Angelique had been given her *congé* three weeks ago. There had been some overlap between her and the alluring Lady Amestable, who insisted on sharing his bed when Lord Amestable was away at his estate, which was quite often. Fortunately for him. And he had enjoyed one riotous night with Mrs Radlow, the golden-haired widow. There was nothing exceptionable in any of them. Unless Lord Amestable had discovered his wife's infidelities and was foolish enough to call him out.

No doubt he would find out, after the lecture was over.

'— how embarrassing it is to have to tell Lady Ponderton every time she asks, that you have not yet settled down. I could understand it if you were still green and wanting to make an impression. But you're thirty. Thirty is beyond the age when an earl starts looking to his responsibilities and thinking about the family line. Just the other day Lady Neyfous was saying that it was such a pity —'

He rose and poured himself a glass of claret from the decanter on the tray. That was the only good part about these encounters. Mama always provided him with the best from her cellars. Perhaps she meant it as a bribe so he would listen. Or as a reward for enduring the lectures.

'— you will stay for dinner, won't you?'

Always the same question. 'Yes, of course, Mama, I'd be delighted.'

She tugged at the bell-pull. The butler entered, a gangly man with no chin and pale-blue eyes.

'Have a place set for Lord Thorwynn, will you?'

'Yes, my lady.' The butler bowed so tightly from the waist that Lionel wondered if he had lumbago.

'Who is this man? What the devil happened to old Matthews?' Thorwynn asked.

His mother sighed. 'His name is Iggleton. He came very highly recommended. Old Matthews has been pensioned off. The poor man was starting to confuse everyone's names. He's gone to live with his sister in Staffordshire, I believe.'

Things would not be the same without him.

'This brings me to why I called you here.'

Ah. Here came the moment he'd been dreading. Despite her penchant for dramatics, his mother usually had good reasons to summon him.

'It's that Neville girl.'

For a moment he could not place the name. Then an image flashed through his mind of a girl lying on the ground very still. He choked on his drink. 'Nothing's happened to her, has it?'

His mother looked puzzled. 'I'm not sure I understand what you mean. If it's one of your cant terms signifying that she is increasing, then I can only say that I am shocked beyond words.'

'Increasing?' he said. He downed the claret in a gulp. He was not slow-witted, but at the moment inspiration escaped him.

'In all the years I brought you up and watched you grow, I never thought for a second you would sink so low.' She was genuinely upset. This was no moral sermon. 'I have tolerated some of your excesses in the spirit that they were done — a young man sowing wild oats. Particularly since much of your youth was spent in the army, fighting Napoleon. You have not spoken to

38

me of it, but I am sure that must have been a terrible ordeal.' She focused her attention on the brocade of the sofa, following one of the patterns with her finger. 'But this time you have crossed the line.'

He rested his glass carefully on the table and went to her. He knelt on the floor, and took her hands.

'I'm very much in the dark, Mama. Could you kindly explain what is going on?'

She took a deep breath.

'Is it possible you have not yet heard? I find that hard to credit. You are always the first to know when you have become the object of gossip.'

His head was still spinning. What possible gossip could there be that would involve Miss Neville?

'I don't see what there is to be done. You will have to marry her.'

'Deuce take it, Mother,' he exploded. 'Stop playing games!' But she wasn't playing games. She didn't like games, except for cards. 'Just tell me what's going on.'

'But I *am* telling you,' she said, bewildered.

'Very well,' he said. 'So why do I have to marry the chit?'

'Because you compromised her, of course. Lady Nattleham, her mother's friend, was riding in Hyde Park and saw her lying on the ground, with you leaning over her, and your hands —' She broke off, embarrassed.

'My hands?' he said, dangerously.

She reddened. Sometimes he wondered if Mama had actually bedded his father. It seemed hard to believe, though his very existence proved it.

'Your hands,' she continued, in a faint voice, 'on her limbs.'

'What nonsense!' He stood up, his hands tearing through his hair. 'I did indeed feel her limbs, as you choose to call them, Mother. Her *legs.*' She looked up in shock. 'But I was in the presence of her groom, and another perfectly respectable young lady. And I felt her legs to ensure that they were not broken. She had *fallen from a horse,* Mother.'

'It was very foolish of you to feel her limbs, even if she had fallen from a horse.' But then the full impact of his words reached her. She rose and drew him to her, to kiss him on the brow. She was smiling.

'I knew it, my foolish boy. I knew you could not be so indifferent to propriety to —'

'Feel a young lady's limbs. In Hyde Park.' She ignored him.

'We must counter this rumour, and set things right immediately.' She paused and looked hard at him. 'Unless you were in the company of some dubious female at the time?'

'No, indeed, Mama. I would not go riding at eight o'clock in the morning with some "dubious" female, as you term it.'

'I beg to differ. Any female who would be riding with you alone in Hyde Park at eight o'clock in the morning can hardly be called respectable.'

He assured her that Miss Swifton was very proper *ton*. 'She's Lady Bullfinch's granddaughter, no less, Mother. I think we can call her respectable.'

Still, there was a nagging doubt in his mind. She had not reacted as any society miss would have reacted when he had pounced on her so very unexpectedly. In fact, now that he thought of it, she had been remarkably unflustered, considering how close he had held her. So close, in fact, that her scent, mingling with a subtle hint of rosewater, had lingered with him.

'Yes, of course, we are well acquainted with Lady Bullfinch. She is a good friend of your grandmother's. And I knew Miss Swifton's mother, Olivia, though she was younger than me. A family of bluestockings, and rather odd, but nothing exceptionable. I will call on Miss Swifton, in that case, and

41

we'll devise a strategy to clear your name. As for Miss Neville, I have heard nothing about her at all, but I cannot help but feel that she must be a scheming nobody.'

'There you wrong her, Mother. She is a perfectly charming and innocent young lady.' A very pretty young lady, in fact. But the direction of his thoughts shifted to Miss Swifton, struggling in his arms; to the moment of awareness, as she jostled against him. His body had reacted, damn it, and jolted him into noticing her. As a woman. Which was certainly odd, because innocents like her usually left him cold. He liked more earthy, older women. It struck him, too, now that he thought about it, that she had remarkable presence of mind, given the fact that he had handled her. He cast a surreptitious glance at his palm. The teeth marks stood out, a clear circle of red.

'If you are planning to call on Miss Swifton, I would be happy to accompany you,' he said.

His mother threw him a quizzing look.

'If she is to help me uncoil this mess, I need to talk to her about it,' he said, surprised to find a hint of defensiveness creeping into his voice. Devil take it, he didn't need to explain himself. 'Anything wrong with that?' he said, voicing it as a challenge.

She smiled, one of those knowing smiles mothers seem to have. 'Nothing at all,' she said. 'I will be glad of your company.'

Julia shifted her legs from under her and looked up from reading *Persuasion.* Lady Bullfinch, of course, was reading a philosophical work by Voltaire, whom she adored, all the more so after she had had a fierce argument with him at a *salon* in Paris.

'It always amazes me how society is so taken in by scoundrels like Mr Elliot,' said Julia. 'You would think someone would have exposed him long before.'

Her grandmother furrowed her brows. 'I'm sure I don't know what you're talking about,' she said. 'But scoundrels are generally tolerated by society if they come from a prominent family.'

Julia sighed. 'And yet the smallest transgression on our part becomes exaggerated beyond belief.'

Lady Bullfinch shrugged. 'That has not always been the case. In my day, young girls were expected to have a romp before they settled down and married, and we had none of this ridiculous white muslin.'

Julia smiled. 'Far better these light muslins than the heavy brocades and hoops you wore. I don't know how you were able to move with all that weight.'

'We didn't think much of it at the time, believe me. I suppose each generation sees itself as more fortunate than the one before,' she said.

'Still, one thing remains consistent,' said Julia. 'In each generation rakes and scoundrels prey on the innocent.'

Grandmother eyed her steadily. 'You mustn't always think of your mother,' she said, gently. 'True, she suffered a great deal when your father abandoned her, but not all gentlemen are like him. Some are quite . . . exciting.'

Julia's cheeks burned, as they generally did, when Grandmother started to talk about her love affairs. There was no convincing her that this topic was considered inappropriate for maidenly ears.

The clunk of the knocker reached her.

'Odd time for someone to come calling,' said Lady Bullfinch, straightening herself. 'I hope it doesn't mean dinner will have to be delayed. Cook will be livid.'

Rumbert appeared in the doorway, a gaunt-looking man who had been the butler since Lady Bullfinch's marriage at twenty. 'Lady Thorwynn and Lord Thorwynn wish to speak to you. Shall I show them in here, or would you prefer to receive them in the

44

drawing-room?'

Julia threw a sharp look, but her grandmother shrugged and shook her head in denial. It seemed too much of a coincidence that Lord Thorwynn himself should seek them out. Not after Grandmother's ultimatum.

'In here,' she said to Rumbert. 'If they call at such an hour they cannot expect to be formally received.' The butler bowed. 'And bring some tea and refreshments.'

Julia went to the mirror, tugged her hair back into its pins and smoothed down her Turkey-red cotton day dress. They were not receiving that day, so she had not given any thought to her clothing. *I really am bird-witted, just as he said.* She was actually preening herself to meet him, a practised rake who had seized her in the park and then walked off with the most casual apology. To make matters worse, the image of the cherub flashed before her, so neat and tidy even after her fall.

Perhaps he was coming to apologize. But somehow she doubted it. It was far more likely he was being pressured by his grandmother. With Grannie's blessing.

Julia did not know what irritated her more — the fact that she was not better dressed, or the scheming.

The moment the door closed behind Rumbert, Julia turned to her. 'I hope you have not spoken to Lady Gragspur already. If you have, you are betraying the terms of our agreement.'

There was no time for an answer. The door opened and Rumbert announced the Thorwynns.

Lady Thorwynn did not resemble her son. There was nothing in her colouring to suggest the piercing blackness of his eyes. Nor in her slight, trim figure to suggest his lithe athletic frame. But they both moved with a fluid grace that made watching them a pleasure. Even if it was rude to stare.

He took her hand, gazed directly into her eyes, and murmured his delight at seeing her for the second time that day. He had the satisfied look of a cat who had stolen a fish out of a tank, as if she had somehow engineered the situation. The impulse to remark that she had invited neither encounter was very strong but she restrained it.

Lady Thorwynn quickly fell into conversation with Lady Bullfinch. Since it involved common acquaintances, friends of Julia's mother whom she did not know, she could not participate. Which left her to entertain Lord Thorwynn.

She knew nothing about him, so she chose

the most innocuous topic she could think of. 'Do you often ride in the park early in the morning, Lord Thorwynn?' she asked. To her astonishment, the question seemed to throw him into confusion.

'Yes, that is — not often.'

For heaven's sake, she was not asking him to give away government secrets. She tried a different direction. 'Did Miss Neville arrive home safely?'

This time he put his tea down with a clatter. 'I believe so,' he said, looking towards his mother for help.

Such a notorious rake could not be tongue-tied. Clearly their visit involved more than a social call. However much she racked her brain, she could not think of a reason.

'And I have heard about your charming granddaughter,' said Lady Thorwynn. She turned in her chair. For a long moment she studied Julia's face, her clothing, and her figure, down to the puce shoes she wore that did not match with her dress.

Would you like to see my teeth, too? Julia submitted to the scrutiny, willing herself not to shuffle her feet and twiddle her thumbs. She kept her eyes on the gold-leaf pattern around the fireplace. What she really wanted to do was wring Grannie out like a wet cloth.

'Which brings me to the purpose of our visit,' said Lady Thorwynn, nodding in a satisfied way. Had Julia won her approval? Heaven forbid. 'Which is, in fact, to enlist your help, Miss Swifton.'

That took her by surprise. In fact, Lady Thorwynn could have knocked her down with one of the ostrich feathers in her turban. Her curiosity running rampant by now, it took remarkable effort to reply calmly, 'I'd be happy to be of assistance, my lady.'

Lady Thorwynn smiled. 'Wait until you know what is required. It is a matter of delicacy. There is perhaps some risk to your involvement.'

Julia did not like risks. In fact, she positively disliked them. Especially if they involved rakes. She glanced towards Lord Thorwynn. He was staring into his teacup like a fortune-teller, trying to read the future. In the growing dusk, she realized there was something gypsy-like about him, with his long black locks tumbling on to his face. She had known a band of gypsies that had frequented their land every year in her childhood. She could imagine him laughing with the women around the camp-fire, his teeth flashing in the moonlight.

He looked up, and their gazes met. He smiled, a small reassuring smile, and without thinking, Julia smiled back. Then she realized that Grannie was watching, so she turned her attention back to Lady Thorwynn.

Lady Thorwynn explained the situation quickly, with a few interruptions from her son.

'So you see, as a witness to the whole affair, you are invaluable in countering the rumours. We must circulate the correct story.'

Julia threw a glance at Lady Bullfinch. For the briefest of moments, she thought of saying no. After all, if he married the cherub, then her grandmother could no longer use him as a threat to force her to marry.

But, to Julia's surprise, Grannie objected. 'You are asking us to circulate a story which may well compromise my niece.'

Lord Thorwynn shook his head. 'That is the risk my mother spoke of. However, if we emphasize that your niece was in your sight the whole time, then there can be no problem. After all, you were only a few minutes behind us.'

Julia thought of the moments when they wrestled on their horses, hidden by the oak trees. It would take only one witness to that scene for a completely different story to circulate. But there could not have been anyone. She had searched for help and seen nobody.

Like a gambler staking his future on his winnings, Julia made her decision. After all, she did not think Lord Thorwynn and the cherub would suit each other at all.

'The rumour is completely unfounded,' she said. 'Neither Miss Neville nor Lord Thorwynn can be sacrificed to such an absurd interpretation of the situation.'

Grannie threw her a complicated look that held both surprise and warning. 'I hope you are fully aware of the risks involved,' she said. 'Think about it before you decide.'

Julia shook her head. 'I am the only one who can help Lord Thorwynn, since I was the only witness to the events. It would be unconscionable to allow the rumour to spread without attempting to put an end to it.' From the corner of her eye she saw Lord Thorwynn make some kind of a gesture. She ignored it, keeping her attention on Lady Thorwynn. 'But we need a plan of action.'

She was amazed at her outer calm. Inwardly, she squirmed like a worm on a hook. She would aid Lord Thorwynn, because she was duty bound to do so, but heaven help him if he tried to ply her with his charms, because she would expend all her energy to make sure he stayed out of her life.

CHAPTER 3

'You missed dinner,' said Conrad, Viscount Benedict.

'I know.' Lionel wrinkled his nose. 'I dined at my mother's. She insisted.'

Benedict raised a thick red eyebrow, but said nothing.

'By the way, I need your company tonight, Benny,' drawled Lionel, spreading his arms on the back of the familiar settee, as far as his starched collar points would permit. The settee seemed almost moulded to his form — he always sat there when it was available. Brooks's was his place of refuge, somewhere to enjoy a quiet interval before moving on to his next activity.

Today, though, Brooks's failed to have that effect. Lionel had a prickling sensation between his shoulder blades. The impulse to look round to make sure no one stared was overwhelming.

He hoped he looked a great deal more at

ease than he felt.

'Certainly,' said Benny, peering at him. 'Something wrong?'

He did not fool Benny, of course, never could. Not even as a thirteen year old at Eton, where they had first met. Benny always saw through him.

Since nothing else would satisfy him, he explained the situation to Benny, glancing around to make sure none of the gentlemen lounging around them could be listening.

'As far as I know, the rumour hasn't reached White's,' remarked Benny, when he'd finished. 'I was there earlier. I'll keep a look out for you, though. Since you won't set foot in the place.'

'You know why,' said Lionel, grimly. 'There are certain . . . people I wish to avoid.'

Benny looked pained. 'I'm very well aware of why you don't go to White's.' His tone made it clear he did not want that particular subject opened. 'I haven't heard anything here, either. So no one's heard at the clubs yet. Perhaps there's nothing to it.'

'Dash it, Benny,' he said. 'If my mother's heard it, you can be sure there is something to it. It'll be in the betting books by tomorrow. "Will I, or will I not, salvage Miss Neville's reputation?" '

'Is she an antidote?' asked his companion.

An image of blonde ringlets, blue eyes and parchment skin rose up and disappeared. 'No, she's quite presentable, in fact.' He considered, rubbing the tip of his nose with his thumb. 'She's pretty enough, but much too debutante for my taste.'

Benny swirled his brandy and nodded. 'Still, better than a girl with a squint.'

'Confound it! I'm not planning to marry her. That's where the Swifton chit comes in. And where you come in.'

Benny set down his glass. 'You're not planning to marry the Swifton girl?'

Lionel guffawed. 'You haven't met her, if you can ask that question.' Unbidden, he recalled her penetrating hazel eyes, a heart-shaped face, and a mouth that was definitely kissable with a deucedly stubborn expression. 'Wouldn't marry me if I went down on my knees and begged. One of those ladies who don't like marriage, I believe. A bluestocking, and a Wollstonecraft follower.' She had never said anything like that, certainly never spewed anything about the Rights of Women during their brief interaction. But he knew her grandmother had been a friend of the notorious Mary Wollstonecraft, and been part of the group that supported her ideas. 'For God's sake,

Benny, all this is beside the point. The point is' — he cleared his throat — 'you need to escort me to Mrs Wadswith's ball tonight.'

Benny let out a bark of laughter and put his hand to his heart. 'What's the world coming to? A ball, for the famous Thorwynn! The Laughing Rake *par excellence!* With a room full of debutantes! Coming it too brown!'

Lionel drained his glass. 'Don't rub it in.' He smiled ruefully. 'I'm afraid I'm going to have to abandon my pedestal for the night and come down to earth,' he said ruefully. 'A temporary condition, I hope. But very indicative of my dire straits.'

'And you can't do without my support?'

'Your support is essential. If only to keep the match-making monsters at bay. The moment they realize I'm not going to marry the Neville girl after all, they'll sink their claws into me, and I'll be done for.' He rose, noting as he did the smirk on Benny's face. 'You might think it funny, but it's no laughing matter for the Neville girl, or for me, if we can't squelch the rumours.'

Benny shrugged. 'Oh, I wouldn't miss the event for anything. It will be the height of amusement to watch you trying to extricate yourself from the old tabbies. And to see Mrs Wadswith's face when she realizes you have chosen her ball to make your first appearance in society since your return from the Continent.'

Julia finished greeting the last person in the receiving line, an elderly man with a red nose and stays that creaked when he bent to take her hand. She surveyed the flamboyant ballroom. Clearly Mrs Wadswith had spared no expense to prepare for the party. She'd put into effect the latest fashion plates from *Ackermann's Repository,* not on a dress, but on the ballroom itself. The dominant colour was Clarence Blue, with several rows of flounces lining the walls. Real wheat ears were set up in Grecian vases throughout the ballroom, and festoons of roses were suspended from the ceiling, windows, and doors. The idea certainly was original, but the execution made the ballroom look like an overcrowded woman's court dress.

The worst of it was that half the hostesses in town would be imitating it.

'You've got to stop fidgeting,' said Grannie.

'I'm not fidgeting.' But her hands betrayed her. Her hands clasped and unclasped of their own volition. She could put them behind her back, she supposed, but it would present an odd appearance.

'Do you want to help Lord Thorwynn or not?' Lady Bullfinch's voice was sharp. 'You won't pull this off if you look so anxious.'

Julia stretched her mouth into a broad smile. 'Better?' she said.

'It's lucky people don't really know you, or they'd know that was a battle grin,' remarked her grandmother sternly. 'Remove that smile from your face at once. You have to look like an innocent young debutante, excited at the chance to dance. Maybe you could manage to simper, as well. Anything other than your ferocious *don't get closer* expression will do.'

Julia grinned, a real smile this time. 'I *am* an innocent debutante. Not precisely young at three and twenty, but not yet on the shelf. And I love to dance.' She could not resist teasing her. 'But no one's invited me yet. My dance card is completely blank.'

'You've only just arrived. I'm sure you'll be surrounded by admirers in a moment. After all, you do have some money to your name,' replied Lady Bullfinch, her fierce black eyes twinkling.

'How delightful to dance with the fortune hunters,' replied Julia, still smiling, but rather more cynically.

A group of young bucks in bright waistcoats and heavily starched shirt collars standing in front of her moved away, no doubt eager to withdraw to the card-room. Lady Thorwynn came into her line of vision, languishing on a puce sofa, right in the centre of the matrons' area. A garland of upside down roses dangled over her head. Lady Sefton and Princess Lieven, patronesses of Almack's, sat close by, watching the younger guests with hawk eyes. Several other prominent personages were seated in the vicinity. She had certainly been able to gather some of Society's most notorious scandalmongers around her.

'Time for battle,' said Julia, indicating Lady Thorwynn, raising her chin and drawing a deep breath.

Grannie reached for her hand and squeezed it. 'Don't worry,' she whispered. 'Everything will go well. It's Lord Thorwynn's future that's at stake, not your own.'

'As long as I don't end up being compromised myself,' she muttered. She had agreed, following the impulse of a moment. But her instincts were screaming for her to back out. The situation could easily veer off in the wrong direction, and she could quickly become the subject of malicious gossip herself.

If her name was associated too closely with the Laughing Rake, she could well find herself forced into the same marriage she was helping him get out of.

But no sooner had she started moving towards Lady Thorwynn when her progress was interrupted.

'Good evening, Miss Swifton.'

An elongated, sausage-like face appeared before her. Mr Eckles was definitely not a fortune hunter, since he stood to inherit a substantial fortune. The matchmakers considered him a fine catch for the young debutantes. Unfortunately, however, his primary passion in life consisted of breeding hunting dogs, an interest Julia did not share.

'Mr Eckles. How delightful to see you.'

'The pleasure is all mine,' he said, bowing. 'Could I put my name down for a dance, perhaps?'

'Certainly.'

He fell into step with her, exchanging pleasantries, and describing to her in great detail his acquisition of a curly-haired retriever. 'Never seen a dog with such an exquisite sense of smell,' he proclaimed, launching into an enthusiastic description.

The moment he realized where Julia and her grandmother were headed, however, he mumbled a quick excuse and disappeared. No young gentleman wanted to be ensnared by a party of matchmakers intent on marrying their charges. She could hardly blame him. She never approached the matrons herself without checking that she did not have a loose tendril of hair or a torn hem or a ribbon out of place. She imagined she would feel the same if she faced a panel of judges for some crime she had committed.

This time, however, Lady Thorwynn's extended arm conveyed approval. She patted the sofa next to her for Lady Bullfinch to sit on, and tugged Julia forward with a warm grip.

'I was just telling Mrs Sefton about the accident in the park this morning. I hope that poor girl wasn't hurt. Miss Neville, I believe she is called. New to town, apparently. You must tell us all about it.'

The matrons closed in around Julia, but their expressions were friendly.

Here we go, she thought. Choosing her words carefully, she launched into the prepared narrative, one in which Grandmother featured prominently.

A quarter of an hour later, Grannie waved her away.

'Go find some of your young friends, girl. You shouldn't waste the whole night dawdling with the matrons.'

Relieved that the first part of her ordeal

60

was over, she put as much distance between the matrons and herself as was possible in a crowded ballroom. An old friend of hers from school, Miss Willaby, waved at her, and she moved in her direction.

She was not destined to reach her.

The sudden change in the tone of the buzzing around her warned her immediately. Lord Thorwynn had arrived. Nothing in his behaviour, however, showed his awareness that he was the centre of attention. He would have been the centre of attention no matter what happened, even if this were an ordinary evening, since he had not set foot in a respectable ballroom for three years. The small smile hovering on his lips seemed genuine, and his dark eyes were amused. She scrutinized his appearance but found nothing to fault. His black curls were fashionably arranged, and his black suit impeccably tailored. He was like a Roman orator, suddenly transposed into modern dress. *A toga would look good on him.* The idea brought a smile to her face.

He caught her examining him, caught her smile. She tried to pretend she was smiling at something someone had said, but since she could find no one to talk to in the vicinity she was forced to abandon the pretence. In two strides he was at her side.

The buzz followed him, growing louder as he approached. The bees were busy. She would know soon enough whether they would be contented with simply buzzing, or whether they would turn on him and start to sting.

'Delighted to see you again, Miss Swifton,' said the earl, taking her hand gracefully and bowing over it. 'I hope you didn't suffer any mishap after our rescue at Hyde Park.' He pitched his voice so that it would carry.

The buzzing diminished to a soft droning. Clearly people were straining to hear her reply.

'None at all,' she said, beginning for some strange reason to enjoy herself. Perhaps it was the influence of her companion. 'But it was extremely lucky that we were at hand to help the unfortunate Miss Neville when she fell.'

His eyes gleamed wickedly.

Buzz, buzz went the crowd around them. Some of the matrons, not Lady Thorwynn's group, fluttered their fans like wings.

'I'm very glad she did not break her . . . limb,' said Thorwynn. 'She was certainly in pain. Have you heard anything regarding her injuries?'

'I believe she has not suffered anything serious,' said Julia. 'My grandmother called on her this afternoon. It appears she hit her head and complains of a bad headache, but nothing more.'

'I'm delighted to hear it. I hope your riding habit survived your kneeling on the wet grass to aid Miss Neville.'

She made a mental note to have a new riding habit made. It would not do to be seen in the old one after this. She gave a short laugh, 'I'm afraid it's beyond repair. Grass stains are very hard to remove.'

'At least it was sacrificed in a good cause,' he said, solemnly.

Julia had to control an impulse to laugh aloud. Luckily, she could allow the hint of laughter in her voice. 'It gives me a perfect excuse to buy a new riding habit. I've been longing for one that I saw in the *Repository of Fashion*. I have the perfect excuse now. I am only sorry my good fortune is at the expense of *Miss Neville's fall*.' Her emphasis was slight, but it was a reminder to those who listened intently.

They were back on topic. 'I wonder what could have caused Miss Neville's horse to bolt like that?' said Thorwynn, on cue, his eyes dancing madly, but his expression completely bland.

'She told me she heard a loud crack, like

a pistol shot. Her horse must be a nervous one.'

'It's difficult to keep horses properly exercised in London. Unless they are exercised regularly, they can become quite skittish. Especially if they are new to town and are not used to the noise.' He launched into a loud discourse on the difficulties of keeping a horse in London.

He was interrupted by the appearance of an impeccably dressed young man with windswept reddish hair.

'Thorwynn,' he said, clapping his hand on the earl's shoulder. 'What brings you here?'

'My mother would not take no for an answer,' said Thorwynn, waving a hand towards Lady Thorwynn. 'She insists it's time I think of marriage.' Then, as if remembering his manners, 'Allow me to introduce Miss Swifton. Miss Swifton, Viscount Benedict.'

She curtsied.

'I met Miss Swifton at Hyde Park this morning,' said Thorwynn, still speaking in that unnaturally loud way. 'Remember I told you about the unfortunate young lady who fell off her horse?'

'Yes. My dear Miss Swifton, I hope you didn't suffer any injuries?'

'You're mistaking the matter, Benny. It

was *Miss Neville* who fell off when her horse bolted. Miss Swifton attempted, very valiantly, to catch up with her horse. As did I. As did Miss Neville's valet. Even Lady Bullfinch tried valiantly to catch her. But none of us succeeded.'

The exchange between the two men was so obviously contrived that Julia began to succumb to a fit of giggles. She smothered it, ruthlessly. She had to control herself; if she started laughing, she would ruin everything.

'It was providential that so many people saw her horse bolt. My grandmother, in spite of a recent set-back in her health, was able to give chase. Miss Neville certainly did not lack people to attend to her.'

'Well, I'm delighted to make the acquaintance of the young lady who was the first on the scene,' said Benedict loudly. He shot her a close look. Something must have alerted him that she was on the verge of losing her composure. 'Perhaps you would do me the honour of dancing the next dance with me? Unless your reputation as heroine has preceded you, and your card is full?'

She gave him her hand, smiling. 'No, indeed, sir, you flatter me. I did not succeed in saving Miss Neville, after all. However, I would be delighted to dance with you.'

■ ■ ■ ■

Lionel watched her as they took their places in the quadrille. The dance began, and he found himself following the fluid motion of her body under her shimmering Pomona green gown. She slid through her steps gracefully, with the certainty of a woman who knew she danced well. He had not noticed before that her auburn hair glimmered with ruby highlights, glinting in the hundreds of candles that lighted the room. Something Benny said made her laugh, and he was surprised at the air of mischief she conveyed. She was not what he had been led to expect. His grandmother had mentioned her many times, usually as an intelligent, no-nonsense young lady who seemed to enjoy earnest conversation. He was clearly seeing another side of her tonight.

She seemed to have taken a liking to Benny. Whenever the dance brought them together, they exchanged a lively remark, and they both moved apart with smiles on their faces.

Her face was open, an honest face in which contriving and trickery did not play a role. He could not help contrasting her to Angelique, his last mistress. Angelique was beautiful, with her expensive perfumes and her sophisticated hairstyles. She knew how to seduce a man, but she had never given him an uncalculated look in her life. As for Mrs Radlow, the Golden Widow, her beauty took his breath away. He still desired her, despite a long and vigorous night they had shared, but her eyes were hardened, and even though she panted in pleasure under his caresses, she had never once looked at him as though she understood him. Unlike Miss Swifton.

He dismissed the thought. The two of them had been brought together by a sense of conspiracy, and the unspoken communication between them came from that. It was as though they were comrades in arms, preparing for battle. They had a common goal to accomplish, and that in itself created a bond which would normally not exist.

There was only one thing wrong with that analogy. In all his years at war, he had never once wished to dance with a comrade in arms.

CHAPTER 4

Julia did not remember enjoying a ball so much in her life.

Certainly she enjoyed the company of Lord Benedict. He put her at ease, and she found conversation with him stimulating. He referred to the Classics, and when she quizzed him on his knowledge, he admitted self-consciously that he had read a first in Classics at Oxford. Before long, they were speaking in Latin, laughing as they translated ballroom inanities into that ancient tongue.

'Well, they must have had some form of "do you come here often?" in Latin,' she said. 'Even if it never made it into the textbooks.'

'I suspect some of the monks copying manuscripts in medieval monasteries decided to leave those parts out.'

She tilted her head as she cut across him. 'They didn't object to some of the more raucous Greek plays.'

'The monks who learned Greek were more . . . enterprising.'

She came off the dance floor laughing. She was still thinking of something Lord Benedict had said when Lord Thorwynn stepped forward and took her hand, teeth flashing.

'I believe the next waltz is promised to me?'

She curtseyed, smiling.

But, as he drew her closer, the laughter died. His dark eyes met hers as his hand settled into the small of her back. His touch was light, but it seared into her, reaching through her gown to caress the skin underneath. He pulled her towards him and for the first time she discovered why the waltz was considered *fast*.

Being so close to a gentleman jumbled her brain. With uncharacteristic clumsiness, she stumbled on to his foot, and — what on earth was happening to her — gave him her left hand instead of her right. Blood rushed into her face and she looked down, trying to hide it. But her head brushed against his chest and she stepped back quickly, stepping on the pink silk shoe of the lady behind her.

'I'm so sorry,' she said to the lady, who frowned and turned her back to her.

She glanced quickly at Thorwynn, doubly flustered now.

'I'm sorry,' she whispered to him. 'Perhaps I shouldn't dance. I think the events of the evening have weakened my nerves.'

What a ninny-headed thing to say. She had nerves like a rock. What had compelled her to make such a statement?

'Nonsense,' he said, guiding her firmly across the dance floor. 'I've seen you dance. You dance exquisitely. Just listen to the music, and set aside everything else.'

She resolved to do just that. The strains from the orchestra floated towards her, and she let herself ride them. The hand that held her at the waist melded into her body, its warmth stirring her blood. The fingers entwined in her own sent quiet ripples of sensation into her body. She lost track of the steps, of the whole ballroom, all her senses focusing on the music and the man who danced so close to her. He led her on a journey that was surely not a dance but a whirl through the air, her feet barely touching the ground. She revelled in it, completely lost to the world around her.

Suddenly, she realized she was no longer moving, and the music was gone.

Her partner was looking down at her, his face inscrutable.

'I can confirm that you know how to waltz,' said Thorwynn. He sounded breathless, his voice rough.

She smiled up at him, still half caught in the flight. 'I can confirm the same about you,' she said.

He bowed to her, offered his arm, and moved her off the floor as other dancers came together, readying themselves for a new dance.

The ballroom came into focus. The faces of the matrons, watching. The inverted roses. The Clarence Blue flounces. The Grecian urns. She stumbled. He steadied her with his hand, and ushered her towards her grandmother. When they arrived, his arm drew away from hers and she felt cold.

'Perhaps you'd care for some refreshment?'

She managed a nod. He disappeared into the crowd.

'I told you you'd enjoy the dancing,' said Grannie, black eyes glinting.

She snapped back to awareness. She was in a ballroom, a social event she generally detested, even if she loved dancing. It was an ordinary night just like any other. All that had happened was that she had danced with the Laughing Rake, and somehow, for one moment, fallen under his spell. She understood better than ever why rakes should be avoided at all cost.

She would tell Grannie in so many words that she would not, under any circumstances, agree to marry this particular rake. He was dangerous, a threat to her peace of mind. She would make sure to avoid him. It would hardly be difficult, in any case, since she did not attend balls very often, preferring the company of a good book to a roomful of chattering magpies. And she knew he generally avoided events organized by the *ton,* preferring more stimulating company.

And she would make a concerted effort to find her husband in a place where a rake like Lord Thorwynn would not be caught dead. In the corridors of the Royal Society at Somerset House, at the exhibits in the Egyptian Hall, at the British Museum, and various lecture halls around London. *Those* were not places where she would even catch a glimpse of him.

Meanwhile, she waited for him to get her a drink. She hoped he would not choose something as insipid as ratafia, a drink she loathed. It always seemed to attach itself to her tongue like a burr, with a sweet fuzzy insistence.

She grew impatient. Of course her impatience meant nothing. Her throat was dry, that was all.

She thought she caught a glimpse of him returning to her corner, but was distracted as Mrs Wadswith, her hostess, approached her. Julia could not help but marvel at the Clarence Blue gown Mrs Wadswith was wearing, the model for the ballroom. She was accompanied by a young officer in a dark-green uniform with black facings. He had a pleasant boyish appearance, with wavy straw-coloured hair and a smattering of freckles on the bridge of his nose. His boy-ish appearance contrasted strongly with the glinting medals that marked him a war hero.

'May I present Captain Neave, Miss Swif-ton? He has expressed a particular desire to be acquainted with you.'

Captain Neave bowed. 'I'm delighted to meet you. I've been hoping to have the pleasure of a dance since the moment I entered the ballroom, but alas, I've had no opportunity to be presented.'

'Faradiddle,' said Julia, laughing at the extravagant compliment.

'On the contrary,' he said, as Mrs Wad-swith moved away, satisfied that she had performed her duty. 'Seeking your acquain-tance is the only sensible thing I have done this evening,' he said. He leaned forward. 'Everything else is faradiddle.' He waved his hand to indicate the flounces and the rose festoons.

A chuckle escaped Julia's lips. She smothered it. 'It's too bad of you,' she said. 'When it was our hostess who was kind enough to introduce you to me.'

'True, and I will be eternally grateful to her.' The musicians struck up a new dance. 'Shall we?' he said.

She needed that drink. But on the other hand, the less she saw of Lord Thorwynn, the better. 'Certainly,' she said, placing her hand in his.

As he led her to the dance floor she made a concerted effort not to look back to see if Thorwynn had returned.

Thorwynn swore and looked down at the two glasses of champagne. She had already found someone to dance with. Devil take it, couldn't she have waited?

Then the green uniform registered, and the unmistakable sand-coloured hair. Just to be sure, in case he was imagining things, he waited until her partner turned in the dance and he could see the man's face. Lionel's blood ran cold. It seemed his luck was out. The man he had spent three years of his life trying to forget had appeared. And, to make matters worse, he was now dancing with Miss Swifton.

He tossed down both glasses of champagne. He disposed of the two glasses on the first surface he could find, and strode off to the card room, in search of Benny.

Benny was in the middle of a game of whist, and the counters that surrounded him indicated that he was on the winning side.

Lionel bent over him and murmured in his ear. 'I think you need to come with me,' he said. 'There's something that needs our urgent attention.'

Benny looked up absently from his game. 'Sorry, Thor, I'm in the middle of a winning streak. Can't stop now.'

'Even,' murmured Lionel, 'if it's about Neave?'

Benny looked up sharply, then surveyed the players round the table.

'I'll join you in a minute, Thorwynn, give me a few minutes to finish.'

Lionel nodded, and stalked back to the ballroom. He found a hidden corner from which he could observe Miss Swifton dancing with Neave. His eyes remained fixed on them, noting every move, every nuance. He took note as Neave bent towards her, smiling, saw her laugh in response. His mouth tightened in disapproval. She lavished the same kind of attention on any man she danced with. She laughed with Neave as she had laughed with Benny. But whereas Benny was an honourable person who would not harm a fly, Neave was —

Bitterness rose up in him as he recalled those weeks after he had returned from the Victory at Waterloo. He had tried to tell his commanding officers about Neave. He had made a cake of himself instead. It took a naive fool to think anyone would care enough to listen, especially when someone was as well connected as Neave. Besides, the war with Napoleon was over. Napoleon was defeated, for the last time. Inflated with the victory, indifferent to the testimony of a minor officer, a mere lieutenant, they had dismissed him. They had given him his honours, his share of the prize money and a promotion. And they had sent him on his way, patting him on the head and urging him not to make trouble.

The sight of Neave brought everything back. The sense of loss, the pain, and the utter humiliation of his pathetic attempt to bring Neave to justice.

He abandoned his post in the corner and went in search of something stiff and strong.

When he returned, four glasses of brandy later, the cotillion was drawing to a close.

He held a brandy in one hand, and a new glass of champagne in the other. Lionel pushed his way through the jostling crowds and waited for Miss Swifton and her partner to walk off the dance floor. He blocked their way. Bowing to Neave without looking in his direction, he handed the glass to Miss Swifton. 'I brought refreshments,' he said.

His sole goal was to draw her away with him, away from Neave.

Her eyes flashed. She did not like his interference. But she was too much of a lady to make a scene. She thanked Neave graciously and allowed Lionel to lead her to the side of the ballroom, a space marginally quieter than the rest.

She spoke quietly, still smiling, so the gossips would not notice her anger. 'You have no right to separate me from my acquaintance that way.' She had spent her life free of the meddling of either brother or father. She did not need a stranger to hover over her. He had misinterpreted her willingness to help him as an invitation to become part of her life. Nothing could be further from her mind.

He shrugged, determined to ride it out. 'I agree that I have no right. However, I would be doing you a disservice if I did not. I wished to warn you: Captain Neave is not all that he appears. I think you would do well to be — careful.'

To his chagrin, the words came out slightly slurred. He normally held his liquor well, was in fact, only a moderate drinker. But the sight of Neave after three years of avoidance had made him lose count.

He downed the glass of champagne.

She examined him closely, a frown lining her brow. He could not help thinking the lines resembled the flounces on the wall. Lines that swayed and dipped. 'You're foxed,' she said, disgust sharpening her voice.

'If I were foxed, Miss Swifton, you would certainly know it. It takes quite a few drinks to get me foxed.' His speech was perhaps a little slow, but what of it? He was not in a hurry.

Certainly not in a hurry to leave her with Captain Neave. 'Really?' she said, her lip curling upwards. 'Well it certainly looks like you've had them.'

His eyes narrowed. Her tone was angry, accusing, and he reacted with anger of his own. Couldn't she see he was trying to help her? 'You need not concern yourself with this matter. I am quite capable of judging how much I need to drink.' He took a deep breath. It would not do for him to quarrel with her. There were many eyes observing them. He pasted a smile on his face. It felt lopsided, for some reason. The whole evening was turning out to be lopsided. Where the devil was Benny?

'Perhaps we can discuss this elsewhere,' he said, in a tone that brooked no argument. 'I will call upon you tomorrow morning and explain the situation.'

She pasted a smile on her face. 'It is kind of you to be concerned about me, but I can assure you I can take care of myself. Although I appreciate your advice, I am not in the habit of consulting with strangers about my actions.'

She took a step away. He could not prevent her leaving, not without causing a stir, and certainly he could not hold her back physically.

'As you wish,' he said, congratulating himself on his calm. 'Won't call on you if you don't wish it. But at least let me tell you something about him. Neave is a rake —'

She laughed. Of all the things he had expected, he had not imagined that she would laugh. 'Isn't it a case of the kettle calling the frying pan black?'

Her words struck him like a hammer. He struggled for words under the onslaught, but found none. She smiled and curtseyed.

'I hope we've solved your problem with Miss Neville in a satisfactory way. We'll know by tomorrow if our story has been accepted by Society. Meanwhile, I hope you'll refrain from treating me with a familiarity that is inappropriate.'

She walked away, leaving him to deal with a wave of emotions that rolled over him. He felt as if he waded in water. The thick air of the ballroom stifled him, and he started to loosen his neck cloth. Then he caught sight of his mother across the ballroom. Better wait until he'd taken his leave. She would probably rearrange the damn thing. He schooled his face into a mask of indifference, and sauntered slowly towards her.

'Leaving so soon, Lionel?' His mother raised a disapproving brow, while one of the old witches surrounding her — he had no idea who she was — raised her quizzing glass to fix her glance on him.

'I have other engagements, Mother.'

'Call on me tomorrow, then.'

He smiled, and bowed. 'I will.' She needed a full report, and he was obliged to give it. If their strategy to stem the gossip had failed, they needed to discuss a new approach.

It took him forever to reach the entrance.

He paused in the doorway to lean on the doorframe and take a few breaths of the pleasantly cool air. A hand landed on his shoulder. He swirled round and peered into his friend's face.

'Oh, it's you, Benny. Terrible timing, I'm afraid.'

'You're foxed,' said Benny. 'It won't do, you know, not at a Society ball.'

'That's what she said,' he muttered. 'The part about being foxed. Not the part about the ball.'

'What happened?' asked Benny. 'I thought we pulled the whole thing off nicely. I told the story to everyone in the card room, with some embellishments of my own. But I think it will be exceedingly hard for anyone to pin the Neville incident on you.'

Lionel tried to remember what the Neville incident was about. The name certainly rang a bell.

He thought of Miss Swifton, turning her back to him.

She would dance again with Neave, he was sure of it. It all came down to Neave, as always. His life seemed to be haunted by him. 'It's Neave again. He's decided to attach himself to Miss Swifton.' He turned his head and stared into the street. It blazed with lanterns that floated to and fro in the wind. He followed the motion of one of them, back and forth, feeling his eyes blur. 'And, as you know only too well, whenever Neave touches something, he destroys it.' He clenched his fingers into a fist. 'I won't let him do it this time, Benny.'

CHAPTER 5

Julia surveyed herself in the mirror. She looked different today. Her brown-green eyes sparkled, her cheeks flushed, and her mouth curled upwards of its own volition. Even her hair seemed to have an extra sheen to it, with little fiery pinpoints dancing in the bright daylight. The excitement of the ball last night lingered. She had enjoyed the company of not one, but three gentlemen, all of them appealing in their own way.

Remarkable, that during two whole seasons of balls and routs she had not found a single gentleman who had not caused her to gaze out of the window, longing for escape. Once the novelty wore off, she realized that the balls were endless repetitions of the same dances, glasses of ratafia, and uninspired conversation. Last year she had refused to attend any but a very select few, those thrown by particular friends of her grandmother that she favoured. She far preferred to attend musical soirées, or the few old-fashioned salons that the older *émigrés* from France still held from time to time. The debates there were lively, at least. Though, of course, there was an inconvenience to it, too. Some of the old *roués* made her the object of their attentions, since she was the only lady under forty who attended.

But last night, she had actually found Mrs Wadswith's ball pleasurable. She relished every minute talking to Lord Benedict, and she found Captain Neave's boyish chatter amusing.

To her annoyance, each time she tried to conjure up either gentleman, she saw Lord Thorwynn's face. What was more irksome, she saw him as he had looked when she had fired that passing shot at him. She knew very little about rakes, having made a point of avoiding them. However, she always vaguely thought that men *liked* being thought rakish. She did not expect that he would be genuinely wounded by the accusation.

She must have mistaken the matter. The candlelight had misled her, flickering in reflection when their glances met. In any case, there was no point in pondering that topic.

She righted a curl that had come loose and went to the window. Captain Neave had invited her for a drive in the Park. He would be here any moment, and she had not ridden with a gentleman for a long time. The day had started with a crystal clear blue sky, a good sign, surely, and no clouds threatened on the horizon. The smell of oak blossoms hung in the air.

A shiny two-seat phaeton clattered to a halt in front of the townhouse. Neave swung down nonchalantly, not waiting for a footman to appear. He ran his fingers through his locks, and pulled down his waistcoat. Apparently satisfied that his appearance was adequate, he strolled towards the townhouse.

She moved away from the window. After all, it was hardly appropriate for him to discover her watching him.

Julia received Neave very properly in the drawing-room with Lady Bullfinch present, a major feat in itself. She refused initially, saying she did not believe in such nonsense. If she couldn't trust her own granddaughter for a few minutes alone in the drawing-room with a gentleman, then she had no business letting Julia go anywhere. Julia had finally convinced her that it was not a matter of trust, but a matter of appearances.

'He might get the wrong idea,' said Julia.

Gran snorted, but agreed to act as chaperon.

Now, however, Julia was faced with a new problem.

'But how is my maid to accompany us when it is a two-seat carriage?' said Julia.

'I believe it is perfectly proper to drive in Hyde Park in a high perch open carriage,' replied Neave. 'Now a closed carriage would be a different matter,' he said, with a smile. The dimples in his cheeks emphasized his boyish appearance. He turned to her grandmother. 'However, if Lady Bullfinch finds the idea objectionable, I will accept her judgment.'

Grannie would not object to such an outing any more than she would object to finding Julia rolling on the floor with a gentleman with half her clothes missing. She frequently recounted stories of her own youth when she had indulged in precisely such liberties.

Julia sighed and looked at her.

'I suppose' — said Lady Bullfinch, at her most arrogant — 'I suppose that I will give my consent. Though I can't say I like these newfangled high perch phaetons. I am convinced they cannot possibly stay upright.

How anyone manages to control them I cannot understand. And I can't help but think that anyone who chooses to drive them is rather reckless.'

'I assure you, Lady Bullfinch, one cannot be reckless driving at the fashionable hour in Hyde Park. It is far too crowded. And the phaetons are quite safe.' When she did not object further, he rose and bowed. 'Thank you, Lady Bullfinch, for granting your permission.' He smiled and kissed her hand gracefully. Then he extended his elbow to Julia. 'Miss Swifton. Are you ready?'

She had thought her grandmother facetious when she talked about the high perch phaetons, but as they set into motion, she realized there was something reckless about them.

'I must confess,' she said, enjoying the sensation, 'I've never ridden so high off the ground before. I suppose riding on the box of a post must be the only similar thing.'

Captain Neave threw her a quick smile, then returned to the delicate task of manoeuvring the team through the thronging street. She studied his gloved hands as he handled the horses. His technique was good, though perhaps rather careless. 'I'm delighted to be the first to provide you with such an experience,' said Neave. 'I hope you're not one of those giddy ladies who are afraid of heights.'

'Not at all,' she said. 'In fact, you'd better not get me too used to riding a high perch, or I'll be asking for a turn with the ribbons before you know it.'

'I'd be delighted to tutor you,' he said, casting her an admiring look. 'I like a lady with spirit.'

'I'm thought quite skilled with a four-in-hand,' she said. 'Our coachman Evans was much admired in his youth for his skill. When I was eight I kept begging him to teach me his technique. He refused for a while, but I was so persistent he eventually agreed. I've driven a two-horse phaeton, but I'm afraid my grandmother won't approve of me buying a high perch.'

'Understandably,' said Captain Neave. 'I'm sure she's concerned for your safety.'

'Well, she needn't be. I never take on something I can't handle.'

As they reached the park, three gentlemen-about-town came riding up to them. Although they were in their late twenties, similar in age to Captain Neave, all three of them were dressed as the Pinkest of Pinks, their clothes conspicuously fashionable, their collars riding high up their cheeks, and their cravats puffed out in front of them like whipped cream. They surrounded the phaeton. One of them, a tall man with icy, sky-blue eyes, heavily pomaded hair, and an elaborate waist coat of bright orange and gold, leered up at Julia, his eyes running down her body and resting on her right ankle, which protruded slightly from under her gown. She quickly tucked the offending ankle away. He noted the gesture and smiled mockingly.

'Nice day for a drive, Neave,' said the one of the gentlemem.

'Yes, indeed,' said her companion, drawing the carriage to a halt. 'I told Marker I'd exercise the horses.'

The three gentlemen examined the horses and gazed admiringly at the phaeton. 'Beautiful steppers,' remarked the ice-eyed man. 'No chance Marker's selling, is there?'

'No chance at all. He's full of juice. Doesn't need to sell.'

Neave made no effort to introduce her to his companions, and, after that initial inspection, and a number of assessing glances cast her way, they ignored her completely.

Julia felt herself left out, and strangely outnumbered. The sensation was uncomfortable, and for some reason she felt unnerved. *You're imagining it,* she told herself firmly. They were in the middle of Hyde Park, surrounded by people, and it was broad daylight.

Eventually, they began to move away, and she breathed a sigh of relief.

'Don't forget,' said the ice-eyed man. 'You have two weeks.'

'I'm hardly likely to, since you keep reminding me,' said Neave, cheerfully.

But as they rode away he watched them. He did not move the phaeton immediately. Instead he sat slumped a little in his seat, his hands twisting and turning the reins, oblivious to his surroundings.

'A penny for your thoughts,' said Julia.

He looked up immediately. For a moment, she thought she saw despair in his eyes. Then, as he registered her presence, he smiled. 'I beg your pardon. I was wool-gathering.'

Whatever he had been pondering was far from wool-gathering. But it was not her concern, after all.

'What would we do without wool-gathering?' she said. She sounded too bright, too brittle. Strange. Nothing had occurred, yet something undefined had changed between them.

He threw her a sidelong glance, then

focused his attention on the horses. He watched them for a while in silence as they moved, then seemed to reach a conclusion.

'May I confide in you?' he asked.

He must be in dire straits if he needs to confide in me. He scarcely knows me.

'Certainly,' said Julia, sitting up straight and preparing to listen.

'I know we are still little more than strangers, but from the moment I met you I felt an affinity with you, as if I have known you all my life. I feel somehow that I can trust you.'

She nodded. She understood the sensation. She had experienced it herself. 'Of course,' she said. 'You can be sure that nothing you say will go further than this carriage.'

'Thank you,' he said, pressing her hand briefly in gratitude. He turned his face away. She thought she saw tears in his eyes.

The hint of tears reached into her and pulled at her heart. 'You *must* tell me what's wrong,' she said, emphatically.

He attempted a weak smile. 'You must be an angel,' he said, 'sent to save me, and I do not deserve it.'

He paused, clearly struggling to put his thoughts together. Then he said, his voice trembling slightly 'My father was a harsh man. I was his only son, but he had certain idea of what a son should be like. I know it's hard to imagine, as a woman, the pressure that a boy can have growing up, but he expected me to be like him — hunting mad, obsessed with outdoor activities, fishing, boxing, fighting all day. I was never physically active. I was an indoor person. I liked to snuggle up near the fire, curl up my legs, and read. My father would have none of it. He forced me to leave the house every morning. If he caught me reading, he would whip me. Hard. I still have the marks on my back.' He looked down at his hands.

Julia exclaimed in horror.

He shook his head. 'I shouldn't be telling you this. I know I shouldn't.' He turned away. 'I've said enough.'

'No,' said Julia. '*Please* go on.'

'Well, the short of it was, I tried my best. I really did try to become the kind of boy my father would like. But I couldn't. I did not enjoy hunting. I did not enjoy fishing. The only thing I excelled in was riding. Fortunately.'

He paused. She waited expectantly as the silence lengthened.

'One day my father decided he had had enough of me. I was a disappointment, you see. So he bought me regimentals and sent me to the Continent. "If anything can teach you to be a man, being a soldier will", he told me.'

Again, a long silence.

'It didn't. I hated the blood. I hated the killing. I could not endure it. But I had no choice. My father cut off my money, every penny of it. I was forced to live on an officer's salary, such as it is.'

Julia knew the salaries were small, though many officers had done very well with prize money once the war was over.

'After the war, I returned to find him still unwilling to receive me, and still unwilling to provide me with funding. I'm lucky enough to have friends who have helped me. And I am still received in society, in spite of my father. I am his heir after all, and he is a viscount with a large fortune,' he said bitterly. 'But meanwhile. . . .'

She felt indignant on his behalf. It was true: society would receive him because of his position. His family was powerful and well established, but without money he could not continue his lifestyle.

It occurred to her suddenly that she could be a solution to his problem, if he married her. Coldness crept into her heart. Was all this a prelude to a proposal?

As if reading her mind, he said, 'I know

the solution to my problem would be to marry into money. Despite my impoverished state, I still have a chance to marry an heiress. But such a thought is abhorrent to me. I can't imagine living my whole life with a wife I do not love, and who does not love me.' He smiled at her, a self-mocking smile. 'Besides, oddly enough, I have my pride.'

The coldness that had gripped her disappeared. Relief flooded through her. He was not a fortune hunter, after all.

'Your feelings do you credit,' she murmured, sincerely.

'You can't imagine how helpful it is to have been able to talk to you this way. Just saying things out loud makes them seem less dire. Already the future looks brighter,' he said. His eyes sought hers. She could read the gratitude in them.

Then his gaze moved from her face to something behind her. He stiffened, and his face turned bland, emotionless.

'Are you well acquainted with Lord Thorwynn?' he asked, his voice formal now.

She started at the name. 'I hardly know him,' she said. 'I met him just yesterday.' Was it only one day ago? It seemed like much longer.

He nodded.

'I know it is not my place to offer suggestions —' Silence.

'Please continue.' He needed encouragement. And she wanted to know more about Lord Thorwynn.

'I would not want you to be hurt. He is a charming man, with easy manners. I admire him in more ways than one. But he has an eye for women. You are too tender-hearted, and I would hate to see him — how shall I put it? — toy with your emotions.'

'I told you before,' she said, smiling. 'I can take care of myself.'

'Indeed you can,' said Neave, smiling as well. 'I am certainly glad to know that you are aware of his inclinations. And I have spoken my conscience.'

'Thank you, Captain Neave,' she said.

'It is I who owe you a debt,' said Neave. 'And please don't call me Captain. Under the circumstances, perhaps you could call me Neave, at least?'

His gaze was earnest, craving acceptance.

'I would be happy to call you Neave.'

He put out his hand to cover hers, thought better of it and drew it back.

When she retired to her room that night, it took her a long time to sleep. Her senses had been awakened, and she tossed about, unable to find a comfortable position to lie in. She fluffed her pillows and rearranged her sheets, but the feather mattress had turned into a bed of pebbles, and she could not find a comfortable position.

Yet she felt more optimistic than she had for a long time. The drive with Neave had been very promising. She no longer felt it would be impossible to find somebody she could marry. If she could find someone like Neave, someone who was not afraid to reveal his inner self. . . .

But later, turbulent dreams roused her. She lay awake in the dark, trying to untangle the threads. She was standing on the grass in Hyde Park, very close to the Serpentine. Neave was in her dream, riding a white horse, though it was spattered with mud. Lord Thorwynn was there too, shouting something urgently to her that she could not hear. He turned and galloped away, his black horse thundering past her.

There was another in her dreams. He was driving a green high perch phaeton. He rode straight towards her. At first she could not see his face. But at the last moment, just before the horses reached her, just before the collision, she saw his face. He was the icy-eyed man who had spoken to Neave.

CHAPTER 6

When Julia woke up the next morning, it was drizzling. Dark angry clouds hung over London, blocking out the light. The darkness had deceived Julia into sleeping until almost noon, something she did very rarely. By the time she descended her grandmother was already taking a light cold luncheon.

'I've been waiting for you to come down,' she said. 'We need to look at the gossip columns again today, just to make sure Lord Thorwynn is out of danger.'

For the next ten minutes, they pored over the pages.

'Nothing, absolutely nothing,' said her ladyship eventually. 'Not a whisper.' She looked pleased, as well she might. Nothing had occurred to disrupt her plans for Julia's marriage.

Little did she know that, now that Julia had met Thorwynn, the idea of marrying him was further from her mind than ever.

'Yes, it does look as if we salvaged the situation.' She *did* feel satisfied that they had beaten the scandalmongers at their game.

'Good.' Granmother put her paper down with a snap. 'Perhaps, in that case, it is about time we visited the infamous Miss Neville.'

It was amazing that a woman like Lady Medlow could have produced the cherub. Her face was small, like her daughter's, but there the resemblance ended.

She seemed especially fond of fur. The shawl draped over her brown morning dress was trimmed with light-brown fur. Her old-fashioned turban, unusually, featured a tail-like strip of brown and black fur. The fur, her sharp teeth and her small round eyes reminded Julia of a weasel she had seen in a book about Canadian trappers.

She and Lady Bullfinch were the only morning callers. Lady Medlow seemed flattered by Lady Bullfinch's visit, and quickly hastened to order refreshment. But her tiny eyes rested critically on Julia, examining her shrewdly. 'I have you to thank for rescuing my Amelia,' she trilled. 'She said you went to great lengths to capture her horse.'

'One can hardly say I rescued her,' replied

Julia, seeing another opportunity to cement her Hyde Park story. 'Lord Thorwynn and I were both at the scene, along with her groom. We were ready to provide assistance if she had been seriously injured. Fortunately, that was not the case. How is she faring?'

'She is completely recovered,' said her mother. 'No doubt due to her youth and agility,' she added. The door opened and the cherub stepped in. 'Here you are, Amelia. Lady Bullfinch has been kind enough to call. She was enquiring about your health.'

'Oh, I am very well recovered, Lady Bullfinch, Miss Swifton,' she said, curtseying politely. 'Just one or two bruises. Nothing to signify.'

Amelia smiled prettily, but the smile did not touch her eyes. She crossed the room and sat next to Julia on the heavy brown velvet sofa. Once the formalities were over, she did not speak. She did not exactly pout, but she looked discontented.

'We are expecting to attend Lady Blackham's ball tonight. Will you be in attendance?' asked Lady Medlow.

'Yes,' said Lady Bullfinch. 'Lady Blackham is a good friend of ours. We would not miss her ball for anything.'

'Good. Then Amelia will have company.' She turned fierce eyes on Julia, daring her to contradict. Julia's eyes turned to Amelia, who shrank into the corner of her chair. 'Of course I will welcome her company,' said Julia, smiling warmly at her.

Amelia did not answer. Lady Medlow frowned. 'Sit up straight, Amelia,' she snapped. 'You're not in the nursery any more. What will people think of you?'

If anything, Amelia shrank back even more. Lady Bullfinch asked Lady Medlow a question, drawing her attention away from the young girl. Julia took the opportunity to start up a different conversation. 'Have you tried the ices at Gunter's?' she asked.

Amelia shook her head.

'Well, then, we'll take you there,' she said. 'Grannie and I are planning to go this very afternoon. Shall we call for you on our way?'

Amelia looked towards her mother, hesitantly. 'You will have to ask Mama. I'm not sure she'll approve.'

She definitely lacked town polish. Normally, Julia was not given to accompanying young debutantes. But with a mother like that, Julia could not help feeling sorry for the cherub.

Meanwhile, it looked like the conversation with Lady Medlow had limped to a halt. Ju-

lia exchanged glances with her grandmother.

'We need to take our leave, Lady Medlow,'
said Grannie, standing. 'We promised to call
on a few of our acquaintances.'

'We would like to call on Amelia later,'
said Julia. 'We're planning to go to Gunter's
for ices.'

Lady Medlow shot her another piercing
glance, this time full of speculation. 'Yes.
Perhaps that would be a very good idea.'

Lionel was not in a good humour. In fact,
his humour was bad enough that he had
forced his valet to change his waistcoat three
times, an unprecedented event, since Lionel
normally trusted his valet's judgement.

His bad humour began the instant he
glimpsed Miss Swifton perched on the shiny
phaeton in Hyde Park, with Neave at her
side.

'Did you see that, Benny?'

Benny watched the phaeton ride out of
sight, his lips pursed grimly. 'We can definitely assume Miss Swifton is his next
victim.'

'Unless he's planning to court her,' said
Lionel.

'Not a chance. His father is sick, I heard,
and not likely to survive until winter. He

doesn't need to shackle himself to an heiress if he's coming into a fortune. Even if his pockets are to let right now.'

Lionel thought he would explode with rage. 'Why am I condemned to witness his villainy and be unable to do anything about it?'

Benny threw him a strange look. 'Don't tell me the Swifton chit has frightened you off?'

'She has forbidden me to meddle in her affairs.'

'You are not meddling in her affairs. This is not really her affair at all. She is, in the scheme of things, completely irrelevant. You are trying to find a way to reveal Neave's real character to the *ton*. Think of this as an opportunity to do so, nothing more.'

'I see no way to uncover Neave without involving Miss Swifton in a scandal.'

'I'm sure if we put our heads together, we'll find a way. A few minutes' reflection should do it.'

Lionel, however, was in no mood for reflection. In fact, he could hardly keep his thoughts straight. The sight of Miss Swifton at that scoundrel's side had thrown reason to the winds. Granted, he did not care for Miss Swifton. Not at all. But Miss Swifton represented all that was honourable in society, while that —'

His horse snorted in protest as his fingers tightened on the bridle.

The responsibility for the situation lay on his head. He was acutely aware of it. Because of him, Miss Swifton had drawn Neave's attention. If it had not been for Miss Swifton's kind willingness to clear his name, Neave would never have had paid her the slightest attention. But Neave had not forgiven him for attempting to instigate an investigation into the Captain's actions during the war. *Even if it had come to nothing.*

And then he had warned her in that tactless manner and brought her hackles up.

An arm held him back as he stepped through the doorway into the brightly lit townhouse.

'For God's sake, Thor! You can't walk into a ballroom with a scowl like that on your face. You look like you're ready to murder somebody.'

'I am ready to murder somebody. I would be very happy to run Neave through with a sword here and now, if that is the only way I can rid the world of his machinations.'

'Unfortunately, you can't. You can't even get away with doing it in a duel, since duels have been inconveniently outlawed. So I'm afraid you're going to have to put on a pleasant face. You're walking into a *ball,* for heaven's sake.'

Which did not improve his humour. He had resolved, after Mrs Wadswith's ball, that he would not grace the *ton* with an appearance for another year at least. Yet here he was, two days later, walking into yet another of those insufferable events arranged for the Marriage Mart. He must have taken leave of his senses.

Devil take it! He could not stand by and let Neave take advantage of Miss Swifton. True, she was not a naive innocent making her first come out into society, but for all her insistence that she could take care of herself, he felt it imperative to protect her against someone of Neave's ilk. He remembered the way she had felt in his arms two nights ago. Eyes closed, she had been moving in a world of her own. It had been difficult to concentrate on the steps of the waltz, with her smiling lips leaning towards him, her round breasts straining through her green gown, her hair glinting close to his face. He had breathed in her elusive scent, rosewater mixed in with something else — something he couldn't recognize but which was unique to her. He wanted nothing more than to run his lips down the side of her neck, then slide them slowly towards those tantalizing mounds, to sink his face into their softness. He compelled himself to keep a distance. To avoid the temptation to use his palm at her back to draw her closer.

No question that she was desirable, though in an unusual way. She was not his type of beauty at all, if beauty he could call it. But that's where her appeal ended. He was not interested in independent women who had no room in their life for men. There were plenty of women who were willing, happy, truth be told, to cast their lots in with him. He had made a cake of himself two days ago when he had tried to tell her about Neave. He had claimed a relationship they did not have. She was not likely to listen to him if he tried yet again to warn her.

But he could not allow her to fall into Neave's hands. And if saving her meant intruding on her independence, so be it. He had no choice in the matter, anymore than she did.

Julia had scarcely entered the ballroom when she was approached by several matrons with young men in tow, wanting to be introduced. She regarded the situation with amusement. She did not know to which of her partners she owed this change in status, but she could think of no other reason. *How ironic, that it is the rakes who have brought me to the attention of the matchmakers, when all the perfectly respectable young gentlemen who had courted me in my first Season did not.* She had never lacked partners at a ball, but among those being presented to her now, she recognized some very distinguished names. She smiled and accepted the attention, all the while wondering if Captain Neave would attend.

Then, as if in response to her wishes, she saw him coming towards her. He approached her with a spring in his step, smiling amiably. There was no trace in his face of the disquiet that had prompted his confidences in the afternoon. He looked simply like a handsome gentleman who found pleasure in her company.

They could not converse properly in a ballroom, surrounded by others who were listening to every word, and he promptly left her to bring some lemonade. Julia sighed. It would be her third glass of lemonade since she arrived. She should have asked for wine, or even champagne.

Neave had barely disappeared into the crowd when Thorwynn bore down on her. Julia stared at him, captivated like a bird staring at a snake. His stride was smooth and elegant, yet he did not seem to move at all, almost as if he lay in wait. She scarcely noticed Lord Benedict, despite his distinctive red hair, loping at Thorwynn's side. Thorwynn's eyes locked into hers, and she could not look away.

Before she knew it, the crowd around her had parted to let him through.

'Good evening, Miss Swifton. I was wondering if you would put me down for a waltz,' he said, his tone brooking no refusal. She lifted her card to look, if only to break the spell of his gaze. At first the letters seemed hopelessly jumbled, as if she'd forgotten how to read. Then letters sorted themselves into words and she was able to locate the empty spaces next to the two waltzes.

'Yes, Lord Thorwynn,' she said, in a voice that managed to sound completely controlled. 'I'd be happy to put your name down.'

'And for the cotillion as well,' he said.

She lifted an eyebrow. He had better not ask her for a third. Even if he did not actually dance with her, it would be all over the ballroom within minutes. A third dance meant that his interest was fixed and he planned to offer for her. It was as good as an engagement.

He didn't ask for a third dance. But in the next instant, Lord Benedict stepped forward and asked for the second waltz. And a second dance.

She laughed. Loudly enough to draw attention to herself from people outside her group. But it was too absurd. Either they were competing for her attention, which was unlikely, or they meant to keep her away from someone else.

That someone else appeared, carrying another glass of lemonade. He managed to break through the circle around her, but she was flanked on both sides by Thorwynn and Benedict.

It would have been funny if it wasn't annoying.

She beamed at Captain Neave, assuring him of her welcome in spite of her boorish companions.

'Thank you,' she said, taking the lemonade, as if he had gifted her a diamond necklace. 'I'm *extremely* thirsty.' But then the lemonade posed a problem. She could not possibly swallow down another glass. She sipped tentatively, managing to cast Neave a warm look over the rim.

He was ill at ease. He was not much smaller than the two men beside him, but he seemed to contract beside them. Their attitude was decidedly menacing. Julia wanted badly to kick them in the shins and tell them to leave her alone. But of course she could not. Not in the middle of the ballroom, surrounded by suitors. It would hardly be ladylike. But perhaps an opportunity would arise later.

Meanwhile, she was cornered. Her smile grew stale as she found herself at an impasse. She could not even glare at them without drawing attention. She prayed for the orchestra to start up quickly. But in the interim, there was nothing to do but chatter.

So, rather than escalate the hostilities, she launched into a monologue. She chose the first topic that sprung to mind.

'It's a pity,' she said, 'that they do not allow ladies into the Four-Horse Club.' There were shocked gasps from the matrons, and one or two laughs from the gentlemen. Not a good choice of topic, perhaps. 'You only have to look around Hyde Park. There are several skilled ladies who drive a barouche and four bays, and for as long as they've been doing it, they've never met with an accident.' There were mutters and murmurs. 'Though I'm not sure I'd like to drive a yellow barouche, which is a requirement of the club.' Some more gasps. Half the gentlemen of the *ton* aspired to drive the yellow barouche that signalled their membership. Those gentlemen who didn't, drove too badly to even dream of it. 'And the rosettes at the head of the horses seem insipid.' She had not set out to shock anybody, but some perverse part of her was determined to do so. A great chasm yawned before her, and she was heading straight towards it. She was sure, before the evening ended, she would be labelled an Eccentric, like her grandmother.

'Perhaps,' said Thorwynn, who was himself a member of the club, 'we can set up a test for those ladies who think themselves skilled enough,' he said, amused. 'And arrange a ladies' branch of the club.'

She examined him suspiciously. Unable to determine whether he was mocking her or supporting her, she resorted to silence.

His statement generated some excitement among the younger bucks. Several of them turned to each other and began to wager on the possibility of any lady being skilled enough to pass.

Just then the orchestra struck its first discordant notes, indicating that they were tuning up and that the dancing would commence soon. Perhaps she would survive the night after all. Salvation was in sight. She peered at her card to see who had claimed her for the first dance, and found the space was empty.

'Allow me to lead you to the dance floor,' said Neave. 'I believe this is my dance.'

She took his hand gratefully, wanting nothing more than to get away from Thorwynn's dark presence.

He was waiting for her as the dance finished. In fact, everywhere she went, all she had to do was turn, and he would be there, waiting.

People were beginning to notice.

She certainly noticed. It irritated her at first. Then it aggravated her. Then it infuriated her.

Finally, incensed, she was goaded into action. She stalked over to where he was standing, trying to appear calm and unconcerned, in case anyone was watching. He was leaning against a wall, pretending to be engrossed in watching a group of young ladies whispering together.

'They're going to bring their mamas over any moment if you persist in singling them out for attention this way,' she said, trying not to sound as prickly as she felt.

He turned to her immediately;. 'Heaven forbid,' he said, lazily, pushing himself away from the wall and standing straight. She expected him to be drinking, but there was no sign of a glass anywhere close. 'But I'm glad you have decided to seek me out.' He smiled, that slow swaggering smile of his that brought an immediate frown to her face.

'I came to seek you out for one reason, and one reason only,' she snapped. 'I wanted to inform you' — she paused, wondering how she could say this politely — 'I would prefer you to keep your distance.' It was very inadequate, considering how furious she felt, but she hoped it was clear enough, at any rate.

'You came all the way across the ballroom to tell me I have to keep my distance?' he said, tweaking an eyebrow.

Subtlety was clearly not his *forte.* She needed a more direct approach.

'I came across the ballroom because I find gentlemen who stand and glower at young ladies in a ballroom very unpleasant. I am asking you to stop watching me. I told you before, and I'll tell you again, I can take care of myself. I do not need a guardian, and I certainly don't need an earl who is in his cups watching over me. So please stop, or I will be forced to speak to my grand-mother, who is, incidentally, my real guardian.'

He stiffened, the smile sliding off his face. The muscles of his face tightened until they became a mask.

'I'm sorry if I have offended you in any way,' he said coldly. 'It was not my intention. My intentions have been solely to make sure you do not come to any harm. You have made your feelings on the matter very clear.' He bowed rigidly. 'Please give my greetings to your grandmother. I hope you will excuse me. I have another engagement to attend.'

He walked off, leaving Julia to reconcile a range of conflicting feelings.

Her first impulse was to run after him and apologize. She should not have been so adamant. She should have waited until she was calmer to speak to him.

A moment later indignation replaced the guilt. How dare he walk off like that, making it appear to anyone observing them that he had snubbed her?

Then she felt pleased with herself. She wanted him to leave, and she had accomplished what she had set out to do. He had left.

Then as a young gentleman approached her to claim the next dance, a strong resolve gripped her.

She would not allow any man, whoever he may be, to control how she lived her life.

CHAPTER 7

An enormous bouquet of blue, white and yellow irises decorated the hallway.

'These came for you earlier this morning, Miss Julia,' said the butler, his face relaxing into a slight smile.

She smiled back affectionately. She had known him since she was three, when she used to beg him to give her rides on his back. 'Thank you, Rumbert,' she said.

Neave must have sent them. She buried her face among them, allowing their perfume to envelop her. It was just like him, to pick something that brought the bright spring weather indoors to her. She picked them up and gazed at the curling petals, at the wonderful contrast of colours.

A card emerged between the flowers. She plucked it out eagerly, wondering what he could have written.

He had chosen a simple card. The writing was strong, the letters clear and sharp.

Dear Miss Swifton

My sincerest apologies for my behaviour yesterday. I realize that I have been an interfering oaf. I would like to make amends. Would you care to ride in the park with me this afternoon?

Sincerely
Thorwynn

Her heart missed a beat at the signature, then settled into rapid, angry pounding.

Did he really think a bunch of flowers was going to mollify her? The only thing that would mollify her was if he stopped interfering in her life.

To add insult to injury, he expects me to go riding with him.

She ran up the stairs to the parlour. Grannie was there, reading *Confessions* by Rousseau.

'Grannie,' she said, interrupting. 'you're always consulting the various dictionaries of flowers. What do irises generally mean?'

Lady Bullfinch balanced her book carefully on her lap, keeping the pages open. 'It can mean several things. The French monarchy, of course, but you're not interested in that. The petals are supposed to stand for faith, valour, and wisdom. And it is named after the Greek goddess of the rainbow. Iris was the gods' messenger, so it often means a message or even a warning.'

A warning. That was it. The flowers were a warning. *Again.*

'Thank you.'

'But sometimes,' she called, as Julia left the room, 'a flower is just that — a flower. Don't go reading meanings into them that they don't have. Anyway, look in the dictionary.'

Everyone knew that flowers had meanings. When everybody was poring over Mme de la Tour's *Language of Flowers,* how could they not?

She strode upstairs to her chamber. There she headed for the mahogany escritoire and sat with a thump, striking her knee against it. The pain only fuelled her indignation. She dipped the quill into the ink pot.

Dear Thorwynn
I would like to know if you are deliberately trying to raise my ire.

No, that was too forward. Besides, it was unlikely he was deliberately trying to anger her. He was simply obtuse.

She tore the page into tiny bits and threw it away.

Dear Thorwynn
I found the flowers and invitation offensive.
Do you think me a giddy green girl to be
distracted by such an obvious ruse?

Again, this would not do. It was extremely
bad form to quarrel with a gentleman on
paper. She crumpled it and tossed it in the
basket.

She took a deep breath, calmed herself
and started again.

Dear Thorwynn
Thank you for your kind invitation. Unfortunately, I must decline, since I have a prior
engagement.

Sincerely
Julia Swifton

She looked it over, dissatisfied. It conveyed
nothing of her anger. But it would have to
do. She could hardly send an incensed note
to someone who had sent her flowers and
invited her for a ride in the park. At least
she had the satisfaction of turning him
down.

To make sure she would not be home if
he ignored her message and called, she sent
a note round to Miss Amelia Neville, asking
if she would like to join her for a ride in

Hyde Park.

Since she arrived first, Julia had the chance to observe Miss Neville on her horse. She had a very good seat, her body straight and at ease in the side-saddle. She chided herself for making assumptions. *Just because her horse bolted, it doesn't make her a clumsy rider.* Her groom followed closely behind her.

The girl's face brightened when she spotted her.

'It was really very *kind* of you to ask me to ride with you,' she said, with emotion. 'You didn't have to. You *already* asked me to accompany you to Gunter's, which was such a *treat.* I never *dreamed* ice cream could come in so many flavours.'

Julia wondered that such a common thing should affect her. 'Don't you have any friends in London you can ride with?'

Amelia shook her head. 'I don't know *anyone* in London. I've never been here before, and Mother hasn't introduced me to anyone my age.' A wistful expression settled over her features. 'I would so like to go around London with some friends of my own. But Mother says I should focus my attention on finding a husband first, and that once I'm married I can explore London to my heart's content. I suppose she knows what's best for me.'

Julia had no doubt the last remark was a quote from Lady Medlow, but refrained from saying so.

'Perhaps. But I am a single lady, and I have explored every corner of London with friends.'

'It's different for you,' she said. 'There is some freedom to being an old maid.' Realizing what she had said, Amelia raised her hand to her mouth, her skin flushing purple.

'I didn't mean — oh, I *didn't* mean to say — don't think — It's just that Mother said —'

The remark jolted Julia. But she quickly realized that the idea did not originate from Amelia herself but from her mother. She smiled reassuringly at the flustered girl.

'Don't worry, I haven't taken offence. It seems your mother has used me as an example of what happens to girls who break the rules.'

Amelia bowed her head. 'I don't wish to speak badly of Mother,' she answered, her voice weak. 'Only she really doesn't *understand* what it's like to be a young girl in her first Season. She has very strict notions, and she is determined I should make a good match. I *know* it's very important, but still,

I *wish* things were otherwise.'

Julia was not sure what to say. She did not want to encourage the young lady to defy her mother, but she could not encourage her to simply obey her mother blindly, either. 'I'm surprised she allowed you to come riding with me,' said Julia.

A small blush crept into Amelia's cheeks. 'She did not know you were meeting me here. She was away when your note arrived. She thinks I am merely exercising my horse.'

A show of spirit, at least. Perhaps there was more to Miss Neville than met the eye.

'Well, in that case, let's take advantage of your respite. Shall we leave the crowds behind, and have a little gallop?'

To her credit, Amelia only hesitated for the briefest moment. Then her eyes glittered with mischief, and she nodded breathlessly.

Julia revised her opinion. *She's a mischievous imp, not a cherub at all.*

Julia left Rotten Row, with Amelia by her side, and the groom following close. They rode at a sedate trot until they reached some large oaks that would hide them from the main path. Immediately, Julia set Hamlet into a gallop. A quick glance behind told her Amelia followed. And behind her, the groom.

In the afternoon, at the fashionable hour,

one did not expect to allow one's horse free rein. But, with some care, one could gallop very fast indeed.

Lionel took a deep sip of his second glass of brandy. Lady Bullfinch and her daughter, Lady Talbrook, were charming, but their company was wearing thin. It was Miss Swifton he had come to visit, not them.

'The Duke of Sherhold really liked your mother, you know,' said Lady Bullfinch. 'He almost proposed. But his father had other ideas for him.' She paused, lost in reflection. 'Too bad, she might have been a duchess.'

'Not that it would have been desirable for Lord Thorwynn,' said Lady Tolbrook, sending him an understanding glance.

He chuckled. 'Definitely not desirable. I'm sorry my mother lost her chance to be a duchess, but with my very existence at stake, you can hardly expect me to be very sympathetic.'

Lady Bullfinch shrugged. 'You would not have known of your loss.' Her expression was grave, but her eyes twinkled. For a brief moment, she reminded him of Miss Swifton.

He wished she was Miss Swifton. He liked Lady Bullfinch's direct ways, but he had not come to visit her, after all.

The door opened, and Miss Swifton stepped in. He stood. She wore a honey-coloured riding dress, cut in military style. She had clearly returned from a ride — in Hyde Park, undoubtedly. Her eyes sparkled with the exercise, her cheeks were ruddy, and long tendrils of hair toppled down on to her face. All in all she had the look of a woman who had experienced an exhilarating interlude. He wondered if she would look like that after he had bedded her.

He stifled the image as quickly as it popped up. He had called on her only because he was trying to rescue her from a villain's intentions. What the devil was he doing thinking of her in his bed?

He distracted himself by speculating whether she rode alone or in company. It was unlikely that she had ridden alone at the fashionable hour. Most likely she had a companion. He felt a sudden twinge as he thought of her riding with some young gentleman, one of her admirers. He restrained the impulse to ask her with whom she had been.

Then it occurred to him that she might have ridden with Neave. The image of them trotting through the park, conversing and laughing, threw him into a rage. While he sat and exchanged *on-dits* with her relations, she was blithely doing exactly what he was trying to prevent. He gritted his teeth.

He realized that she was standing in front of him, and he was practically growling at her.

'Lord Thorwynn?'

'I'm sorry,' he replied, not having heard a word she said. 'I'm afraid I did not hear you.' He sounded very brusque. That would not do at all.

'I simply said that it was an unexpected pleasure.'

'Hardly unexpected, since I sent you notice that I would call.'

Her eyebrows came together in a frown. 'You did not receive my note? I sent a reply immediately.'

He had received it, of course, and ignored it, but she was offering him a way to explain his presence, so he took it.

'I left home early this morning to take care of business, and I have not been back since.'

One auburn eyebrow flicked up, but she said nothing to contradict him. He had a distinct feeling that she did not believe him.

'Pray take a seat, Lord Thorwynn,' she said. 'If you will give me just a minute, I will rejoin you. I don't wish to sit in the parlour smelling of horses.'

'You could never smell of horses,' he said gallantly. He could have kicked himself in the next moment when she raised yet another eyebrow. Well, there was no rescuing the situation. Might as was well just grin and bear it.

He grinned. 'I meant,' he said, laying his cards on the table and hoping she would be willing to let it pass, 'that a fresh outdoor horse smell never hurt anyone.'

Her mouth twitched, and a small spark lit up her eyes. 'Indeed? Would you care to wager on my chances if I attended a ball smelling of horses?'

'In my days,' said Lady Bullfinch, intervening, 'no one bothered with baths. They were thought unhealthy. And they were, since it was nearly impossible to find clean water anywhere near London. I remember my parents telling me that when Queen Caroline decided to set aside a special room for a bath tub, and proceeded to bathe once a week, she was thought extremely odd. Of course, even she, daring as she was, bathed with the protection of a linen shift.'

The expression on Lady Talbrook's face left no doubt as to her opinion on that matter.

Lady Bullfinch laughed. 'We did use more perfumes than people do these days. I could say, in fact, that we washed ourselves in cologne,' she said. 'But I admit bathing is much more pleasant.'

'Well, I would not give up my baths for anything,' said Julia.

The vision of Miss Swifton naked in her bath intruded in his mind. He followed her every move as she soaped herself languidly.

They had all turned to him, waiting for an answer. To what? What had they asked?

'I,' he said, 'I agree.' What was happening to him? Perhaps it was time to pay a visit to the Golden Widow. It had been a while since their last frolic.

'Since the general opinion seems to be that I need not change, I'll remain downstairs.' She settled down on a settee, as far away, Lionel noted, as she could possibly be from him.

Now that he had her attention, he realized, he did not know what to say to her. Confound it! He had only one thing to say. He wanted her to stay away from Neave. But that was the very thing he *couldn't* tell her. It occurred to him that he should have appealed to her grandmother for help while he had the chance.

Meanwhile, while he waited for her, she had been out with Neave. Ridiculous was hardly the word. He had been on a fool's errand, and he had accomplished nothing.

Irritation flared up and grabbed him by the throat.

He really had nothing to say, and he had stayed long past the time acceptable for a social call. Throwing a quick glance at the dragon-footed mantel clock, he came to his feet.

'I hadn't realized it was so late,' he said, smiling smoothly at the elder ladies. 'It was a pleasure talking to you.' He turned to Miss Swifton. 'I promised to meet Lord Benedict at Brooks's.'

For the third time in just a few minutes, Miss Swifton raised her eyebrow. The gesture annoyed him. Even if it was a good sign. It showed that she was not easily deceived.

CHAPTER 8

The London Season was in full swing, and Julia kept busy. The Grosvenor Square house received a new stream of visitors. Mamas and grandmamas wished to reacquaint themselves with their dear friend Lady Bullfinch — and to remind her that their sons were eligible bachelors. Gentlemen callers arrived with bouquets and poems. There was even one marriage proposal, which her ladyship declined. Julia only discovered this after the fact, when she spoke to her about it over breakfast.

'You aren't interested in Mr Eckles, by any chance, are you?' she asked, putting her blue china teacup down with a clatter and eyeing her doubtfully.

'No, of course not,' said Julia.

'That settles it, then,' said her ladyship. She immediately launched into another topic of conversation, something about a new exhibit at the Egyptian Hall.

'Wait,' said Julia, breaking in before the force of the torrent carried her away. 'Why did you ask about Mr Eckles?'

Lady Bullfinch turned her hands over and examined the palms closely. 'If you must know,' she said, 'the fool offered for you.'

It was Julia's turn to put down her teacup, very slowly. 'I gather you turned him down?'

'Naturally.'

'I would be grateful if you would consult with me first, before declining anyone else. I needn't remind you that I have the right to make my own choices.'

'Of course I know that,' said her grand-mother. 'I was just trying to spare you un-necessary embarrassment.'

I'm tired of everyone wanting to spare me something or the other. Why did she always find herself saying the same thing? Did she really appear so fragile?

'I know you are acting with the best of intentions, but I would rather deal with any awkward proposals myself. Surely you think me capable of that?'

The old lady sat perfectly still, her eyes fixed on Julia.

Julia sighed. 'It's nothing that can't be mended,' said Julia. She smiled as she thought of Mr Eckles and his curly-coated retriever. 'I'm glad you got rid of poor Mr

Eckles. He's convinced I want to know everything about his breeding programme.'

'I hope not,' said her ladyship, blandly.

Julia chuckled as she caught her meaning, for once not feeling embarrassed. 'Not his personal one,' she said, playfully, 'just his dogs.' He was not a bad person. Simply a bore. 'I hope he manages to find a wife who *is* interested. For her sake, at least.'

Lord Neave was among the callers. His visit was formal, and he did not stay beyond the requisite twenty minutes. During that time he offered to escort her to the shops to buy material for her new riding habit. This time he arrived in a barouche with matching greys, and they set out accompanied by Julia's maid. Before long he had convinced her to buy any number of fripperies — new lace, a green ribbon which he insisted matched her eyes, and a new bonnet trimmed in lavender. Julia was amazed at his involvement in her purchases.

'Very few gentlemen will spend the time to advise a lady what to buy. Most gentlemen would be consumed by boredom at the sight of the first ribbons.'

'But you must know by now, Miss Swifton, that I am interested in most things that interest you. You have a lively mind, and turn the dreariest shopping expedition into' — he searched for a word — 'a picnic.'

'La, Lord Neave,' she replied, 'now you are being a flatterer, and you know I dislike it.'

'Then I'll cease immediately.'

His light-hearted mood resonated with hers, and she was more inclined than ever to view him favourably. True, he flirted a great deal, but that was only to be expected. She did not take his remarks seriously, but enjoyed them in the spirit that they were meant.

Lord Benedict called on her, too, one morning, and since he was a solitary caller, he and Lady Bullfinch spent a pleasant twenty minutes discussing gardening, a topic obviously familiar to him. His older sister Emily had forced him as a boy to spend many hours helping her with pruning and picking flowers, and he proved to be quite knowledgeable.

'I was only twelve, and never thought of saying no to her. Then one day my father caught me at it and my poor sister was at the receiving end of his wrath. At that time I was happy enough to abandon the thorns and nettles to her, so I strutted away with my father. But later I would watch her from the window and wish I could join her.'

Of Lord Thorwynn there was no sign. *Perhaps I have finally succeeded in driving him away.* The irises wilted, and had to be thrown away. *Good riddance.* She had many other, sweeter smelling flowers.

Lionel leaned against the wall at the Kinleighs' townhouse, concealed by a gigantic terracotta pot with a squat palm tree growing out of it. Not for the first time that evening, he swore. If it was not for that Swifton hoyden, he would be dining comfortably in Brooks's, before setting out for a night of far more pleasurable activity than escaping scheming matrons. By showing up several times at society balls, he had sent the wrong message. Every mother with an eligible daughter descended upon him the moment he arrived.

Of course, the real question that hammered at him was why on earth he couldn't leave well enough alone?

True, Neave needed to be brought to justice, and the *ton* needed to know the truth about him. But why had he taken it upon himself to pursue him, when he had already failed before? And when Miss Swifton had made it perfectly clear she did not appreciate his attempts?

The sound of his name broke into his

reflections. A footman waited a few steps away, with a folded note on a silver salver. Lionel took the paper and glanced down at the writing. His name was scribbled on the front, in a hurried, almost unintelligible hand.

He dismissed the footman and opened the letter. The scrawl inside, if possible, was even worse. Someone in a great hurry had penned it.

Lord Thorwynn
Forgive me these hasty lines, but I need to speak to you urgently. Something serious has come up. I need your help. I will wait for you in the library.

It was unsigned. He prided himself on remembering people's handwriting, and he had not encountered this writing before.

He crushed it into a ball and tossed it on to a tray with empty glasses. It must be from some unknown married lady, bored with her husband and looking for some adventure.

Neave could wait. At least for the moment. He was more than glad to abandon the boredom of the ballroom.

Similar situations had happened before. He liked it when the lady took the first step

— the element of surprise heightened the pleasure. As long as it was a pleasant surprise, of course. However it turned out, the prospect of some new amusement would compensate for being forced to attend these endless balls.

He drained his glass and added it to the tray. With a spring in his step, he headed for his rendezvous.

He was not one to disappoint a lady.

Julia knew it was unwise to go out into the darkness of the garden, but she had to breathe some fresh air or she would explode. One of the reasons she had given up going to balls was the crush. She disliked being in a room with so many people pressed together. In the larger townhouses that had formal ballrooms, there was always some corner where one could escape. But tonight the only empty corner was behind a palm tree, and that was occupied by Lord Thorwynn.

Not a trace of moonlight lightened the shadows. The only illumination came from inside the windows. She did not want to be seen, outlined against the house, so she turned and took a path that led her just out of the light. She did not go far. She simply wanted a private moment to breathe away from the din of the ball. She stood under a tree, leaning her arm carefully against the bark and removing her silk slippers to stretch her cramped toes.

She let the darkness enfold her. The sweet aroma of jasmine wafted towards her, and she drank in the scent, relishing the gentle warmth of the May night.

But not for long. Men's voices moved towards her. Quickly, she withdrew behind a hedge, into the darker shadows. She crouched a little, hoping her head would not show above it. She could not risk an encounter with a group of strange men, especially if they were in their cups. Most likely they would be, if they were frolicking in the garden in the dark.

She expected them to continue past the bush back to the ballroom. Instead, they stopped just a few feet away. Her heart beat faster. Had they seen her hiding? She waited, scarcely breathing, the rush of blood pounding in her ears.

Then someone spoke. The familiar voice startled her. He was so close she expected him to reach into the bushes and take hold of her arm. Relief flooded through her and she started to step out.

'I promise you, she's mine.' Something in the way he spoke was different. His voice had a hard edge to it that stopped her in her tracks. She kept very still, waiting for him to finish before revealing her presence. 'I have her exactly where I want her. I'll bring her outside tonight, and you'll witness the event.'

One of the men sniggered. 'I for one wouldn't mind watching.' She could not mistake the ice-eyed man they had met in Hyde Park. He had hardly spoken, but she would know that voice anywhere. 'She's a tasty morsel. Perhaps she'll consent to have me after you're done with her.'

Neave hissed. 'You must remember, we're not talking about a common whore. This one's a lady.'

'Not after you've finished with her,' said a third man. Appreciative male laughter followed.

'Remember that my goal isn't to ruin her. The wager only specified that I would bed her, with you as witnesses. Nothing more,' said Neave.

'Getting cold feet, are you?' sneered the ice man. 'You're running out of time. If you want to win that wager, you had better move tonight.'

'The agreement stipulated two weeks. I still have three days, according to the wager.'

'We can't keep following you wherever you

136

go in case you manage to lift her skirts. We're here tonight, so this is your chance, win or lose.'

'Better get back to the ballroom, then,' said the third man. 'I need a few drinks if I'm to skulk in the bushes waiting for you to deliver the goods.'

'I for one am not intending to get foxed,' said another man, beginning to move away. 'I don't intend to ruin the sport by stumbling about in the dark. Might interrupt something.' Some more laughter followed.

Their voices grew dimmer. She did not move. She had not heard Neave's voice as they moved away, and she was afraid he had stayed behind, that he had caught sight of her. Her mouth felt dry, but she didn't want to swallow. She scarcely dared to breathe.

Nothing happened. Only silence on the other side of the bush. She tried to peer through the gaps in the branches, but she could see nothing.

She waited, stomach twisting into coils, heart like a clock gone wild. He would have to move first. She would not give him the satisfaction of stepping out.

Time lengthened. She had no idea how long she stood behind that hedge. Eventually she began to realize that if he wanted he could have seized her and pulled her out.

He did not need to wait for her to come out.

Her heart resumed its normal speed, and the pain in her stomach receded. She discovered she had crushed a handful of leaves in her hand, their bitter odour filling her nose. No doubt her gloves would be stained. She tried to slide soundlessly from her hiding place, but her muscles refused to obey. She crashed into the side of the bush and stepped out, watching for any movement. There was no-one around. She lifted her gown and darted back to the French doors of the ballroom.

The clamour and the heat hit her as she stepped inside, but she did not feel safer. She imagined Neave and his friends watching her, closing in. Scores of faces rose up in front of her and they all looked the same. She was afraid any moment Neave would come up to her and ask her to dance. She could not have faced him, not without giving herself away.

She escaped to the ladies' retiring room. There, perhaps, she could recover some of her calm. Enough at least to walk over to her grandmother and tell her she needed to go home.

But, too flustered to notice her direction, she went too far, or took the wrong turn.

She imagined Neave following her. She hurried down the dim corridor, looking frantically for the door. The fall of footsteps sounded behind her. She turned round the corner and threw open the first door she found. She entered and shut it quietly behind her.

She started to tremble. She didn't think she could stop. Their words had not fully registered until this moment. At first she thought they could not be talking about her, but then she remembered she had met Neave exactly ten days ago. It could not have been someone else.

After that, she had been too intent on getting inside safely to think about it. But now the whole scene flashed before her. She realized she was fortunate to have escaped. Only that reckless desire for fresh air had saved her.

She wondered if he would have succeeded. Would she have gone with him into the garden alone? She did not know. Perhaps he might have drawn her out by claiming the need to confide to her. She would have accompanied him, if he had done so.

She thought of all those things he had told her. About his father. About the army. All lies, all meant only to engage her sympathy. She should have known that someone with such a dark past could not move through life so lightly, laughter in every step.

She ran shaking fingers over her face. She was disturbed, true, but after all, she had escaped. She did not know to what lengths he would go to win the wager, but she would take every precaution. He only had three days. And if he planned to abduct her, he would not find her unprepared.

She grew calmer. She took a deep shuddering breath and looked around her.

She was alone in the library. Fool that she was. Planning precautions yet standing there like a sitting duck. She turned quickly, anxious to join the crowds in the ballroom. There was safety in numbers, after all.

Then the door handle began to move. Slowly.

She whirled around to find a place to hide. Her gaze fell on the curtains and she darted behind them. If they moved, of course, he would find her. But the library was poorly lit, and perhaps he had not actually seen her come in. If he was just searching for her without being certain, he might see an empty room and leave.

Someone grabbed the curtains and pulled them away violently.

She clutched them close, struggling to maintain her grip.

He tried to pull the curtains again; she continued to grip them. He let go, giving up on wrestling them from her.

Instead, his hands began to wander over her body, touching her through the curtains. She squirmed, trying to dodge those probing hands.

It took her some time to realize that his hands were not violent.

The person in front of the curtains was *tickling* her.

It could not be Neave unless he was using some strange method she did not know to subdue her.

She threw the curtains back, bracing herself.

And came face to face with a grinning Thorwynn.

CHAPTER 9

She stared at him in shock. This day was quickly becoming a succession of nightmares.

'You?' she said.

His mouth fell open. *'You?'* He made no move to approach her. In fact he took a giant step backwards.

'Yes, it's me. Who did you think I was?' she said.

He opened his mouth to reply then shut it again. 'Never mind.'

Relief flooded into her. He was not Neave, and he did not mean to attack her. She headed for the closest settee and collapsed on to it. The seat was harder than she expected, and it jarred her back.

She sat up straight, waiting for the pain to subside.

Thorwynn took a seat opposite her, regarding her soberly. 'Perhaps you'd care to tell me what this is all about?' he said.

'Why do you think there's something to tell?' she asked. She could not endure the humiliation of telling him, on top of everything else.

'Do you usually hide behind curtains in the library when there is a ball in progress?'

'Ah. Yes. The curtains.' She struggled to find some explanation. 'I lost a pin. I was searching for it.'

'Really?' he said.

'Really,' she replied, injecting her voice with conviction.

'You lost your pin behind the curtains,' he said, perfectly blandly.

He stared at her. His unmoving gaze made it impossible for her to remain still. She brought a fingernail to her mouth to bite it, remembered she was wearing gloves, and dropped her hand. It flopped into her lap. In an effort to look unperturbed, she perched her hand on the arm of the sofa. The curved wood dug into her and she shifted again.

Still he watched.

'Well?' he asked.

She could not possibly tell him what had happened. Especially when he had warned her about Neave's nature. Especially *because* he had warned her. And she had rejected his advice so rudely. He would sneer at her and enjoy every moment of her discomfort. He would tell his friend Lord Benedict about it. They would gloat together, and her loss of face would be complete.

Then she remembered Neave and his companions. She heard the ice-eyed man's voice floating to her in the darkness. She shuddered.

Thorwynn's bland gaze changed to concern.

'Are you cold? Perhaps you are on the verge of falling sick. Would you like me to give you my coat?'

She was shivering, but not from cold. He took her silence as an answer and moved next to her on the settee, stripping down to his waistcoat and wrapping her in his coat. It still held the warmth of his body. It encircled her and gave her some comfort.

'Would you like me to send for your carriage?'

She thought of the townhouse, plunged into darkness, with just a few candles. The servants would be asleep. And she would be alone.

'No,' she said. 'No. I need to stay here.'

'But if you have a fever —'

'I do not have a fever,' she said, clenching her teeth.

144

'That's more like it,' he said, grinning.

He had a pleasant grin. She had never thought of grins as kind, but this one radiated reassurance. She felt her body relax, and the shivering subside.

She decided abruptly that, even if he mocked her, she would tell him.

The mahogany clock boomed, indicating midnight. The night was just beginning.

She took a steadying breath, and braced herself. Her ribs pressed inwards, blocking her breath. She lacked the courage to speak.

But she owed it to him, after the way she had treated him. After she had refused to listen.

She could not look at him while she spoke. So she centred her gaze on her hands, examining the lines that crisscrossed her palms. She did not want to see his face when he found out.

'You were right about Neave.'

'Ah,' he said.

There was a touch of triumph in his voice. But she ploughed on. 'I was lucky enough to overhear a conversation he had with some companions of his,' she said. 'Apparently he has an agreement with his friends, a wager.' She paused, not sure how to express it. Heat rushed up through her face to the very roots of her hair, and her cheeks positively glowed.

145

'He was to' — she tripped over the words, even now — 'seduce me by next Thursday, in return for a certain sum of money.' The words sounded flat, stripped of meaning. Said that way, they did not convey anything of what this meant to her.

The molten iron ball inside her had gone cold, leaving a heavy lump in her stomach. The leaden taste of betrayal.

Her companion said nothing.

She sent him a glance, questioning, wanting to know his reaction.

He moved nearer, took her hands in his, and brought his face level to hers so she could not look away.

'I'm sorry. I wish I could have spared you this. But this is nothing compared to what you would have suffered if you had not heard his plans. You had a very fortunate escape.'

Of course. Through her gloves the touch of his fingers sent soothing ripples of calm through her. He was right. Nothing had happened. She had been in danger, but she had found out in time, and she would be spared.

'You'll recover,' he said. 'It always seems like you never will, when you are in love, but believe me, you will. I've seen it happen countless times.' His mouth twisted. 'Even

146

experienced it a time or two myself.'

She pulled her hands away sharply.

'Is that what you think?' she said, angrily. 'That I love him?'

He seemed genuinely puzzled. Her anger died down. Despite his kindness, he still managed to anger her. She needed to curb that temper of hers. 'I'm sorry,' she said. 'It's nothing like that. I didn't love him. I didn't have the chance. Perhaps if I had spent more time with him. . . . I simply enjoyed his company — fool that I was.'

The creases in his face smoothed out, and the strain disappeared. He leaned back in the chair, threw out an arm to rest on the back of the sofa, and extended his legs.

'Good heavens!' he said. 'To judge by your determination to seek his company, one would have thought you must have been madly in love with him.'

'You were so nettled that I did not jump at your command that you conjured up the wildest explanations for my defiance,' she replied, her temper rising in spite of her resolve.

'Hah!' he said. 'I did not conjure up anything. Half the *ton* is aware of the *tendre* you have conceived for him.'

The blood drained from her face. 'Is there — ?' she asked, struggling to speak. Matters went from bad to worse. 'Has there been a great deal of gossip?'

He shrugged. 'Hardly as bad as that. But there was an entry at White's concerning upcoming nuptials between you.'

Nuptials were never part of it. She did not regret that. She had not had a chance yet to dream of a future with him. But it was still a sour pill to swallow. It stuck in her throat.

'Cheer up,' said Thorwynn. He appeared considerably cheered himself. 'You're only suffering the pangs of wounded pride. There's no real damage done.'

She nodded. 'Yes. When I think of what might have happened —' A shiver passed through her very bones. The dread that had overcome her before Thorwynn's arrival returned. 'But he might still make another attempt. The wager is not yet over.'

He jerked into alertness. 'You're right,' he said, 'he won't give up so easily. And he doesn't know that you're aware of his scheme. He'll persist.'

'Perhaps I should confront him,' she said.

'No. That will only drive him to more desperate measures,' he said. 'Better to keep him off guard, thinking you are unaware of his scheme. It depends how much he needs to win. I had thought that he was coming into an inheritance, but his affairs must be

148

worse than we thought.'

She shrugged. 'I know nothing of his finances.' She knew nothing, nothing at all about him.

She turned to her companion. 'Clearly you know more about him than I.'

Thorwynn's face shuttered. He leaned away from her again, sprawling in the seat. But his body was taut, a clockwork figure wound all the way up, ready to spring.

'I know more about him than I could ever care to.'

She waited. She did not press him to speak. But she could sense his turmoil.

He closed his eyes. 'It's a long story, and I can only give you the briefest details. I knew Neave at Eton, but our paths did not cross much. His pursuits and mine were a little different. I was a year older than him, in any case.' He pursed his lips. 'After one too many offences, this time involving the daughter of one of the school tutors, no less, he was sent down permanently. His father decided that forcing him to fight on the Continent might tame the wildness in him.'

'I don't how he fared in his army career. His uncle the Duke of Lattimore's influence bought him a very good rank, far higher than mine. I finished my degree in Oxford and joined the army, eager to fight

Napoleon. When they assigned me my regimentals I found I was to serve under his command.'

His hands clenched. His face, closed to her until now, twisted in distress.

'We were in the midst of a skirmish. The French were pressing us on three sides. The fighting was fierce, the situation rather desperate. I asked him if we should sound a retreat, before we were surrounded completely. He said no, that we were to continue. At that point we were about seventy, and we were severely outnumbered. Eventually, the French began to close in. I looked to him to sound a command, to give us orders. He was nowhere to be found. Then I located him. He was partly concealed behind a tree. He was stripping the uniform off a dead or wounded French soldier. The next thing I knew, he had undressed, and changed into the French uniform. Then a French soldier attacked me and I had to turn round. The next time I looked he had disappeared.'

He fell silent, lost in his memories.

'Only ten of us survived the slaughter. By the time I realized that Neave had deserted, it was too late to do anything.'

He covered his face with his hands. 'I still dream about those men, their dead faces staring up at me. In my dreams I take command and save them.' His voice was a hoarse whisper. 'But then I wake up to discover that nothing has changed.'

'Wasn't he punished for his desertion?'

He laughed, a bitter, ugly laugh. 'I did my best to instigate a hearing. But his uncle intervened, and it was blocked. I never got a chance.'

He passed his palms over his face. 'The worst of it is that he's still in the army, in an elite unit. They call them the Riflemen, now. But since we're no longer at war with Napoleon, he can enjoy his privileges without any of the inconveniences of war. He has taken up a licentious lifestyle with a vengeance. He particularly enjoys seducing very young virgins. If you ask Lord Benedict, he will tell you of a young relative of his, barely fourteen years old. Luckily, they were able to marry her off quickly.'

She did not need to hear more. Her situation was trivial when compared to those women whose lives were ruined by Neave.

'I don't understand,' she said, 'why, if he is so short of money, he doesn't marry into a fortune.'

'I can't answer that. There are rumours that his father is dying, and that he is coming into a large fortune very soon. But perhaps it is not ultimately money that drives him, but the challenge. Who knows?'

They sat together on the sofa, ruminating in silence. His grief communicated itself to her and she pondered those dead men, lying on the ground. She drew closer to him and took his hands as he had done with her. Their eyes met. The despair in his eyes changed, replaced by a flare of something else. He pulled her to him and his lips sought hers, probing at first, then persistent. The urgency in him awoke an impulse she had never known. She drew his head closer, wanting more.

The door of the library swung open.

They sprang apart. But there was no hiding his coat that had slid down to the floor. Or the shirtsleeves that no gentleman should reveal before a lady. Or the two of them sitting close on the settee, alone in the library.

The gasp from the doorway told her what she needed to know.

Two women stepped in. Lady Medlow pinned Julia with her small eyes. She did not seem to recognize her at first. Julia knew the moment she did because her expression changed. Her mouth twisted with malice, and she made a strangled sound in her throat, almost a squeal.

The other was Lady Telway. She raised her quizzing glass and studied the couple through it.

Neither woman said a word.

They walked out, and shut the door firmly behind them.

In a few minutes, it would be all over the ballroom.

'I cannot tell you,' said Thorwynn, 'how deeply I regret what just occurred.'

Julia shrugged. One way or the other, this was going to be the night when her life would fall into tatters. She knew what had just occurred could not be forgiven in Society. As scandals went, it was not the worst that could possibly occur. But it was a scandal, nevertheless.

She comforted herself with the thought that it was better than what could have happened, with Neave.

Thorwynn struggled with his coat. It fitted too well for him to put it on without a valet. She moved to help.

'Better not,' he said. His voice was harsh.

'It doesn't matter now. Even if they see me helping you with your coat, it will not make the situation worse.'

He considered that. 'Then I would appreciate your help. I despise this fashion which makes one dependent on one's servants.' With some effort, he was once again the elegant earl. Julia admired the solid width of his shoulders under the tight-fitting superfine.

She smiled at him, and he smiled back.

'Ready to face the wolves?' he said. 'If we leave quickly enough, we can escape before the tale has circulated very far.'

She nodded. 'I need to find my grandmother.'

'We'll find her together.'

He paused in the doorway. 'Before we go, however, we should come to an agreement. I don't trust Neave. I don't believe he'll give up on winning his wager. I think it would be safer if you spend the night at my mother's house.'

She frowned. 'You can't just arrive with me in the middle of the night and hand me over to your mother.'

'I was planning for your grandmother to come with you.'

'Ah. That will be very reassuring to your mother, especially if she is already asleep. Imagine her surprise if she wakes up to find she acquired two visitors while she was sleeping. Not to mention having the servants prepare two bedchambers in the dead of the night.'

He regarded her with amusement.

'You clearly don't know my mother. It will give her a wonderful opportunity to fall into hysterics, which she very much enjoys. And you need not be afraid she is asleep at this time. More likely she is playing faro somewhere and will return long after you are asleep.'

'Still —'

'Still, you have little choice in the matter. You cannot return to Grosvenor Square. You have thwarted Neave's plans, and he will not be happy about it. I am certain he will move against you, if not tonight, then in the next three days.'

She groaned.

'But to involve your mother . . .'

'Mama is the soul of discretion, I assure you. And you need not worry that you will have to deal with her tonight. You will not see her. I'll write her a message, explaining that you might be in danger, and that you need to stay somewhere other than your normal residence. And I'll contrive to pay a visit to her as early as possible tomorrow morning to explain what I can. Does that satisfy you?'

She was too tired to make any decisions. If he could convince her grandmother to accompany her, then she would go. At least for tonight.

Tomorrow her mind would be clearer, and she would deal with her life in a calm and logical manner. The way she always did.

CHAPTER 10

Lionel delivered Miss Swifton and Lady Bullfinch to his mother's townhouse. As he suspected, she had not yet returned from her evening out. Having assured himself that everything had been done to take care of their comfort, he left, returning to the ball. Forced to slow down to greet acquaintances, his progress to the card room proved painfully slow. He gritted his teeth. He could not afford to alienate anyone, especially in the circumstances. In the card room, Benny clutched his cards close to him, slumped in his chair.

'We're going, Benny,' said Lionel, placing his hand heavily on his friend's shoulder.

'Thorwynn, must you persist in interrupting my games?'

'You're losing anyway,' said Lionel. 'I'm doing you a favour.' Under the guise of looking at Benny's cards, he bent down and murmured, 'There have been

157

developments.'

Trust Benny to react immediately. He sprang to his feet and took his leave politely.

'Has Neave made a move?' said Benny, lengthening his stride to match Lionel's.

'Walls have ears,' muttered Thorwynn.

Judging by the number of people who greeted him again on the way out, the scandal had not yet spread far.

In the safety of his carriage, Lionel recounted the events of the evening. He could trust his coachman with his life.

'It's a relief, at any rate, to know that Miss Swifton was not hurt,' said Benny gravely. 'You realize, of course, you'll have to offer for her. Under the circumstances.'

'Of course I know it,' said Lionel. 'I have compromised her, and unlike others who shall remain unnamed, I am a gentleman and a man of honour.'

They relapsed into gloom. Thorwynn had sometimes imagined getting married. This happy event always occurred sometime in some very distant future. But he had never imagined it like this.

'You could do worse, I suppose,' said Benny.

'True enough.' His spirits were sinking further by the minute.

'If you sink any lower,' said Benny, 'you'll

fall off the seat.'

'You can't expect anything else from me, the night before a proposal. Don't you realize? This is for life. I'll be leg-shackled to a chit I've spoken to half-a-dozen times at the most. Before I know it, I'll be stumbling over a brood of brats with runny noses who'll call me Father and think I have something to teach them. All because I was caught kissing a lady.' He groaned and ran his fingers through his hair. 'What did I do to deserve this? It's enough for me to want to disappear into my bedchamber with three dozen bottles of gin and never come out again.'

Benny laughed, damn him. It was no laughing matter. 'Not gin, surely. No point in slumming it in your own bedroom. At least drink something decent.'

'I don't want something decent. The point is to ruin myself, not to enjoy drinking.'

'In that case, blue ruin will do the job,' said Benny, in a deucedly cheerful tone.

'You don't seem to comprehend the situation,' said Thorwynn. 'The parson's noose is round my neck. My life is over.'

'Bound to happen sooner or later,' said Benny. 'It just happened to you sooner.'

Thorwynn grunted.

'The way I see it,' continued Benny,

completely oblivious to his misery, 'today is your last day of utter and complete freedom. You can indulge in a fit of blue devils swigging down gin in your bedchamber, or we can make the best of it and indulge in a night of pleasure. You will certainly be able to enjoy a night or two out when you're married, but they won't have the sense of careless abandon that you can have now.' He surveyed his friend, slouching on the carriage seat. 'So which will it be?'

A growl rose up from deep within him. 'Let's go to Brooks's. I'll decide once I'm there what I wish to do.'

Lionel handed his hat to — what the devil was the new butler's name? He preferred old Matthew — and made his way through the shadowy hallway. His head felt so heavy he was sure it would fall off. A footman opened the door to the parlour and bright light pierced his eyes. He used his hands to filter out the invading daylight and made his way to his mother.

Lady Thorwynn lounged on her usual settee. There were only two herbal concoctions next to her. So Miss Swifton and Lady Bullfinch's arrival had not caused too much excitement. 'Good morning, Mama,' he said. She pouted her lips and he stumbled forward to give her a light kiss on the cheek. 'You're looking well today.'

'You're a scoundrel, but I can't help liking you,' said his mother, smiling.

He backed towards a sofa, sitting down carefully so his head would not fall off.

'To what do I owe this early visit?' she asked.

He glanced towards the clock. He could just make out the hands through the blur in his brain. 'It's one o'clock in the afternoon, Mama.'

His mother smiled a secret smile. 'Did you sleep at all last night?' she asked.

'I'm not going to give you an account of my activities last night,' he said, stiffly. 'It's hardly appropriate for a son to explain his nocturnal activities to his mother.'

'I didn't want an account of your activities. I'm more concerned about your appearance. You could at least get your neckcloth in order,' she observed. 'Especially if you're planning to see Miss Swifton.'

He looked up quickly at the name, then regretted it as his head tilted dangerously.

'You're foxed, Lionel,' said his mother. God, he hated That Tone. That Tone always meant she was going to start on a lecture.

'I'm not foxed,' said Lionel, quickly, hoping to stave it off. 'And I don't know why you don't like my cravat. I changed my clothing before I came. My valet assisted me.' He rose and tried to peer into the gilded mirror to straighten his cravat, but his fingers kept going the opposite direction. He frowned in concentration, but he could not get them to work.

'I suggest you go home and sleep it off,' said his mother.

'Can't,' he muttered. He gave up on the cursed cravat and groped his way back to the sofa. Perhaps he could take a nap there. After all, he had a right to sleep wherever he liked in his mother's place.

He drifted into a confused jumble of images. It was good to put his head down. . . .

Then he remembered he was there to see Miss Swifton. He struggled to an upright position. 'Is she awake yet?'

'I suppose you mean Miss Swifton. Yes, she's awake, but she has gone with her grandmother to the lending library. Friday, apparently, is their day to borrow books.'

Why was the chit never there when he needed her? And confound it, wasn't she supposed to be in danger?

'They assured me they wouldn't be long,' said his mother. 'But I would still advise you to go home and come back later, when you've slept some of it off.'

He groaned. The last thing he wanted was to negotiate his way back to the doorway and find his way back home. He wondered if he'd already dismissed the coachman. He should send someone to see. No sense in making the fellow wait if Miss Swifton wasn't in. He started to say something about it to his mother, but his tongue got in the way.

'I think some coffee might be in order,' said his mother.

'Already had some,' he muttered. Those blue flowers on the sofa — was there such a thing as blue flowers? — drew his attention. If he could just put his head on them, he knew, he would feel better. There was a reason he shouldn't do it, but he couldn't think what it was.

He laid his cheek down, and went out cold.

Julia wished she did not have to stay at Lady Thorwynn's. She hardly knew her, and it was always awkward, staying in someone else's house. And in this case, the situation was downright embarrassing. Bad enough that she could not explain to Lady Thorwynn why she was sheltering in her house. Then add to it the scandal of being discovered kissing her son in the library. Julia's cheeks flamed. She did not know which was worse.

She hesitated as the footman approached the parlour door where she would have to face Lady Thorwynn. She was tempted to retreat to her chamber and avoid her entirely. But that would be replacing kindness with rudeness. She was too well-bred to do that. And her conscience would not allow it.

So when the footman opened the door she breezed through it, trying to appear far more confident than she felt.

'Lady Thorwynn,' she said, 'I'm sorry we left the house before you had come downstairs. Grandmother insisted on returning some books she had borrowed. She left me at the door and went to visit some friends.'

'I hope you will make yourself at home,' said Lady Thorwynn, gently. 'As you can see, my son already has.'

It was then that Julia realized that the strange strangled noise she had been hearing since she entered the room was actually the sound of snoring. Thorwynn was sprawled in a very undignified manner, mouth wide open, one leg hanging off the sofa, and one arm thrown back behind his head. He was snoring sonorously.

She had never yet encountered a gentleman sleeping in the middle of the parlour during one of her visits. On the other hand, she was staying under their roof, so surely she need not stand on ceremony. She hesitated, not sure whether to go or to stay. She cast an uneasy glance in Thorwynn's direction.

'The maids are preparing a chamber for him. I'll have two of the footmen take him upstairs,' said Lady Thorwynn, obviously realizing her discomfort. 'Then we can have a quiet talk.'

Thorwynn descended the stairs grimly. He was bathed and shaved and now felt ready to face the world, even if the pain in his head made it difficult to see clearly. The footman who assisted him told him it was early evening. He had wasted enough time already. He needed to move fast, before Miss Swifton thought he had abandoned her to her fate.

Miss Swifton occupied the parlour, along with Lady Bullfinch and his mother. He cursed his luck. If the situation had not been so urgent, he would have retreated and waited for another opportunity. But by now he was berating himself so harshly for having slept off the day that he could not be too delicate about it. Besides, the situation was clear enough.

'Good afternoon, ladies.' He hoped his grin didn't look like a grimace. It felt like one.

A chorus of greetings returned to him.

He bowed in Miss Swifton's direction. 'Miss Swifton, I wonder if you will do me the honour of a private word in the library, please?'

There were mutters and raised brows as three faces turned to him expectantly.

Miss Swifton looked towards Lady Bullfinch. If it was a plea for assistance, she did not receive it. Lady Bullfinch just regarded her gravely. Julia rose and moved slowly in his direction. He signalled for her to precede him, opened the door and closed it behind them.

The way to the library seemed to stretch the whole length of the house, even if it was a mere doorway away. He watched the back of her head, the woman he would soon call his wife. In a few minutes, it would be done, and the trap would shut on him for ever.

Inside the library, the dark wood and the crowded volumes hemmed him in. The books squinted down at him, silent witnesses of this moment. How many other moments like these had they witnessed, he wondered?

She was watching him expectantly. She had seated herself in an upright burgundy leather chair. The pendulum of the carved oak grandfather clock swung from side to side. He followed its movement, reflecting for the first time how strange it was that such a movement defined what people call time. But enough.

He cleared his throat. 'This will not come to you as a surprise, Miss Swifton, I am sure.' Her face revealed nothing. 'I wish the circumstances could have been different, but they are not.' Still nothing in her face. How did one do this without simply blurting it out? He would not go so far as to go on his knee. The gesture had always struck him as trite, and completely pointless. But some gesture was needed, he felt, to distract from the stark reality of the question.

He bowed. It was a formal enough thing, after all. 'I'm sure you don't wish to listen to some long speeches about how delighted I am at this opportunity and other such things. We are both perfectly aware of the circumstances.' He took a deep, deep breath. 'Miss Swifton, will you do me the honour of marrying me?'

There. He had said it. It hung on the air, heavy and dark like the oak around him.

She rose. There was an odd refinement in

her bearing, a quiet dignity that he had not noticed before.

'I thank you for your rational approach to the matter. It makes things much simpler, does it not?'

He nodded curtly.

'I will deal with you the same way. When no feelings are involved, it is easier to be direct.'

Confound it, woman. If you wanted to be direct, a simple yes would have been enough.

'I am happy to inform you that there is no need for you to trap yourself into this marriage. I have given the matter some thought. I have decided that, in spite of the circumstances, I do not wish to marry you.'

It took Lionel some time to unravel what seemed to be a very convoluted speech. Had she said she was happy to, or that she did not wish to?

If only this headache would go away, then perhaps her answer would be clearer.

He repeated the sentence in his head.

She had said no.

Never for one moment had he imagined such a thing. It was so beyond his comprehension that he just stared at her, his mouth open. Then, realizing it was open, he clamped it shut. But he still stared.

'B— b— b— but . . .' He had never stammered in his life. The words, however, refused to come out. She stood in the middle of the library, hands grasped in front of her, absolutely poised, while he could hardly get a word out. He tried again. 'But —' Hardly an improvement on his previous effort.

'You have done the honourable thing, Lord Thorwynn, and I am truly grateful to you. And I know you wish to protect me from scandal. You have been more than kind.' The smallest smile touched her lips. 'But the fact is,' she said, 'I can take care of myself.'

She marched out of the room. The thump of her feet on the floor echoed in his head. Thankfully, she closed the door softly.

Julia knew Grannie would eventually seek her out. Thorwynn would tell them about her refusal. Or the absence of both of them for a long time would provoke a reaction. They would come knocking at the library door, if only to see if the two of them were writhing on the ground in unbridled passion.

So when she barged through the door, Julia was prepared. She sat in a comfortable chair by the window, an open book in her lap. She had not read a word of it, since the words had suddenly turned into jumbled ciphers. But holding a book made the world seem like its usual self.

Her ladyship settled on the bed. Her face indicated that Something Serious was happening.

'Thorwynn tells us you turned him down,' she said.

Julia nodded.

'He seemed very puzzled.'

Julia shrugged. The movement shifted the book in her lap.

'Can you explain this folly to me?'

Julia said nothing. Was there any point in trying to explain?

'I'd like to know why you turned him down. I'm sure you have good reasons,' said her ladyship gently.

Other than that the gentleman in question was a rake, and he was clearly very miserable at the idea of marrying her? That he had a habit of getting so foxed he passed out in his mother's parlour? Other than she had always planned not to marry, rather than suffer like her mother in a joyless marriage? That she wanted at least a choice in the most important decision of her life?

She gave the only answer she could give. 'Lord Thorwynn is not the kind of person I envisioned as a husband. Even if you picked him out for me from the start.'

'Perhaps not,' said her ladyship, 'but he'd make a decent kind of husband.'

She thought of him as he had been earlier, his clothes dishevelled after a long night of revelry. 'What kind of a husband does a rake make?'

'Youthful indiscretions, nothing more.' Her tone did not allow for argument.

'He's *thirty*. Hardly a boy of twenty.'

'He has good character. He'll settle down, once he finds the right person.' Lady Bullfinch examined her closely. 'Don't forget he's experienced a great deal during the War. It takes time for a man to recover.'

'Three years?' said Julia. But she felt a guilty pang as she remembered his confession in the library. *He never had the chance to sow his wild oats at twenty, as other young men did.* Perhaps she *was* judging him too harshly.

'Whether he's a dissolute rake or not — all that is irrelevant,' said her grandmother sharply. 'It's the *circumstances* that count now. What matters is that he's willing to do the decent thing.'

'Why is it all about how decent and honourable he is? Why is it no one is asking how *I* feel?' She looked at her in appeal. 'I thought you at least would understand that I can't just give up my right to choose because of a little gossip. You were always dismissive enough about gossip, and always harping on how easily cowed young girls are these days.'

Her ladyship shook her head. 'When a girl is ruined,' she said, gently, 'she *has* no choice.'

Those words, gently spoken, struck her like a lash.

'In this case, what you do will affect the whole family. Your cousin Miranda will be coming out next year. She will need to weather the scandal, if you don't marry. Why should she pay for your foolishness? And, although I will pull through, I am sure, I will be forced to survive the backlash. Something I will hardly relish at my age.'

Down came the whip, again, biting into her conscience.

Conventional words. Yet they had the force of destiny behind them.

All her life she had believed herself separate from convention in some way. Not in any grandiose way, of course. She had learned to be a lady in the finishing school her grandmother had sent her to. Established by a French *émigrée,* an aristocrat known before the revolution for her salons and her intellectual pursuits, it was an unusual school. It gave young ladies a real education, not a smattering of accomplishments that were skin deep. The girls at the school debated philosophy, read from the masters in the original languages, and learned the principles of rational thinking. She learned there that while she could not openly defy society, there were many ways in which women could retain some independence while still being part of it.

But it was not really true. There were too many pressures to withstand.

She rose, wearily, allowing the book to fall on the floor, not caring to pick it up.

'I need some time to think,' she said. 'I need to be alone.'

She nodded. Julia could see she would have preferred to stay. But she had to reach her decision by herself. At least she could still hold on to that, in the midst of her crumbling dreams.

She watched her ladyship pace to the doorway, watched the door shut behind her.

She was alone.

Cummings rarely took offence. He was the best valet a gentleman could expect, though a touch too arrogant for his own good. But the fact was, he was the envy of his valet cronies. He had told Lionel so. Because no matter what Lionel wore, he still managed to do his valet credit.

But today Lionel did not like any of his suggestions. The waistcoat he chose was inappropriate to wear for an evening at the theatre. The shirt he gave him had wrinkles, tiny lines that marred the perfection of his coat. And his cravats were not starched enough. They hung limply no matter what he did with them.

Cummings finally abandoned him to his fate. 'In all the years I've dressed you, I've never had such difficulty with your clothing,' he said, testily. 'If you are *dissatisfied* with my *service*,' he continued haughtily, 'perhaps you would like me to seek another position and employ *another* in my place.' He raised his long nose and looked at the ceiling.

Lionel was in no mood to put up with his hurt sensibilities. 'Perhaps,' he drawled. 'It is of course up to you.'

Cummings's nose came down quickly enough. 'I am not desirous of leaving your service, as it so happens,' he said, 'though Lord Wrexham has offered me a position in his establishment.'

Lionel ignored him.

'If you're all finished, my lord, I will

withdraw downstairs.' He managed to fill the words with wounded pride.

Lionel flicked a dismissive hand. 'Go, for heaven's sake!'

Glad to have a few minutes to himself, he examined himself in the mirror. Normally, he liked what he saw. His hair had the perfect tousled look, and was thick and shiny. His lips were well shaped, full and masculine. Women had told him they were very sensuous. His nose perhaps was not perfect, a little crooked from when he slid off the roof of the stables as a child and broke it. His eyes were black, a good strong colour. Overall, he was considered by most to be an attractive man.

Perhaps she did not like darker men. It would account for the dislike she had taken of him from the start.

Someone scratched at the door. Confound it! Could he never have a moment of peace in his own chamber?

It was one of the footmen. He handed Lionel an envelope.

He recognized her writing immediately. He opened the note, read it quickly, and tossed it on to his bed.

She had changed her mind. She had agreed to marry him.

She had given in. Of course no woman in

her sane mind could reject such a proposal, under the circumstances. No woman in her sane mind could refuse *him.* He knew she would rethink it. No doubt her contrary nature had provoked her to turn him down immediately, in the library.

But with a little thought, she had come round. She had recognized that marriage to him was an opportunity she would be foolish to pass over.

She wanted him to keep it confidential for the moment. She was nervous about announcing it. She did not want to break the news to Lady Bullfinch or his mother. Perhaps she still had the tiniest seed of doubt.

But she would come round.

He sank down into his armchair and settled his legs on the stool in front of him, cupping his hands behind his head. A big smile settled on his face, reaching from ear to ear.

He was crowing.

CHAPTER 11

Thorwynn waited at the bottom of the stairs, observing his future wife as she headed towards the gilded staircase. She wore a white and blue evening dress made of some shimmering material that glimmered and flowed as she walked. An odd thing, the way she came alive when she moved. If she sat still, one could overlook her, but not when she was in motion. It had a fluidity about it that forced him to follow her with his eyes.

Which was precisely what he did. He watched as she glided down the stairs, took in the gentle curves of her body, the graceful unfolding of her arms as she reached for the banister, the confident sensuality of her legs as they reached down for the next step.

He had not done so badly for himself, after all.

But then he caught sight of her face. It matched her clothing. The particular shade of blue which ice had when it was very cold.

She looked down upon him from the height of the stairs as if she wished he would just suffer an apoplexy and fall to the ground. It would not do at all. They were supposed to be betrothed, for heaven's sake, even if it was a secret at the moment. Weren't they supposed to enjoy each other's company, at least until they were married? Well, he had melted much harder ice than this. No reason why he should not succeed in this situation.

But meanwhile, the easiest way to bring her off her high horse was to shock her.

He grinned at her as she reached that last step, and took her hand. His eyes gleamed. 'So you thought better of your rejection,' he said, with a deliberate drawl, allowing some of his gloating to seep through.

Her eyes flashed. She started to say something, then thought better of it. 'The circumstances demanded it,' she said, tonelessly.

She stepped down on to the ground. He tugged at her hand to bring her closer, then leaned forward and whispered in her ear. 'I can't say this aloud, since we have not yet announced the engagement. But I can't help noticing that you look different tonight. Perhaps more *feminine?*' he said.

She pulled her hand away from his angrily and whirled around. But not before he was able to glimpse the pink flush that stained her cheeks. He was rubbing her nose in the dirt. Hardly a gentlemanly thing to do. But at least the frozen expression was gone.

Which was just as well. If they were to go to the Theatre Royal to face the gossip-mongers, then she could not afford to seem too high in the instep. It would only alienate whatever few friends she had.

The next step was to get her to look as if she liked him. That would be a harder task, since he did not have much time. But he was sure, if he really put his mind to it, that it was not impossible.

Julia braced herself as she entered the box. They had arrived late, so they met nobody upon entering. She was certain their arrival would cause a stir, nevertheless. But with none other than Mr Kean performing, everyone's eyes were glued to the stage. Especially since the role of Othello was generally considered to be his best.

She heaved a sigh of relief. She could relax and watch the performance, at least until the intermission. She had not wanted to come in the first place, but first her grandmother and then Lady Thorwynn had convinced her it was necessary. Lady Thorwynn, in fact, had been unusually tactless.

'It wouldn't do at all,' she had said, in that soft-voiced way of hers, 'for you to stay at home. The *ton* will think you are being cowardly. And much as I sympathize with you, I would think the same.'

The remark surprised her all the more since it came from a person she scarcely knew. Someone she had thought of, somehow, as being quiet spoken and delicate.

It had certainly been effective. Julia had lifted her chin and excused herself, claiming to need extra time to dress. But Lady Thorwynn's words had not improved her temper, and the knowledge that she would have to face Thorwynn as well as the whole of the ton weighed heavily on her.

She had regretted her note as soon as she sent it, wondering what he would think of her when she seemed unable to make up her mind about something as important as a marriage. She had certainly made a fool of herself in the library when she had turned him down so carelessly. And then again when she sent her message. Why had she not waited until she saw him, at least?

His gloating had not improved the situation.

She shot him a sideways glance. He appeared to be focusing on the performance, which surprised her, as she did not think Shakespeare would interest him. But then, most people seemed to like *Othello.* Perhaps because it was set in an exotic locale. Or perhaps it was Mr Kean alone who commanded attention with his powerful presence.

Nevertheless she was forced to admit that, apart from his initial remarks, Thorwynn's behaviour had been perfectly gentlemanly. He had even tried to put her at ease by relating an anecdote about a childhood mishap with a horse. He had certainly made Grannie laugh in the carriage when he imitated an old master of his with whom she was acquainted.

Julia sighed. There were advantages to having a betrothed who was a rake, she supposed. Rakes were by their very nature amusing and charming. It was who they were, and what they did best.

She turned her attention to the performance. She might as well enjoy what she could of it, before the lights went up and she became the centre of the latest scandal.

The interval had hardly begun when Lady Medlow appeared in the doorway of the Thorwynn box. She had a fur wrap around her shoulders, and her small eyes gleamed in the light of the crystal candelabra hanging from the ceiling. Her daughter hovered behind her, twisting the folds of her dress uneasily.

Lady Bullfinch and Lady Thorwynn gathered around Julia, a solid wall of protection. Grannie gave her a secret pat on the hand.

She waited for the sword to fall.

But apart from a rigid nod, Lady Medlow ignored her. She greeted the older ladies politely. Then, having completed the formalities, she squeezed through the defensive wall to greet Thorwynn with a squeal.

'Don't you think Shakespeare is *incredible?*' she said enthusiastically, beaming at him. 'I find him so *refreshing!*'

'Indeed, Lady Medlow? Refreshing? In what way?'

His eyes met Julia's and she had to look away.

Lady Medlow's smile faltered just a little, but she rallied quickly. 'La, Lord Thorwynn, you're funning me. Why *everyone* knows Shakespeare is refreshing.' She gestured to her daughter to come closer. 'I was just talking to Amelia about it. What was it you were telling me, my dear, about Shakespeare?'

Amelia flushed and looked at Julia for help. 'Well, yes, that is to say . . .' she stuttered. She swallowed and ploughed forward.

'I was telling Mama I thought Shakespeare quite clever, the way his personages come to life on stage.' She looked towards Julia for approval. She nodded.

'That was it. Precisely what I said,' beamed Lady Medlow. 'A refreshing dramatist.'

Thorwynn pretended he had not heard Lady Medlow. 'Is this your first Shakespeare performance, Miss Neville?'

'Yes,' she said. 'And it's far better than I would have thought. I've read all the plays in *Family Shakespeare,* but I never imagined they could seem so real on the stage.'

Thorwynn smiled. 'If you are so fond of Shakespeare,' he said gently, 'we'll have to make sure you attend all performances of Shakespeare.'

Her mother intervened. 'She is not *that* interested in Shakespeare, I assure you. Nobody could accuse my beautiful Amelia of being a bluestocking.' She darted a cold look at Julia. 'Unlike some young ladies nowadays. But I have always believed that girls should not have too much education. It makes them likely to become old maids.'

Her remark puzzled Julia. She did not know, of course, that she and Thorwynn were engaged. But surely, having caught them in such a compromising situation, she expected something of an announcement?

'Besides, I believe literature inflames the passions, and makes impressionable ladies more forward than they should be.' Again, her round eyes turned toward Julia.

Thorwynn bowed. 'I think above all it is poetry that inflames the passions,' he said mildly. 'Especially poetry by that scoundrel, Lord Byron.'

He knew very well Julia liked Lord Byron. She refused to be drawn into the fray. She did not know what game Lady Medlow was playing, but she preferred to observe it, not to participate.

To her surprise, Amelia came to Lord Byron's defence. 'When a man is such a genius,' she said, 'much can be forgiven him.'

Lady Medlow gasped, and pressed her long pointed fingers to her heart. 'Surely I have not nursed a viper in my bosom!' She glanced towards Thorwynn. 'I had no knowledge that she was reading such things, or I would have thrown the book in the fire.'

Amelia, however, was not to be cowed. 'Everyone reads Lord Byron, Mama. It would have been a pity, indeed, if you had thrown the book in the fire, since it belonged to the lending library, and I would have been compelled to explain.'

Lady Medlow's eyes grew larger. Realizing the situation was rapidly deteriorating, her eyes darted towards one of the other balconies. She let out a squeak. 'Look, I see Lady Cumbridge waving to us. Come child, we must hurry, or the performance will begin.' She gripped her daughter's hand in her own and dragged her away.

Thorwynn's gaze met Julia's. His eyes danced. Despite her resolve to keep him at a distance, bubbles of laughter rose up. She grinned, and he grinned back. The shared laughter relieved some of her tension.

'Since you named your horse Hamlet,' said Thorwynn, his manner friendly, 'I assume you enjoy Shakespeare.'

'My grandmother gave the horse his name. Her mount is called Malvolio.' He raised his brows in astonishment. 'Difficult to believe, but true. She made Shakespearean names a tradition in the family. My mother was Olivia, my aunt is Viola, and my uncle Horatio.'

'Clearly her influence did not extend so far as to force your parents to name you Juliet instead of Julia.'

She laughed. 'You may ask her yourself,' she said, gesturing towards Lady Bullfinch, who was engaged with two of her friends who were visiting the box. 'But the story is that my mother called me Julia as a compromise. Thank heavens. I can't think of anyone in Shakespeare who is more insipid. Except poor Ophelia.'

'You don't wish to drift down a river with flowers in your hair? Though if you have read the *Family Shakespeare* as Miss Neville has, you would know that she is no longer poor Ophelia. In Mr Bowdler's new version, she does not commit suicide. She drowns by accident.'

'Why does that not surprise me?' she said. 'Mr Bowdler has taken the spirit out of Shakespeare and reduced it to a shell. But I did not imagine that you were a reader of Shakespeare.'

His face suddenly shuttered. He shrugged with studied nonchalance. 'Perhaps I have been spending too much time with actresses of late. It must have rubbed off.' He smiled cynically at her indrawn breath. 'I apologize if I have offended your delicate sensibilities, Miss Swifton.' He stepped away abruptly. 'I must see to the refreshments before the curtain rises,' he said, and disappeared from the box.

When the play started again she found herself unable to understand a word spoken by Mr Kean.

Lady Medlow's visit had destroyed that possibility. She was sure that Lady Medlow and her friend Lady Telway planned to reveal her indiscretion before the night was over. The rows of boxes stared at her like accusing eyes, and the bright candles seemed to focus their light on the Thorwynn box. She felt that it was she, not Mr Kean, who was on stage.

She shuddered each time the glint of an open glass was directed towards them.

One particular lady, a woman in a primrose evening dress and a lilac turban, seemed to direct her attention towards them repeatedly. Julia's hands grew hot and moist under the blue gloves, and she longed to peel them off. She braced for the storm. Surely that lady was only the first of many to stare at them.

Then her curiosity gained the upper hand, and she trained her glass on the primrose-clad lady. She wanted to know the worst.

But instead of a group of gossiping matrons, she found the turbaned lady sitting alone, with an elderly couple one seat away from her on one side. The couple were both engrossed in the performance. They were certainly not exchanging the latest *on-dits*.

As for the turbaned lady, she was certainly not paying attention to the performance.

She noticed immediately when Julia turned her glass on her. She responded by bowing her head, her mouth puckering in amusement. Julia quickly lowered her glass. In turn, the turbaned lady raised her glass with calm deliberation and stared at Thorwynn, sitting to the right of Julia, as though to stake a claim.

Julia let out her breath in relief. Clearly, the unknown lady knew nothing about the scandal. Her sole interest was Thorwynn himself. Nothing to concern her, then.

Seconds later, however, reality hit her with an iron fist. This lady was one of Thorwynn's admirers. Thorwynn, who was betrothed to Julia. Marrying him made ladies like that very much her concern. She was marrying a *rake,* after all. No doubt he had a whole entourage of women hankering after him.

The thought dismayed her. Her father had been such a man, by all accounts. She had never known him, although he was alive somewhere, living a riotous life on the Continent, after being driven by a series of scandals to leave England. When she was younger she used to dream that he would return to visit his daughter, that he would regret leaving Julia to her fate and come back to ensure that she was well cared for.

She had told Lady Bullfinch of her dreams

one day. Her confession had distressed her grandmother. 'I hope you are happy with me,' she had said.

Julia had hugged her tightly. 'Of course I'm happy with you. You know I am. But to think that my father is somewhere out there . . .'

She had shaken her head. 'You must not think of that. You are far better off with your father far away. From what I know of him, he is too selfish to care for anyone but himself.'

'Mama must have thought him charming.'

'So did many other women. He could charm a cat's whiskers from its face. However, his charm brought your mother nothing but misery.' She had closed her eyes in pain, remembering the daughter she had lost. 'I'm convinced her unhappiness weakened her constitution. That was why such a mild cold was able to kill her. No-one would have thought it.' She had taken Julia's head and pulled the child towards her. 'You must push aside any thoughts of your father.'

Over the years, Julia resolved not to make her mother's mistake. She had promised herself she would never fall victim to a charming rogue.

It was ironic, indeed, that she was about to marry one. One who acknowledged, quite openly to her, his future wife, that he consorted regularly with actresses.

At least I'm not in love with him.

In the shuffle of the crowds leaving the theatre, Julia was separated briefly from her group.

Almost immediately, someone grasped her arm from behind. She knew without turning who it was. Her heart sped up, and her throat grew so dry she could not swallow. His grip was not painful, but it was like iron, cold and inescapable. She could not tear it away without provoking an incident.

She chastized herself for her irrational fear. He could not do anything to her here, in the midst of the theatre crowds.

She decided to play his game. He did not know that she had discovered his intentions. So she allowed her eyes to flutter, and turned to face him, a flirtatious smile on her face. At least, she hoped that it was flirtatious. 'Why, Lord Neave. What an unexpected pleasure,' she said. 'I did not know you enjoyed Shakespeare.'

'Everyone enjoys Kean,' he said, lightly. 'And one does not go to the theatre merely to watch a play. In my case, I came to see if I could discover your direction.'

She kept smiling, even though her teeth

ached. 'Whatever do you need my direction for?' she said, playfully.

'I've looked for you everywhere,' said Neave, gazing at her intensely. 'I called on you this morning, but you were not in.'

'Yes, I left early today.'

'I saw some trunks being loaded into a carriage,' he said, watching her closely. 'I was afraid you might be going on a journey.'

She fumbled for an easy lie. Why had they not discussed the possibility of running into Neave in the theatre? She could have come up with some convincing story about her sudden absence from the townhouse. 'An old schoolfriend of mine has taken sick,' she said. 'I have offered to keep her company during her illness. She's a widow, you see, and she's alone in the house.'

His eyes gleamed like a wolf's, no doubt at the knowledge that her friend lived alone. 'You must give me the address of your friend, then, so I may call on you.'

'It would hardly be appropriate, Lord Neave, to call on me when my grandmother is not present as chaperon.'

His eyes hardened briefly at her words. Then his expression shifted back its former intensity.

'The fact is,' he said, lowering his voice, 'I am unable to put you out of my mind.' He sent her an ardent glance, then looked away, as if embarrassed. 'I would very much like to ask your grandmother's permission for your hand.'

She opened her mouth to reply, but he hushed her. 'Don't answer me now. I would like to call on you tomorrow morning to discuss this subject, if you will give me your friend's directions.'

Julia shook her head. 'I'm sorry, but I really must catch up with my party. When my friend is recovered, I will send a note around to let you know. Until then I'm afraid I can think of little else. I am afraid for her.' She was surprised how convincing she sounded. Her voice even held a little tremor when she spoke of her fear. Of course, she really was afraid, but for other reasons.

'Oh, I hope to see you before then.' He said it lightly, but his eyes were predatory. 'Meanwhile, I can only wish your friend a very speedy recovery.' He bowed, stiffly, and melted into the crowd.

CHAPTER 12

Julia sprang up in her bed. Pitch dark surrounded her, boxing her in.

She reached for a candle at her bedside. The nightmare rolled off her, following the perspiration that trickled down her face. She wiped it with her sleeve, struggling to banish the all-too vivid scene.

She ran through the trees. It felt more as though she was riding because the trees were becoming a blur. Her bare feet tore, pierced by bramble and thorns and branches. Her lungs wheezed with effort. Blood dripped into her eyes from a cut in her head. It blocked her vision, but there was no time even to brush it away.

She knew the house she sought was straight ahead. If she could reach it, she would be safe. If she could keep running those few steps. . . .

An arm snaked round from behind a tree. Her feet kept moving. But her body was suspended, jerked back and upwards by the steel muscles of her assailant. A hand descended on her mouth, smothering her. She could not breathe. . . .

She struggled to control her breathing. It was only a nightmare. It was not real. She was safe, here, in Lady Thorwynn's house. No one knew her location.

She wondered if Neave huddled in the shadows of the street outside her window, watching her.

She shuddered and pushed the thought away. He did not know her location.

Tomorrow was the last day of the wager. Tomorrow she would be free of him, and she would return to a life of sanity. Between waking and sleeping, she pictured herself searching for a husband in the lecture halls and the museums, someone who did not think her a bluestocking or an oddity.

When she woke up, the sun poured into the room like a halo around the edges of the drawn curtains. It was late — very late. She drew aside the scarlet damask curtains and pushed open the window. The sky was a vast canvas of contented blue, interrupted by solitary clouds that drifted lazily around. A warm breeze carrying the giddy aroma of blossoms rippled over her skin. Birds chattered and gossiped and flirted, screeching and tweeting to their life's content.

On a day like this, her nightmare receded so far it seemed a figment of her imagination.

Then reality came crashing in around her. She was engaged to be married. To Lord Thorwynn. What had she been thinking of last night? She had forgotten entirely that there would be no other husband. Her bed had been made and she would have to lie in it. Or at least, grow accustomed to seeing it around.

The engagement would have to be announced sometime, perhaps today, if Lady Medlow had spread the rumours at the theatre. Perhaps she was holding on to her little titbit, waiting for the right moment, for full dramatic effect.

She rang for Bethany, her maid, to help her change. She picked out a peach walking dress with rows of Vandyke trimming at the bottom and a peach muslin sash. Not that she was planning to go walking.

A walking dress, however, was more appropriate than a plain morning dress for someone whose engagement may be announced any moment.

She could barely wait for Bethany to finish arranging her hair. She wanted desperately to read the gossip columns, to confront the abyss waiting for her.

She found Lady Thorwynn in the parlour, sipping a mustard-coloured tonic and grimacing at the taste.

'I'm surprised to see you awake already, Lady Thorwynn. You were out until late yesterday. It is barely eleven o'clock.'

Lady Thorwynn sighed, and then, holding her nose, disposed of the rest of the yellow-green liquid with a gulp and a quick shudder of distaste. 'Alas,' she said, sighing tragically, 'I wish I could sleep longer. But the slightest noise disturbs me. It's impossible to sleep with the commotion of the servants in the morning. The clatter of pots and dishes alone is more than enough to wake me. Nerves, you know.'

Julia doubted very much that Lady Thorwynn could hear the clatter of pots and dishes all the way from the basement kitchen to her room on the third floor, but there were times in her life when she had found sleeping difficult, and she could understand her discomfort.

'Have you tried chamomile? I've heard that it does wonders for sleep.'

'I have tried it. I've tried every herbal concoction under the sun. But nothing has helped,' said Lady Thorwynn.

Julia, having no other advice to offer, raised the issue of the gossip columns. 'I'd like to look at them,' she said, trying to hide her anxiety.

Lady Thorwynn was not fooled, however. 'I have already perused them,' she said, 'and there is absolutely nothing pertaining to you or my son.'

Julia frowned in perplexity. What was Lady Medlow waiting for? If she waited much longer, the news would become stale. For how could an event that took place in a ball three days ago stir the imagination of the *ton?*

She was still pondering the matter when Lady Thorwynn left the house for an appointment with her *modiste.* She was beginning to wonder if there had been some strange mistake. Had Lady Medlow and Lady Telway actually seen her and Thorwynn in the Kinleigh library? Perhaps the library was too dark. Perhaps they were looking for something and didn't notice them. Unlikely as it seemed, she could see no other explanation for this protracted silence.

With no one to talk to, and her grandmother still asleep, she decided to retreat to her room, where she attempted to read, though with very little success.

An urgent scratch at the door surprised her out of her meditations.

'Enter,' she said. The door almost flew open. Mary, Lady Thorwynn's maid, rushed into the room, her face pale, clutching her apron and muttering a prayer under her breath.

'You've got to come, Miss Swifton. I don't know what to do. Lady Bullfinch has taken very ill. She can't breathe.'

Julia ran down the corridor. Her footsteps as they fell made a rhythm. *Please don't die, Grannie, please don't die.* A terrible rhythm of fear and panic. *Please don't die, Grannie, please don't die.*

Even from outside the bedchamber, she could hear the laboured breathing.

'Send Bethany for Dr Lincoln,' she ordered, spitting the words out as she ran. 'She'll know where to find him. Tell her to run.' The coachman was not there, so she could not send her by coach. 'And send to the stables for a horse.'

Lady Bullfinch lay on the bed, clutching her chest, her eyes wide with effort as she wheezed in a desperate attempt to breathe. Julia rushed to her bedside to look for the medicine Dr Lincoln had given her. It was on the floor, the bottle broken, the dark liquid staining the carpet. Desperately, she tried to wipe up the liquid on to her hands, to bring some of it to her tongue, but there was too little of it.

She struggled to bring her upright, thinking it might ease her breathing. It seemed to help, just a little, but the terrible wheezing did not cease. She did not know what else to do.

Mary appeared in the doorway. 'Bethany's gone for Dr. Lincoln, my lady, but the groom's not in the stable, and the coachman's gone. There is a horse in the stable, I'm told, but it's not saddled. One of the footmen can get it ready, but it will take a while.'

Julia shook her head. 'There's no time. Someone needs to take a message to Lord Thorwynn. Tell him he needs to come, urgently. And send up whoever prepares Lady Thorwynn's concoctions.'

Meanwhile, Julia convinced herself, the only thing to do was to stay calm. And to try and help her grandmother breathe.

'Grannie, you're going to be all right,' she said, trying not to show her dismay as she rolled up her shoulders, grasping for breath. She needed to reassure her, not frighten her. 'Lean on me,' she said. 'Perhaps if you lean forward a bit it will help you.'

She took a slow, deep breath herself, hoping it would encourage her to breathe. *Breathe, Grannie, breathe.* A slow, deep breath.

Something she did seemed to help. Her ladyship took a shuddering breath, then coughed violently. Another painstaking breath, then some more coughing.

She was still grasping for breath, but the situation seemed less desperate.

The housekeeper appeared. 'Do you have any stramonium?' asked Julia, reluctant to stop that slow, deep breathing.

The housekeeper shook her head.

Julia groaned inwardly. They had a supply of stramonium at the townhouse. She had used inhaled infusions to help Lady Bullfinch during her illness. Julia turned back to help her grandmother breathe. Deep breath. Another deep breath.

She relaxed a little in her arms. Julia peered into her face, alarmed, wondering if she had grown too tired to breathe. But the wheezing had become less pronounced, and her shoulders had gone back to their normal position. She rubbed her back to help the muscles relax. *Deep breath, another deep breath. Keep going, Grannie. Keep going.*

By some miracle, the attack was subsiding.

By the time Dr Lincoln arrived, her grandmother's chest rose and fell normally.

'Do you have any stramonium?' Julia asked, rather abruptly. He looked at her blankly.

'There is no longer any need to be concerned,' he said. 'The attack is over. I'll give her something to drink that will help her. It looks like she experienced a contraction of the lungs, but she is quite recovered, now.'

In fact, she looked almost her usual self. The colour had returned to her cheeks, and her eyes had regained their normal lustre, even if they were somewhat bloodshot.

'Go get yourself something to eat,' said her ladyship, with a half smile. 'And stop fussing around me. I'm perfectly well now.'

The last thing Julia wanted to do was to eat. Now that the urgency was over, she realized how terrified she had been. Her knees felt weak, her thoughts jumbled.

How could there have been no stramonium in a household whose mistress was known for her herbal concoctions? Suppose she had stopped breathing?

She had to visit an apothecary immediately. What if there was another attack, this time more severe?

Dr Lincoln was certainly competent, but she did not put too much faith in doctors.

Her own mother had died with her doctor beside her, claiming she would recover soon.

She slipped into her room, wrapped herself in a cashmere shawl, and took out her reticule.

As for Neave, he could not be any danger to her. He did not even know where she was staying. In the short trip to the apothecary's it was hardly likely she would run into him.

He appeared out of the shadows, taking her elbow firmly in his hand.

'I was a fool to trust you,' hissed Neave. 'To think I believed in that cock-and-bull story you concocted about your friend, when all the time you were staying in Lady Thorwynn's house.'

Very briefly, almost too fast for her to follow, a knife glinted, then disappeared.

Panic froze her. He was a desperate man and she did not know what he was capable of. Her heartbeat thundered in her ears. Should she just surrender to him, let him win his wager? Supposing she gave in, and he stabbed her afterwards and threw her body into the Thames?

She tried to calm herself. She would never escape if she did not gather her wits about her. What could she say to convince him to let her go? Nothing came to mind. 'I'll call a hack,' he said. 'And you'll come with me, nicely and quietly.'

Nicely and quietly. The words echoed in her head. She needed to try and get away from now until they reached the main road, where the hacks could be found. What would be the best thing to do? She could scream, of course, but that could well result in a scandal that she might never live down.

She wondered if there was any way to make him trip, or to make him fall down one of the steep servants' stairs. They would pass by several more townhouses on the way to the main road — surely the wrought-iron gate would be open at one of them. If not, she could pretend to fall, open the gate, and push him so he fell down the stairs. She would make him lose his footing, using one of the iron boot scrapers. She strained with her eyes down the row of houses to see which entrance would best serve her purpose.

She was so engrossed in her thoughts, it took her a minute to realize he was making no move to walk down the street. He stood there, just a few steps away from Lady Thorwynn's townhouse, waiting.

An acute desire to laugh rose up in her and she smothered it. The laughter cleared her brain and she grew absolutely lucid.

There were no hacks in this street. George Yard, where Lady Thorwynn's townhouse was located, was not a through way. It terminated in a large mansion that blocked any other exit. It was difficult for carriages to turn round, so they came this way only to drop off passengers if they had to. In order to call a hack, one had to walk to Duke Street, or to Grosvenor Square through a connecting narrow lane. It was an inconvenience Lady Thorwynn often deplored, at the same time declaring how glad she was to be free of the constant rattle of carriages.

They would stand there forever, waiting.

She went over everything Thorwynn had told her about Neave, especially the scene at the battlefield with him running away. She considered the knife, hidden somewhere in the folds of his overcoat. Would he use it if she tried to run away?

'Damnation!' he said, giving the iron railing a sharp kick. 'Have all the wretched hacks in London gone to the devil?'

She said nothing.

'I should have brought my own carriage.'

She could not help taunting him, partly because she wanted to know how far he would go. 'It would hardly have served, to have your carriage standing on the street with your crest visible for all to see, while you waited for me to come out.'

'Silence!' he said, flashing the knife again.

They stood awkwardly by the side of the road. An old-fashioned gentleman came in their direction. He wore a green and pink taffeta frock coat, long hair tied with a ribbon, and high red-heeled shoes with buckles. Julia recognized him as one of Lady Bullfinch's acquaintances, Lord Yarfolk. He sauntered lazily towards them, waving his walking stick.

She wondered how to draw attention to her situation without causing an even greater problem. She did not want a confrontation between Neave and Lord Yarfolk, particularly since the latter was hardly in his youth. But she was not going to allow Lord Yarfolk to amble right on by and leave her to her own devices.

As he drew closer, she smiled warmly, clearly intending to engage him in conversation. Neave's hand tightened warningly, but she ignored it.

'Good morning, Miss Swifton,' said Lord Yarfolk. 'A beautiful morning, is it not?'

Julia opened her mouth to speak. Neave pinched her arm hard, and she shut it with a gulp. 'Yes, indeed, sir,' said Neave. 'We are awaiting a hackney. Miss Swifton and I are planning to go shopping for a new hat.'

He gave them an odd look. 'Perhaps you might be more successful if you walked to the bottom of the road,' he said, mildly. 'Hacks generally do not travel this way.'

'Thank you, that's precisely what we'll do,' said Neave, pulling at Julia's arm. Deliberately, she made a move to free her arm from his grasp. He was forced to release her, aware of Lord Yarfolk's presence.

'You know, Captain Neave,' she said sweetly, 'I've just remembered something I left behind in Lady Thorwynn's townhouse.' She turned to Lord Yarfolk. 'I'm staying there with Grandmother at the moment,' she said, by way of explanation. 'I do believe I'll go back inside to retrieve it. Why don't you find a hack?' she said to Neave, with an arch smile, 'I can wait for you on the steps.'

He glared, and looked from her to Lord Yarfolk. She took advantage of his confusion to move away from him. 'Lord Yarfolk,' she said, putting out her hand. 'It is quite providential that you arrived.' Neave stiffened, the hand inside his coat shifting. 'I'm aware this is a rather improper suggestion, but I would appreciate it if you could come inside to keep Grannie company. She is rather unwell, and I'm sure a visit from you would revive her spirits.'

'Why, certainly,' said Lord Yarfolk, offering her his arm with elaborate old-fashioned courtesy.

Neave's hand emerged from his coat.

She halted, in the midst of taking Lord Yarfolk's arm.

Neave's fingers were empty. There was no knife. She heaved a sigh of relief. He would not risk a confrontation, then. After all, he had as much to lose from a scandal as Julia would. More in fact, if he pulled a knife on a member of the *ton.*

Neave was fuming. But there was little he could do. He was not desperate enough to pull out his knife and stab her in broad daylight, with Lord Yarfolk as witness. He had relied on her being too afraid to say anything.

She tried to walk at a leisurely pace as Lord Yarfolk minced along in his high-heeled shoes. Although she knew it was unlikely, an irrational part of her half-expected a knife to come flying through the air and land in her back.

But in the end, it was only his gaze that bore into her back, filled with angry despair.

'I hope I didn't interrupt anything, m'dear,' said Lord Yarfolk, as they climbed the steps into the house.

'No. On the contrary. I was glad you came along. He was being a little . . . insistent.'

'I take it you're not planning to take a ride in the hack?' He stopped and faced her, handing the footman his walking stick. Their eyes met. His glimmered with intelligence.

'No, I have no intention of doing so.'

'Perhaps, then, he has no intention of bringing a hack?'

'No, indeed.'

Nothing more was said.

'Is Lady Bullfinch truly indisposed?'

'Yes, my lord. She is, and she would be happy to have your company.'

She had barely deposited Lord Yarfolk in Lady Bullfinch's bedchamber when Thorwynn arrived, his cravat hanging loose, and his clothes hastily thrown on. He came forward quickly when he saw her.

'What the devil has happened? The man you sent over said it was an emergency!'

She was on the verge of reassuring him that all was well, when the knocker sounded and Iggleton admitted Lady Thorwynn.

She paused as she noticed Thorwynn's appearance. 'Lionel, my dear boy, are you making it a habit of appearing at my steps in crumpled clothes?'

His eyes gleamed dangerously. 'Not by

choice. However, since I was woken from my sleep by an urgent summons, I must assume something serious has occurred.'

Lady Thorwynn shifted her glance to Julia in alarm.

It seemed such a long time since Julia had summoned Thorwynn. So much had happened since then. It had not occurred to her to have someone inform him he was no longer needed.

'Fortunately, the situation is under control,' she said. '*Both* situations.'

She realized abruptly that she had not had anything to eat that morning. 'If you'll come into the parlour,' she said, apologetically, 'I'll explain everything. But you'll have to forgive me if I ask for a tray to be brought. I'm afraid I'm rather hungry.'

Thorwynn nodded. 'Make it for two. I was forced to forgo breakfast when I was called here so urgently.'

Thorwynn listened to her sympathetically as she recounted, between mouthfuls, the story of her grandmother's attack. Lady Thorwynn appeared visibly upset.

'If only I had not gone to that wretched *modiste*,' she exclaimed.

'Really, there was nothing more that could have been done,' said Julia, reassuringly.

'You can't blame yourself. How were you to know?'

Nothing Julia said, however, had any effect on Lady Thorwynn, who rang for a posset to soothe her agitation.

'You said at the beginning that there were two incidents,' remarked Thorwynn.

Julia had avoided mention of Neave's attempt at abduction in deference to Lady Thorwynn, who was certain to be overset to hear anything more. She tried to signal to Thorwynn that she would tell him later, but Lady Thorwynn intercepted her gesture.

'You need not worry that I will be upset by any other unpleasant incident,' she said. 'I have already reached breaking point. One more unfortunate happening will not make any difference,' she said, piteously.

'For heaven's sake, Mama, if you continue in this manner the poor girl will go running for a doctor,' he said, smiling ruefully. 'Mama's strong as an ox, Miss Swifton, so you need not spare her feelings.'

Urged by the two of them, Julia gave them a detailed account of her encounter with Neave.

Lady Thorwynn put her hand to her heart. 'To think what would have happened if Lord Yarfolk had not happened along! And to think he is even now comforting your

210

grandmother. I must make an effort and go upstairs to thank him personally.'

She did not appear capable of rising by herself. Julia went over to her side and, after a great deal of sighing and fussing, she finally stood on her feet. Her shawl gripped tightly around her, she sailed out of the room.

Alone with Lionel, she watched him peer out of the window for signs of Neave.

'I don't think he'll return,' remarked Julia, 'at least during the daytime.'

Swivelling around quickly, he confronted her with narrowed eyes. 'What did you think you were doing,' he said, tightlipped, 'leaving the house alone when you knew you were in danger?'

'I was going to the apothecary to bring some medicine for Grandmother,' she replied, coldly. 'I did not imagine Neave knew where I was. He must have followed us after the theatre last night.'

'I thought we had agreed you would take no risks.' He no longer sounded angry. 'The whole idea of moving you here was to keep you safe.'

'I'm well aware of that,' she said. 'But these were exceptional circumstances.'

Lady Thorwynn reappeared. 'Lord Yarfolk will be joining us downstairs. He is reading to your grandmother, some bawdy tale that I would blush to even hear mentioned. I left immediately after hearing just a few sentences. I do not understand these older folk. They do not seem to have the delicacy of sentiment our generation has.'

No one reacted to her statement. Thorwynn had returned to staring out of the window, and Julia finished the last of her cold cuts.

Thorwynn suddenly slammed his fist down on the window sill. 'Why does that measly blackguard always manage to get away?'

His vehemence startled Julia, who dropped her fork. His mother shook her head reprovingly, though Julia was not sure if it was because of the falling fork or her son's manners.

'Can't we bring him to justice for attempted abduction?' asked Julia.

'I'm afraid not,' said Thorwynn. 'Unless you can produce witnesses to the attempt. It is only your word against his.'

He did not add that, of course, a woman's testimony was worth only half a man's in court.

'If you had actually been taken into the carriage by force, and held somewhere, we could have brought a Bow Street Runner with us as a witness. But as it is . . .'

'So you think I should have just gone with him, so you could have had the satisfaction of rescuing me? With a Bow Street Runner?' she said sarcastically. She glared at him.

'No one is suggesting that,' said Lady Thorwynn, gently. 'You are just a little overwrought. Of course we are very happy you were not abducted. Lionel was speaking *hypothetically*. Is that not so, Lionel?'

He waved his hand impatiently. 'Of course.' But he was lost in his own thoughts, and Julia did not think he was being completely hypothetical.

'In any case,' said Lady Thorwynn. 'I believe what Julia needs now is a bath and some rest. And a tonic to calm her nerves. I will tell the housekeeper to prepare one.'

Lord Thorwynn emerged from his thoughts. 'Not one of your tonics, Mama!' he said. 'I absolutely forbid you to impose them on her.'

'You're in no position to forbid anything,' said his mama, mildly. 'I am certain a tonic will do her a world of good.'

'I would love one of your tonics, Lady Thorwynn,' said Julia.

She had the doubtful satisfaction of receiving one of his glares.

CHAPTER 13

With all that had occurred in the past several days, Julia could no longer claim herself a calm, completely unruffled kind of person. A few days earlier, she would have said that she was the exact opposite of Lady Thorwynn. Julia was proud of her logical way of approaching things. She did not like an excess of sentiment. These days, however, some of that cool logic seemed to be escaping her.

She needed to regain her tranquillity. Since books always had the ability to soothe her, she decided to explore the Thorwynn library. She liked the sharp scent of leather bindings, and the dusty nose-tickling smell of old, yellowing paper. It made her feel in her element.

A quick perusal revealed several handsomely bound volumes of Lord Byron's poetry. She took *The Corsair* off the shelf, and leafed through it. There were notations in the margins. She swallowed a quick laugh. *Someone* was reading Lord Byron. It could be Lady Thorwynn, but she did not think she was the type to write notes in the margins.

The hypocrite! Denouncing Lord Byron in public while scribbling notes to his poems in private. Perhaps he had merely memorized a few lines to impress the ladies. That was more like him. She started to decipher one of his comments, then snapped the book shut. Reading his notes struck her as an intrusion, somehow like reading someone's diary. She did not have the right to it. True, she needed to know more about the man soon to be her husband, but she preferred him to reveal himself to her, rather than snooping behind his back.

Well, she knew at least one thing about him now. He read poetry.

Other than that, she knew nothing about him. Nothing about his interests, his concerns, his dreams. Nothing about his childhood. They had never talked, in fact. It struck her as singularly odd that she, of all people, would end up marrying someone with whom she had never even had a real conversation.

Perhaps because it was impossible to have a conversation with a rake. After all, rakes characteristically were superficial, devious, and manipulative. In which case, how much could one believe a word of what they said?

Neave was a case in point.

She had been completely taken in by him. She had thought the conversation in the park was real, Neave had spoken about his father, about his childhood. But how much of it was true?

She pushed the question away. She had no interest in discovering more about him. Most probably he used his revelations as a ploy to awaken young girls' sympathy, something he repeated to each girl before he seduced her.

Lionel, however, had made no attempt to gain her confidence. He had told her of his experience of the war, but it was in the context of Neave's villainy. He had not wanted sympathy for himself. He would have spurned any such gesture on her part.

He cared deeply about his men, about the fate they had suffered. That, at least, was genuine.

She rose impatiently and walked to the window. It was no use going over every word he had said. It would not make him better known to her.

The only certainty she had was that he drew women to him like moths to a light on a sultry summer night. And she was not completely immune to that ill-advised attraction. She had flailed in his arms when they waltzed. And she had succumbed completely to his kiss, that ill-fated night in the library. She had enjoyed every moment of it.

Unfortunately for her, as his wife, however, she would be compelled to watch as women fluttered to him, and he accepted their homage.

An hour later she was still on the first page of Sir Walter Scott's *Rob Roy*. She tried yet again to reread the first paragraph, but in vain.

The sound of footsteps reached her. The door opened. It was Thorwynn.

He strode across the room, grinning. The grin was so candid, so open, she almost relented towards him. Perhaps their marriage would not be so bad after all.

'Have you been waiting for me to return?' he asked, amiably.

His vanity soared as high as a hot air balloon. She could not resist driving a hole in it. 'On the contrary,' she said, throwing him a painted smile. 'Since I know you don't like to read, I took refuge in the library. I did not think you would follow me here.'

His smile wavered, then reasserted itself. 'I can't say I particularly appreciate your wit, but I am glad you are more cheerful than yesterday. I took the liberty of calling at Rundell and Bridge and procuring an engagement ring for you. I hope you'll find it to your taste.'

He held out the ring in its little maroon box. It was a dainty ring, with entwined gold leaves that twisted cleverly to hold small diamonds in them like dew drops. She took it, and placed it experimentally on her finger.

'It fits exactly,' she said, surprised.

He looked pleased with himself. 'That was because there was a lady in the shop whose fingers looked just the same size as yours. I asked her to try the ring, and she did. Shows I'm a good judge, eh?'

A good judge of women, as of horseflesh. Was that how rakes viewed women? As they viewed a pair of steppers?

She did not want to appear ungracious. But she was tempted to give him the ring back. She could just imagine him, looking into the young lady's eyes, smiling into them, and slowly drawing her glove off before sliding the ring on to her finger. She would, of course, have been happy to oblige, her fingers tingling as he brushed lightly

218

against them.

'Thank you, Lord Thorwynn,' she said, making a strong effort not to sound churlish.

'Do you like it?' he asked, smiling widely.

'It's very delicate,' she said. His taste surprised her. She would have imagined a more heavily ornamented ring, something much more elaborate. This elegant little ring was too understated.

His smile disappeared. 'If there's something wrong,' he said, 'I'd like to know it.'

'There's nothing wrong, my lord,' she said.

'I think Lionel would be more appropriate at this point, don't you think?'

She shrugged. 'Lionel.' She liked the name, but it felt uncomfortable. It created too much of a bond between them, an intimacy that she was not ready to accept.

He sat on the armchair closest to her sofa, then leaned towards her. The scent of soap reached her, and a more subtle trace that was his own. 'I know we scarcely know each other,' he said, 'but successful marriages have been built on less.'

She nodded. 'I think I simply need to grow accustomed to the idea.'

He surveyed her for a moment. Then he changed places and sat close to her. 'I believe a kiss is customary when two people are betrothed.'

Before she could protest, he touched his lips to hers. The barest moment of contact. It felt like the brush of a butterfly wing against her skin, but warmer.

The kiss was so brief, she wondered if she had imagined it. She closed her eyes and strained forward, wanting more.

But he'd already moved away. She opened his eyes to find him sitting back, his hands clasped behind his head. He was grinning again.

Heat rushed to her face. She did not want to feed his arrogance. She raised her eyebrow in challenge. 'For a betrothal kiss, wouldn't you say that was rather — unsatisfactory? Hardly a sign of commitment.'

He laughed and passed his gaze lazily over her mouth. She had to restrain herself not to lick her lips. 'Sometimes a light touch can achieve a lot more than an excess of ardour,' he said, languidly.

'I should remind you, Lord Thorwynn — Lionel — that I am not a lady you are attempting to seduce, or a light-skirt you are dallying with. I am your future wife.'

He lifted an eyebrow, regarding her steadily. 'Precisely. All the more important that I seduce you properly.'

Julia knew by now she could not win this

conversation. She floundered, helplessly out of her depth. But there was no escape. She was stuck in his mother's house, and could not simply walk away. She was a fish caught on his hook, trying not to struggle.

She looked down at the ring. It served as a reminder that her future was in this man's hands. 'No doubt you know best,' she said. 'You most certainly have plenty of experience in the matter.'

His mouth twitched. 'Yes, I do have experience,' he drawled, 'but unfortunately, not in marriage.' He reached out and took her hand. Not as a lover would, but in friendship. 'You may not believe it, but this is not an easy thing for me, either. True, I can draw on my past experience with women, but, as you so aptly put it, marriage is a very different game than dealing with a mistress.' He looked serious now, his eyes seeking her in an earnest attempt to communicate.

She nodded. He was meeting her part of the way, at least. 'Then we must muddle through together as best we can,' she said.

The musical soirée at Lady Pitton's had been mercifully short. They excused themselves early, citing Lady Bullfinch's illness as an excuse. For Julia, of course, it had not been an excuse at all. The first thing she did when she arrived at the house was run upstairs to make sure her grandmother had not experienced any recurrence.

For him, the soirée had been interminably long. Normally he enjoyed musical performances, but today he had other things on his mind. It became clear immediately that no scandalous gossip had circulated. Everyone greeted Lionel as they normally did, and Julia received the usual kind of attention. It was becoming abundantly obvious that there was to be no scandal.

Mercifully.

Which left him with a dilemma. He had offered to marry Julia because of the scandal. Now that they had been spared, there was no real reason to marry her except that he had already given her the betrothal ring, and they had reached an agreement.

But I don't have to marry her. He could be free once again to resume his normal life. His life as a rake, Julia would call it. Well, what was wrong with that? He had been happy enough living that life, until a few days ago. Now he would be able to pursue that lifestyle again, without a care in the world. He did not have to become a tenant for life.

The problem was, he would have to tell

her and he did not want her to think him cold blooded and uncaring. He especially did not want her to feel jilted. It was hardly gentlemanly to offer for a lady and then withdraw the offer two days later. It was the devil's own scrape.

The door of the library creaked open slowly. Julia's eyes — amber tonight, because of the gold trimming on her dress — combed the room, then rested on him. She nodded, satisfied, and stepped in.

'Your mother said you had not left yet,' she said. 'She said I would find you here.'

He smiled. 'I needed to reflect on things, particularly our marriage plans.' He managed to keep his words vague enough, until he had actually decided to speak to her.

His gaze went to her ring finger where he placed the ring earlier. She had taken it off, of course, before anyone else noticed it and knew of their engagement. But the very emptiness there seemed an indication. Why had she not worn the ring and announced their betrothal to the world?

Perhaps she was not yet completely convinced. In which case, he could broach the subject without hurting her feelings.

He took a deep breath. There was no easy way to do this. But he had to.

He started to speak, only to find she had already started saying something. 'I have something to —'

'I wish to discuss —'

He threw her a wry smile. 'Ladies first, I believe.'

'Very well,' she said. The small maroon box was in her hand: the ring box. She twirled it around absently between her fingers. 'It is only that — What I would like to say —'

'Yes?' he said, prompting her.

'There is no way of saying this without causing offence, but I would like to end our engagement.' The words came out in a rush. 'The circumstances that led to its formation are no longer there. No one knows of it, so there can be no embarrassment. You did not offer because of an attachment, and I am not attached, so —'

She was making a hash of it, but he would not help her out. Now that the boot was quite on the other foot, he found the situation intolerable. It infuriated him that she could stand there so calmly and toss away a chance at a marriage that had a great deal to offer her.

'Let me make sure I understand you correctly,' he said, coldly. 'You wish to end the engagement.' He said it with emphasis, as if she was saying something absurd instead of the very thing he had been planning to say just minutes ago.

She lifted her chin. 'We both know that we were pushed into our engagement by circumstances. We did not go into it blindly. You were a gentleman and you offered to protect my reputation. But such a radical step is no longer required. No one knows of the engagement' — she cast him an examining glance — 'at least I hope no one does, since I did not even inform anyone, not even Grandmother. So it is simply a matter to be settled between the two of us.' She placed the ring box decisively on a table in front of them.

It was logical, of course. It was what he wanted. But, devil take it, she could have at least waited a day before bounding into the room to break off the engagement.

Of course, nothing had really changed. If they declared their association over, no one would be any wiser. And he would be exactly where he was, just a few days ago. Which was where? On the verge of developing a longer standing arrangement with the Golden Widow. She had ogled him quite noticeably at the theatre, during Kean's performance. She was a morsel he had tasted, but would not mind tasting again.

Provided she did not become indiscreet.

He examined his companion and the soft changing brown-green of her eyes, the fiery highlights that flickered in her hair, the way her chin curved into a pronounced, obstinate edge. It was very clear from the way she held that chin right now that she expected him to consent.

Well, he would consent, and devil take her. He hoped never to set eyes on the obstinate chit again.

'I am hardly the type of gentleman to compel a lady against her will,' he said, trying to keep the sullenness out of his voice. 'You are, of course, free. However, I hope you will continue to take advantage of my mother's hospitality until you are certain you are completely safe from Neave.'

'Today was the last day of the wager. Surely after today I will be safe?'

'I cannot answer for his actions. It is possible. But it might be better not to tempt fate.' He recognized her hesitation. 'You need not worry that I will embarrass you with my presence,' he said, his voice laden with irony. 'Now that we have nothing more to fear, there is no longer any reason to escort you to any events.' He paused and examined her. 'You will have what you have requested time and again. I will leave you alone.'

She shook her head. 'I am sorry if I was impatient with you,' she said. 'I am aware that I am greatly indebted to you in more ways than one. I know that I have behaved badly. I hope you will forgive me.' She offered him her hand.

Her confession touched him unexpectedly. He took her hand and raised it to his lips. 'Perhaps, if things had not started as they did,' he said, 'our connection might have gone in a different direction. As it stands . . .'

She nodded. 'Yes.' He wanted to ask her what she meant. But she pulled her hand away, gently. 'Thank you for everything,' she said. She slid away, across the floor, out of his grasp, out of the room.

What was it about the way she moved that drew his attention?

He supposed he was not likely to find out.

The thought should have brought with it relief. Instead, he felt an unaccustomed sadness, as though something warm and sunny had disappeared from his life.

CHAPTER 14

Julia waited one more day before returning to her home in Grosvenor Square. She preferred to take no risks, and besides, Lady Bullfinch needed rest. Lionel, true to his word, stayed away, despite Lady Thorwynn's assertion that he was expected for dinner. A place was set for him, but he did not appear. The empty seat remained throughout the dinner, a reminder of his absence. Julia could not help feeling that the dinner conversation flagged a little, without him.

Lady Thorwynn had been the best of hostesses, and her kindness unlimited, but Julia was glad to return to her home, to be on familiar ground again. She had lived in her grandmother's townhouse from the time she was three, except for occasional stays in the country with friends of her family. The familiar picture of her mother stared down at her from the top of the wide stairway and a pang passed through her.

She mounted the steps and gazed into her mother's warm honey-brown eyes. It was a picture painted before her mother had met Julia's father. 'I did the right thing, Mother. You would have been proud of me,' she whispered. The expression in the honey eyes did not change. Julia stood still for a long moment, waiting. Then, with a sigh, she turned away.

As though she had been away for a year, not a few days, Julia inspected the house, making a list of work that needed to be done. She fell into neglected household tasks with unusual energy, throwing the household into a frenzy of spring cleaning.

She was in the dining-room arranging flowers when Rumbert announced a visitor.

'Miss Neville to see you,' said Rumbert. 'I took her to the parlour.'

'Thank you, Rumbert,' she said.

She found the young woman pacing the parlour, obviously in a state of agitation.

'What is it?' cried Julia.

Amelia crossed the room quickly. 'Thank *goodness* you are home,' she said, her brow wrinkled with anxiety. 'I came as quickly as I could when I learned what had happened. I had no idea you were involved in their schemes, you see, so didn't say anything before, but when I heard them talking —'

Clearly it was not an emergency. Relieved, Julia put her arm around the girl's shoulder, and led her to the settee.

'Come, sit down. I'll ring for some tea, and then you can tell me all about it,' she said, reassuringly.

'Oh, but you don't know —'

'I know you'll tell me, by and by,' she said. She tugged the bell pull. 'Whatever it is, it can wait until we have some tea.'

Despite her soothing attempts, Miss Neville stood up again and began to wander around the room, picking up objects and staring at them, then putting them down again. Perhaps she should not have called for the tea. Julia doubted she would drink any of it.

The tea tray arrived. Julia poured and handed Amelia a cup.

'Perhaps you would like to tell me what this agitation is about?'

She began an incoherent narrative that Julia could not make head or tail of. All she understood was that her parents would force her to marry an ogre — an earl — a very ugly old man with half his teeth missing and warts on his face — if she did not obey her mother. By marrying another earl, also an ogre, but quite young.

'If you don't sit down, Amelia, I'm afraid I won't comprehend a word that you're saying.'

She sat down then. Julia supposed that now that she had started the narrative, she was growing calmer.

'Could you start again? With the ogre — I mean old man earl?'

'If you saw him,' said Miss Neville, leaning forward in an effort to convince Julia, 'you would know why I could never, never marry him, apart from being very old.' She stopped to consider this. 'Some people who are very old look nice and kind. But this man doesn't look kind at all. He just looks ugly and *beastly*.' She shuddered. 'He used to be one of Prinny's friends, before they quarrelled. At least, that's what Papa said. I think that is why he wants me to marry him. Because he has a lot of influence at court.'

'Not if he's quarrelled with the Prince Regent,' said Julia. 'Look what happened to Beau Brummell.'

'That's what I thought. Not about Beau Brummell, but the other part. But Papa has political ambitions, you see, and he'd do *anything* to get closer to Prinny. He has some plans he wants implemented, and he is constantly seeking to get close to the Regent. You know how they are saying King

George cannot live long —'

'Yes, yes, I know that,' interrupted Julia. She did not want to hear Lord Medlow's opinion on the court or the royal family.

'Anyway, my father was adamant. He went so far as wanting to draw up the papers. But Mama objected.'

That surprised Julia. She would have imagined Lady Medlow delighted to sink her teeth into someone so powerful.

'Mama thinks he smells of the shop,' Amelia explained. 'There's a grocer somewhere in his ancestry, she says, or something like that. Anyway, she managed to make Papa promise to put the whole thing off. She convinced him that there was no hurry. I hadn't even had a Season, you see. Mama is sure I'll find someone just as good. They brought me to London, to make my come out, and be presented at court, which is, of course, important to Papa. And if I receive an equal or better offer of marriage, then I would not need to marry Lord Frugford.'

Julia had heard of Lord Frugford, though she had not met him. According to the *on-dits,* he was a lecher.

'That day in Hyde Park.' She took a deep breath and looked at her hands. 'I swear to you it was not my idea at all. My mother threatened me if I did not do it.' She rose again and began to pace. 'It was no accident. My fall, I mean. At least, I did *really* fall. But it was because I pricked poor Stargaze with a nail, and he went wild. I was sorry to hurt him, but Mama insisted it was necessary.' She looked hopelessly at Julia. 'You hate me now, don't you?'

Julia shook her head. But her thoughts were racing. That explained at lot of things that seemed odd at the time.

'She was with me at the park, you see, and she sent the groom to fetch something, so he couldn't immediately catch up with me. We knew Thorwynn was riding in the park. All he had to do was chase after me and Lady Nattleham would do the rest.'

'But you *fell*,' I said. 'Suppose you had fallen badly and hurt yourself?'

Amelia grinned. 'I am an *excellent* horse-woman. I can do tricks on a horse. One of the grooms in the stable used to belong to a circus, and when I was small he taught me how to slide down to either side of the horse without falling.' Her eyes gleamed. 'That's what I did. I slid off the horse and crumpled to the ground.'

'Did your mother know this?'

'Of course.'

Julia thought better of her for this at least. If she knew her daughter would come to no harm, then her actions were less despicable.

'And then you happened upon us and the whole thing came to nothing.' She frowned. 'I was very glad of it, for I don't wish to marry Lord Thorwynn, either.'

Julia looked puzzled. 'Surely he's a better option than Frugford.'

'Oh, much better,' said Amelia, quickly. 'I know he's your friend, and I'm sure he is very agreeable, but he — he frightens me.'

'Frightens you?'

'He has a way of looking at you as if you are an insect below his notice. I like him a bit better now, after we talked in the theatre, for he was quite kind there. But I still don't want to marry him. Especially *now.*'

She tried to puzzle out what Amelia meant by that last statement, but decided she did not know everything yet.

'What I fail to understand,' Julia said, 'is why you came to tell me this so suddenly, and why it threw you into such agitation.'

Amelia grew confused. 'Agitation?' she asked, puzzled. Something must have occurred to her, because she gave a little laugh. 'No, *that* wasn't what made me agitated,' she said, as though it was perfectly obvious.

So there was more. Julia had a sinking feeling in her stomach.

'My mother was very vexed when the attempt did not succeed. She had put a great deal of planning into it. She did not want to give up. So she planned for Lord Thorwynn to be caught in a compromising situation with me.'

'In the library, at the Kinleigh ball,' said Julia.

Amelia nodded. 'Yes. My mother wrote a note suggesting an assignation by a lady. I was to be very naughty and soft talk him and somehow bring him to embrace me or kiss me, though I had no idea how I would accomplish that. But when I opened the door of the library I found you were there already. You had your back to me and didn't see me.'

Julia remembered that moment's panic and despair. It was a wonder she had not noticed the door opening. She had been jumping at shadows.

'So I crept away and went to find Mama and Lady Telway to warn them. I couldn't find them, and someone claimed me for a dance. It was someone Mama didn't approve of — Captain Neave, whom I think you know — so I took advantage of her absence.' Her eyes lit up and her face brightened. 'He's a very amiable gentleman, not at all silly like so many of the others. I think I may come to like him.' Then she remembered why she was here, and the brightness disappeared. She pouted. 'Mama remonstrated with me *all the way* home in the carriage. How she couldn't rely on me for anything and other such things. But how could I have made Lord Thorwynn kiss *me* when *you* were already in the library? It stands to reason. But there was no convincing her. No use explaining *anything* to her when she's irrational.' She grimaced. 'She said *I'd* put her in an awkward situation. As if I *planned* it all. She saw you with Lord Thorwynn, and would have so loved to embroil you in a big scandal, but she's determined not to let you have him.'

Well, that explained why there had been no scandal. 'What is it, then, that brought you to me today?'

'I heard them discussing something about using you to make Lord Thorwynn offer for me. I felt I had to warn you. I *can't* continue to play her game. And I *don't* want lose your friendship. I value it highly.'

Julia smiled at her warmly, glad of her affection.

Amelia paused, frowned, and added, naively, 'Apart from the fact that I have no other friends in London, I wouldn't have *anyone* to go out with.'

Julia's mouth twisted ruefully. 'Don't worry,' she said, 'I won't hold you responsible for your mother's plans. I know you don't agree with them.'

'Not at all,' cried the girl, anxiety clouding her face. 'The problem is, they're hatching another plot. *That's* why I came. I don't know what it is, and this time they aren't going to tell me, so it may be more difficult to thwart their plans. I know you have some interest in Lord Thorwynn, and I wouldn't ruin that for *anything*.' She walked to the window, looked outside briefly, and then turned. 'Besides,' she said, with a mischievous twinkle, 'as I said before, I have no desire to marry Lord Thorwynn.' She shuddered elaborately.

Had Amelia actually called him an ogre, earlier? It seemed incredible. But meanwhile, Julia really needed to clarify matters with the young debutante, once and for all. 'As for Lord Thorwynn, I have no interest —'

'You don't need to pretend with me,' said Amelia, looking mischievous. She took a seat close to Julia on the settee. 'Don't worry. Your secret is *safe*. I would never mention a word to anybody.'

It was no use arguing. Amelia had made up her mind. In any case she was discreet, and she liked Julia well enough not to wish her harm.

They parted on the best of terms. The confession had taken a load off Amelia's back, to judge by the way she almost skipped down the stairs as she walked out. Not a cherub at all. More like a kitten, with some good, healthy claws.

Meanwhile, Julia puzzled over Amelia's certainty that she had an interest in Lionel. She shrugged. She supposed Amelia was basing it on the kiss her mother had interrupted in the library.

The memory of the kiss evoked a small quiver that passed through every inch of her. Odd, that she should remember it now that the relationship between them had ended. She found herself lingering over that kiss. Reliving the sensations that had passed through her at the time, interrupted so abruptly by Lady Medlow. And to her dismay, she found herself longing for more.

Lionel downed his third glass of brandy. It burned its way through his throat. Damn, but it was good to rid himself of all those entanglements. The last two weeks had been like some strange nightmare in which he played a role, but didn't understand the rules. That Swifton hoyden had led him on a merry chase. Well, he was certainly glad it was over. Now he could enjoy life again.

'You're very distracted this evening,' remarked Benny, amusement plain on his face. 'I've called you twice, but you haven't heard me.'

'I very much doubt it,' said Lionel. He picked up the decanter, and saw that it was empty. 'You've been drinking rather a lot,' he commented to Benny, and signalled the waiter for another bottle. 'I'm simply relishing my lack of commitments.'

'Why are you scowling so darkly, in that case?' asked Benny. 'And why are you hunched up over your brandy like a miser?'

Lionel drew himself to his full height, or as close he could, given that he was seated, and that he had swallowed down his brandy very quickly. 'I'm scowling because I know if I see that Swifton chit again, I'm going to strangle her.'

'Well, you need not see her again. Not for a very long time. You are hardly on visiting terms, and you have no more reason to attend any balls. It's unlikely you'll run into her. That should cheer you up.'

It should have, but it didn't. He tried to account for that lingering feeling of — something he couldn't put his finger on. *Malaise?* No, hardly that. *Agitation?* No, why should he be agitated? *Unease?* That was it.

He searched about for a reason. He found one. Aha. 'I'm not yet sure she's safe from that snivelling scoundrel,' he said.

To Lionel's astonishment, Benny threw his head backwards and laughed.

'What's so funny about that?' he said, feeling thunderously angry. 'I would think that you, of all people, would understand what she went through.' He rose. He was not going to sit here and let that whey-faced grinning idiot make fun of Julia's misfortunes. 'I'd better leave, before I land you a facer and my membership in Brooks's is brought into question.'

Instead of drawing back, Benny's grin grew even wider. 'I can't believe it. You're besotted. Totally besotted.'

'I'm not besotted,' growled Lionel, irritated beyond reason by Benny's remarks. He wondered why he had ever regarded such an addle-headed muttonhead as a friend.

'Sit down then and let's discuss it like gentlemen, shall we?' said Benny, still grinning.

The waiter arrived with the brandy. He eyed Lionel uncertainly, wondering no doubt if he was going to ask him to take it back.

He sat down reluctantly. There was absolutely nothing to discuss. But he could not think of anything else to do that night. He may as well stay and drink the brandy.

'Since this topic is so irritating to you,' said Benny, 'let's talk about something else. It'll give you time to a take a hold on your temper.'

'There is nothing whatsoever wrong with my temper,' said Lionel, between gritted teeth.

Benny looked at the ceiling. Fortunately, he kept quiet.

'Any thoughts on what we are going to do with Neave?' asked Benny.

This was hardly an improvement on the last topic. In fact, Benny seemed bent on provoking him. 'If I had any ideas I would have implemented them already,' he snapped.

Julia's face in the library as she emerged from behind the curtains came back to him. He would never forget the mix of emotions there. Terror, horror, suspicion and uncertainty all at once. Then relief when it registered that he had been doing nothing worse than tickling her. Fortunately, she had never asked him who he thought he was tickling behind the curtain. Maybe she had reached her own conclusions.

In any case, it didn't matter. But Neave's

intentions mattered a great deal. Lionel wanted more than ever to haul him by the throat and toss him into some filthy cesspool to drown.

Yet he was doomed to fail, mainly because there was no way to accuse him without bringing ruination on the lady involved. And he knew it. Lionel's fingers twisted into fists. If there was some way to bring him to justice. . . .

'You're doing it again,' said Benny.

'Doing what?' said Lionel, taking the carafe and sloshing the liquid into his glass. It was the colour of dried blood. He had never noticed. He put his glass down with a thump.

'Scowling,' said Benny, 'horribly.'

'What do you expect if you bring up Neave?' he said, not growling now, just talking through his teeth.

Benny had the grace to look contrite. 'Yes, that wasn't very good of me, was it? It's just that I wanted to see how far I could push you before you cracked and admitted it.'

Lionel blew out a heavy breath. 'I thought we weren't going to discuss that topic.'

'Which topic?' Benny asked, false innocence written all over his face. 'Oh, yes, now I recall: the Swifton chit.'

'Don't call her that.'

'The Swifton chit?' He was grinning again.

Lionel lunged for him and gripped him by the neckcloth. The conversation at the tables around them ceased. Those gentlemen who had their backs to him turned and craned their necks.

He let go. 'Truce?'

Benny rubbed his neck pointedly, although Lionel had only touched his cravat, which looked slightly crumpled. 'Truce. Remind me not to mention her again.'

The moment he said that Lionel felt an almost overwhelming compulsion to talk about her.

'She's not so bad. Not really a hoyden, you know. Quite level-headed in fact. Just doesn't like men very much.' He winced as he said it.

'Men, or rakes?' said Benny, leaning back and watching him with a half smirk. Lionel ignored the question.

'I'll concede to you that it seems to be rakes she objects to.' Even as he said it, a heavy gloom seemed to descend on him and pin him to the armchair. He eyed the thick russet liquid in his glass.

He could not change who he was, any more than that brandy in the glass could turn to something else. Ratafia, for example. That's what she wanted. She wanted him to become docile ratafia, when he was a fine, well-honed brandy. How much more unfair could the situation be?

'Perhaps you could convince her otherwise.' He looked up to find Benny watching him. He was more earnest now.

'Convince her?' asked Lionel, having lost thread of the conversation.

'Not to object to rakes. Or at least, not to object to this one particular rake.'

He raised his brow. 'How do you propose that I do that?'

'Talk to her.'

It seemed such a simple thing, when one said it like that. So simple it was doomed to failure. But the more Lionel thought of it, the more appealing it seemed to be. Why not? It would not hurt. It might even do some good.

He put the glass down. 'I think, for once, Benny, you've made a sensible suggestion. Let's go.'

'Go?' he asked. 'Where to?'

'To the Coppertons' ball. To see Miss Swifton. To talk to her.'

Julia was driven by the same restless energy that drove her earlier into obsessive cleaning. She was surrounded by suitors the moment she entered the ballroom, and she had not yet sat down for a dance. Her card was almost full.

Almost, because she had left the spaces beside two of the waltzes empty. She glanced at those empty spaces now and wondered what had prompted her to leave them open. The blank whiteness of those unclaimed lines seemed a chastisement, a reminder of the many follies she had committed in the last two weeks.

The strains of the waltz floated towards her. The chatter of the young men around her irritated her nerves like pepper on an inflamed cut. She needed a moment to herself, or she would snap at them. 'Excuse me, gentlemen, but I'm feeling rather faint. I need to find my grandmother and withdraw to the retiring room.'

There were a few murmurs of protest, and a few offers of assistance, but she declined them with a tight smile and moved away to where she had last seen Lady Bullfinch.

A dark wall rose up before her and she slammed into it, the very breath knocked out of her.

Strong arms steadied her. The heady aroma of a familiar perfume filled her nostrils.

She allowed the arms to hold her, just for one moment. Then she stepped back.

'I am very sorry, Lord Thorwynn,' she muttered.

'My apologies, Miss Swifton,' he murmured, in unison.

She kept her eyes down. His touch had provoked a riot of feeling and she did not want to look at him until the sensations had subsided, which was difficult when he was standing so close.

'Good evening, Miss Swifton.'

Startled, she looked around Lionel's shoulder, which was very much in the way.

'Lord Benedict,' she said, smiling at him warmly. He was a wonderful distraction. Her heart calmed down and her breathing returned to normal.

'Why don't I get such a pleasant smile?' said Lionel, in a pretence of wounded pride.

'Perhaps you don't deserve one. Whereas I . . .' said Lord Benedict.

She smiled at Lord Benedict. 'Do deserve one. Of course you do. As for your friend,' she said, unable to resist teasing Thorwynn, 'he doesn't need my smile. There are enough young misses throwing smiles in his direction in one evening to last him the next two years.'

Lionel looked around him, as if noticing the smiles for the first time. 'The simpering smiles of girls ordered to smile by scheming mamas hardly count.'

'I have only now realized my disadvantage,' replied Julia. 'I have no scheming mama to tell me to smile at you.'

She expected him to laugh, or at least smile, but his brows knotted and he seemed displeased by her statement.

'I would not tease Thorwynn tonight, if I were you,' said Lord Benedict. 'He is in a thunderous temper.' He paused and rubbed his neck dramatically. 'He might even decide to grab you by the neck as he did with me earlier in the evening, so beware.'

Thorwynn confirmed Benny's statement by sending him a murderous glance that promised future retaliation.

'Then perhaps I should avoid him altogether, as I would avoid a wounded bear,' she said, still talking to Benny.

'As I have never seen a wounded bear, I cannot comment on that comparison, but it seems to me a good way to describe Thorwynn.'

Thorwynn simply glowered.

Julia, in contrast, began to experience that strange bubbly feeling again, laughter rising to the surface.

'Well, then, I'd better disappear from here in full haste, before the bear decides to pounce.'

She excused herself, a little smile playing on her lips. The ballroom no longer seemed oppressive, and she looked forward to supper with anticipation.

'I thought you were going to talk to her,' said Benny. 'Instead you stand there scowling at her as if her very sight disgusts you.'

'Who appointed you as my keeper? If I wish to glare at a lady, I do not need your permission to do so.' In fact he wished he had not brought his friend to the ball. He had always been aware of his friend's good looks, and was well aware that many young women found Benny very attractive, even though he rarely made the slightest effort to deliberately attract attention. But tonight he found Benny's handsome face distinctly unpleasant.

'I thought you wanted to talk to her,' said Benny.

'I didn't exactly have a chance,' remarked Lionel, coldly. 'You seemed to be manipulating the conversation yourself. I could hardly get in a word myself.'

Benny looked at him incredulously, then burst into laughter. 'I think you'd better go somewhere else tonight. Or better still, go home and sleep it off. Perhaps tomorrow you'll be more rational.'

'I'm perfectly rational,' said Lionel. He watched as a young man waylaid Julia and led her to the dance floor. 'What does that puppy think he's doing? I distinctly heard her say she's feeling faint.'

'She seems to have recovered,' said Benny.

And in fact she looked quite animated. The pallor that had marked her face just a few minutes ago had disappeared. She appeared very pleased about something. A huge smile lit up her face.

Lionel followed the line of her vision, and cursed inwardly.

A young athletic-looking gentleman was heading towards her, and he was clearly very welcome.

Lionel decided to retreat. Benny seemed for once to have the right of it. Tonight he would accomplish nothing.

He turned on his heels, prepared to ram his way out through the crush of people. An instant later, however, he came to a complete standstill, his eyes narrowing on a figure dressed in the elite green uniform.

Neave stood in the shadows, observing Julia, his face twisted with malice.

Lionel changed direction, hovering near the dance area. The next dance was a waltz, and by God, Julia was going to dance it with him.

Chapter 15

He summoned up his most charming manner. He would not permit her to turn him down.

She had scarcely left the dance floor when he stepped up to her, bowing gracefully and smiling his most dazzling smile.

'I believe this waltz is ours, Miss Swifton?'

She looked down at her dance card.

'I think you put my name down earlier,' he said, quickly, before she could say anything, before she had time to read someone else's name. He took her hand, trying to make the gesture graceful so it would not look as if he was grabbing her.

Her eyes swept up from under heavy lashes. Dark and thick, they framed those fluid eyes. For an endless moment he found himself drawn inside them. Then the music started and he sought a place for them on the dance floor.

Her hand rested delicately on his. He

swept her into the dance, noting with satisfaction that this time she did not resist as he drew her just a little closer, perhaps, than he should.

By the time he realized it was a mistake, it was too late.

He could not very well push her away. But he eased her away from him, because to hold her so close strained every muscle in his body that seemed to be determined to crush her to him. His body reacted to every small move of hers; her fingers flickering lightly on his shoulder; the edge of her thigh grazing his; her foot touching his calf when she missed a step; even her breath as it stirred against his cheek. Every tiniest action caused a rush of desire in him.

His senses had become so attuned to her presence that he could almost hear her heartbeat, without actually being close enough.

When had that happened? Just two days ago he sat serenely in the library of his mother's house as she told him she did not want to marry him. So why was he reacting this way?

He edged away from her, leaning backwards, striving to avoid all contact. The waltz that had started so gracefully turned into a stiff march across the ballroom, his arms hard and his body unyielding. He would have laughed if he could, but he was incapable of laughter. She must think him no better than a lump of metal. Which is what he had become. He had no choice in the matter. It was either that, or finding himself swept out of the ballroom into the darkest corner he could find.

After what seemed like a year, the waltz ended. They parted awkwardly, wordlessly. He bowed formally to her and made his escape, looking for the quickest route out of the room.

He had not counted on the old tabbies, however. They waited. They hovered in the ready, their eyes fixed on him. The moment he left the dance floor, they steered their young debutantes straight at him. A flock of white-clad girls fluttered and twittered around him, and he was forced to be civil because, God forbid he should offend the sensibilities of these young innocent buds. It was Benny, of course, who had pointed that out during one of the numerous balls he seemed to be attending. He had reminded him there was no call for him to be uncivil to them, when it was his fault for coming to the ball in the first place.

His glance went over their heads, ignoring the diffident smiles in front of him. His mouth somehow produced words that must have been appropriate because no-one looked shocked. His eyes attempted to pierce through a group of young gentlemen thronging around Julia, but all he could see was the top of her brown head.

Well, there were other fish to fry. The surge of lust he had experienced as he danced with her was simply the result of being without a woman for several days. He would remedy that as quickly as possible.

Still making meaningless conversation, he searched round the room for someone to amuse himself with. He noticed in passing the Neville girl, who also had a handful of admirers, and to all appearances she flirted quite comfortably.

A familiar throaty laugh reached his ears and he turned around languidly, a half-formed smile on his lips. By God, his luck was finally turning. Mrs Catherine Radlow was here, the Golden Widow. It was certainly a stroke of good fortune. He had not seen her since that night they had spent together and he had every intention of renewing their acquaintance.

He disentangled himself from the twittering girls with a polite apology and strode towards her.

Catherine was speaking to Captain Abbot,

a man Lionel knew from his army days. Perhaps she had set up with him, after his own absence from the scene. But, as he approached, he noticed her quick sideways glance at him, the way her hand moved to her throat. He was in his element here. He was a good enough judge of women to know that she was fully aware of his approach, and that Captain Abbott did not really signify.

'Good evening, Mrs Radlow,' he said, smiling lazily and drawing her gloved hand into his. 'You've brought sunshine into this very dim occasion, thank heavens.'

He bowed to Captain Abbott. The latter gave him a quick grin, exchanged a few remarks with him about mutual acquaintances, and excused himself.

'I haven't frightened him off, have I?' asked Lionel. He kept his gaze fixed on her face, seeking information on her mood, looking for an implicit invitation.

She shook her head and lowered her eyes briefly, but did not laugh. She was not going to make it easy for him.

She was piqued at him for neglecting her. Damned unfair, when she had made no attempt to get in touch with him either.

His eyes went to Julia. A scrawny young man with substantial shoulder padding was

254

leading her to the dance floor. She probably did not know about the padding. She did not have any brothers, so she probably did not know that men resorted to such things.

He turned his attention to Catherine Radlow. Why did women like to complicate things? He could lay a wager that he would be in her bed later tonight, but she was going to make him work for it. He was not even sure he *wanted* to work for it. She was a tigress in bed, and he had enjoyed every moment of their one wild frolic. But he was tired of catering to women's sullen fits.

Across the room, Julia laughed at something her partner said. What had that puppy said that was so funny? He tried to think of the times he had made her laugh. Had she ever truly laughed when she was with him? All the more reason to find out what that stunted weakling was saying to make her laugh.

'Would you like to dance, Mrs Radlow?'

She looked a bit surprised.

'The dance is almost finished. Did you mean this dance, or the next?'

Next dance Miss Swifton would not be laughing at this man's jokes, and he would not be able to overhear what she thought was funny. 'This dance. I find the tune very agreeable, don't you?'

She gave him a quizzical look and took his offered arm. 'The music is agreeable,' she acknowledged. 'I can't say I took particular notice of it.'

The dance floor was crowded, and the dancing wavered as several couples were forced to adjust to their entry. More than one person glared at them, and Lionel thought he saw a tiny frown cross Julia's face from the corner of his eye as they squeezed in next to her. Apart from a quick nod in her direction, however, he did not acknowledge her presence.

Instead, he focused his efforts on coaxing Mrs Radlow into a better humour, and into his bed.

Meanwhile, his ears strained to overhear Julia's conversation with her partner.

The music stopped.

He had to restrain himself from throwing hostile glances at Julia's lanky partner. He concentrated fully on smiling at Catherine. He bowed to her with exquisite graciousness. He put out his hand, took hers, and tucked it under his elbow with an exaggerated flourish and moved off the dance floor.

With Catherine as his partner, Lionel lost at a game of whist. She laughed it off, though she had held her end up. Benny, who was teamed with a charming widow named Laura Elware, called him a milksop.

'If you can't play any better,' he said, 'don't insult me by playing another game.'

Lionel tossed down his cards. 'I know when I'm not wanted,' he remarked, giving Lady Elware a broad smile. 'Come, Mrs Radlow. Let's withdraw to the ballroom.'

The moment they reached the ballroom, his eyes sought out Julia. He found her quickly. She stood alone. It was coming close to suppertime, and if he sat next to her at supper, that would give him an opportunity to converse with her. He excused himself from Catherine under the pretence of going to fetch something to drink, and approached Julia.

'Are you engaged for the supper dance?' he asked, at his most appealing.

'I'm sorry, Lord Thorwynn,' she said, with a sugary smile. 'I'm afraid I'm already promised to Lord Talbrook.'

Lord Talbrook chose that moment to reappear, carrying two glasses of wine. 'I'd like you to meet my cousin, Nicholas Flint, Lord Talbrook,' said Julia. 'He's recently returned from a long trip to the Continent, and has been amusing me with tales about his travels.'

Lionel bowed and greeted him civilly,

examining him from under his lids. Merry blue eyes, light-brown hair with just a hint of curl, a wide, honest face. He exuded an era of fitness and health which Lionel found particularly irritating. He noted with satisfaction that though handsome, Lord Talbrook was much shorter than him.

'Perhaps we can compare notes,' said Lionel. 'I've spent time on the Continent, although much of it involved fighting against Napoleon. It would be pleasant to talk about some of the places I've been.'

Talbrook bowed, smiling amiably enough. Miss Swifton shuffled her feet, perhaps feeling excluded from the conversation. Good.

'Here's my card,' said Thorwynn. 'Send me a note if you wish to have a drink tomorrow. Are you a member of Brooks's?'

'Why, thank you,' replied Talbrook. 'I have not been to Brooks's since my return, but I'd be delighted to join you there.'

Any hope that he might be too negligible to be a member disappeared.

Lionel bowed and moved away, making sure Julia saw him joining Mrs Radlow.

Her eyes followed him as he strode away. He was not behaving so much like a bear as like a bull. She had read about bullfights in Spain, and seen a picture of a bull ready to charge. For some reason it reminded her of Lionel as he had borne down upon her to invite her to supper.

She turned to Nicholas, taking the glass of wine from him. She sipped it slowly.

'I know it's rude of me, when you have so many other things to tell me, and I *do* want to hear them all, but you mentioned seeing my father.'

She realized she was clasping her glass so hard it might break. She willed her fingers to loosen, and tried to control the clenching in the pit of her stomach. Some part of her had thought her father dead — had hoped, in many ways, that that was the case, especially since he had never responded to any attempt on her part to contact him. She had accidentally found his address one day in her ladyship's desk, when she was about nine. With the help of Aunt Viola, Nicholas's mother, she had sent him a string of letters telling him about her. After more than a year of receiving no reply, she had convinced herself her father was no longer alive.

But now Nicholas had seen him and the time for make-believe was over.

'Let's find a quiet corner to converse,' said her cousin.

They moved to an area that was partially concealed by a row of blossoming orange trees in large Wedgwood pots. Several benches were set up there to create the illusion of a park setting. The fragrance of the blossoms filled the air. Julia sat down on an empty bench, and for a moment simply drank in the delicate fragrance. Then she turned to her cousin expectantly.

Nicholas was ill at ease. 'I saw your father in Vienna. In fact, I made a particular attempt to enquire after him, once the reports reached me that he was there. He owns a very successful gambling establishment frequented by people of fashion. I sought him out, and explained who I was.' He hesitated.

She knew he wanted to spare her, but she needed to lay to rest this particular ghost. 'You must tell me the truth, Cousin,' she said, her voice scarcely above a whisper.

'He's married,' said Nicholas, 'to a very rich widow. An opera singer whose husband died and left her a fortune. She helped him start up the gambling house. I believe he has several children with her.' He frowned, as if remembering something unpleasant.

'Go on, Cousin.'

'There is nothing more,' he said.

'You have not told me how he reacted to your introduction of yourself.' She knew she was pushing, but she wanted to know the whole story.

'This is hardly the place to be talking about such a serious matter,' said her cousin, surveying the crowds around them. 'I'll call on you tomorrow, and we will speak more privately.'

'By all means call on me tomorrow. But you will condemn me to a sleepless night imagining all the terrible things my father said, when perhaps it was not that bad after all?'

He gave her a pale smile. 'You've always been stubborn, Cousin, which is a good quality at times. But sometimes you tread in murky waters.'

She refused to be distracted. 'Tell me what he said.'

Her cousin sighed. 'He told me his marriage to your mother had been nothing but youthful folly, and that it was so far in the past he could scarcely remember her.'

She could see from the way he chose his words carefully that he was not telling her everything that her father had said. She imagined her father had expressed himself far less politely.

'He said he knew your grandmother took good care of you, that she would make sure you had everything you need. You are well provided for, both with the money you inherited from your mother, and your grandmother's wealth. That is all he needed to know about you. He did not understand why I wanted to dredge up the past. England is nothing but a distant nightmare to him, and he wants nothing to do with it.'

Or with her. The words were unspoken, but they hung in the air between them.

Bitterness and sorrow rose up to form a large, sharp-edged pebble in her throat. It threatened to choke her. She did not see how she could join the others for supper. She did not even know how she would get to the front entrance of the house from where she was.

'I was afraid of this,' said her cousin, peering at her closely. 'Perhaps it would be better if I took you home.'

On the verge of accepting his offer, she caught sight of Lionel with the blonde-haired lady on his arm. Julia had recognized her immediately as the turbaned lady at the theatre. They talked in the way of intimates, heads together and bodies close, though not so close as to be improper. The sight stung Julia, sending her thoughts in a completely different direction.

She would not simply disappear. She had told Lionel she was going in with her cousin, and did not want to appear a liar by not even going in to supper.

She pulled herself together. She had heard the truth about her father, and the truth hurt. But it was nothing new, after all. She had never actually known him, had no recollection of ever meeting him, so she could not really mourn his loss. She swallowed down the pebble. It settled in her stomach, hard and heavy.

She turned to her companion. 'Shall we?' she asked, chin up and back like a stake. She rested her hand on his elbow. His solid familiarity reassured her, and some of her sorrow slid away.

She would think about Nicholas's news later.

In the darkness of the carriage, Catherine leaned against him. He inhaled her seductive perfume, heavy and promising, and passed his lips along her hair. She turned and raised her head. Her hands moved up to his face. She caressed his cheek, gently, then, licking her lips, she passed her thumb across his lower lip.

He pulled her towards him, too impatient to wait. He wanted to take her, here and now. His lips closed down on hers.

She pushed him away, laughing.

'What's the hurry?' she said. 'We've got all night.'

Again she outlined his face with the tips of her fingers. He took her hand gently in his, and held it. She peered at him through the dim light shining through the windows.

He examined her beautiful face, ghostly and shadowed in the darkness. Her lips were perfect, curved and sensuous. Her large blue eyes brimmed with life. Her delicate nose curved just slightly at the tip, the nose of a fairy-tale princess.

He thought of the time they had spent the night together. It brought a smile to his lips.

He kissed her again, lightly this time, and then let her go.

The carriage stopped in front of her house. She started to rise.

He did not stir.

'So, are you joining me later?' she asked, laughter in her eyes.

He opened his mouth to say, yes, of course. Instead, he said, 'I don't think so.'

She sat back down on the carriage seat and regarded him intently.

'When did this change of mind happen?'

He shook his head. 'I'm not sure. I'm sorry.' He had not expected this at all. In fact, he had prepared himself for a long night of enjoyment.

'It's that brown-haired girl, isn't it?' asked Catherine, with a touch of sadness.

'What brown-haired girl?'

'The one you kept watching all through supper.'

He wanted to deny it. He wanted to tell her she didn't know what she was talking about. He examined her face. There was no malice there, no anger, only ruefulness.

He ran his fingers through his unruly locks, stared out of the window. Anything rather than look at her.

'I don't know. Perhaps.'

She smiled, putting her hand to his cheek. 'You don't have to spare my feelings, Lionel. They are not engaged. I simply enjoy your company.'

He appreciated her warmth and her generosity. He put his arms out and drew her into them, a tight embrace full of affection.

'You're a fine lady, Catherine,' said Lionel. 'I hope you will find someone worthy of you some day.'

'Perhaps,' she said, echoing his words. But she sounded uncertain.

He watched her descend from the carriage and walk slowly to the townhouse, watched the footman open the door. It was not until the door had closed completely behind her that he signalled the coachman to move.

CHAPTER 16

The carriage creaked, a thin, high-pitched whine that strained her nerves to screaming point. The horses' feet struck the pavement, clip clopping in her ears. Even with all the padding and velvet, the seat was hard, so every time the carriage jolted, it rattled her to her very teeth. And Grandmother was entirely uninterested.

'You heard what I told you,' she said. 'Nicholas saw my father.'

'Yes,' she replied.

'And he isn't in the least interested in me.' Her voice came out as a petulant bleat. She did not like petulant bleating. She despised it, in fact.

'Yes.'

Julia turned on her. 'Don't you have anything else to say?'

'No, I'm afraid not,' said Lady Bullfinch, unperturbed.

Julia threw her head back against the seat

in disgust. She would have thought Grannie would understand what she was going through. Instead, she just sat there like — like a *fish,* staring, with big round eyes and no expression. Fish didn't care for anything except opening their mouths and swallowing food.

She had never cared about her father. Had never tried to help her find him.

A particularly deep rut in the road caused the carriage to lurch unpleasantly. She rubbed a bruised elbow. Why couldn't anyone have invented something more comfortable for people to ride in?

She wanted nothing more than to fling open the door and jump out. She needed to walk, to clear her thoughts. But it was three o'clock in the morning.

She would have to wait until she could go riding, later.

As if to convince her, a handful of raindrops flung themselves against the window, followed by another. Within moments, long teardrops raced down the window.

A childhood dream, destroyed. Her father had found another wife, another set of children to care for. She had followed a pipe-dream, nothing more, and she had only herself to blame.

Grandmother had always told her to

forget about her father. Yet she had persisted in wanting something from him that he could never give.

'Did he ever hold me?' she said, abruptly, into the darkness.

Her ladyship did not pretend not to know whom she meant. 'I believe he did. He remained with your mother until you were about one and a half, after all, even though he dallied with other women.'

'How could he just forget about me, in that case?'

Grandmother regarded her evenly. 'Some people are simply selfish. Men or women. They aren't capable of true love. They're too taken up with their own needs to care for those of others.' She sighed into the darkness. 'Don't try to puzzle them out, child, because you can't.'

Julia remembered her little girl self, the nine year old who thought she would remind her father of her existence by writing a few letters.

Her cheeks burned for that little girl.

Her eyes fell on the old lady. Huddled in the corner of the carriage, she appeared frail and tired. Julia's heart went out to her.

Much as the information Nicholas had revealed had upset her, he had told her nothing new: nothing had changed. She had

Grannie. Grannie who had cared for her every step of the road.

'Thank you, for being there,' she whispered.

Silence met her, then a gentle snore. She was asleep.

Thorwynn's grandmother returned to London from her country residence, and Lady Bullfinch went immediately to call on her. Left to her own devices, Julia took the opportunity to go out. She needed to overcome the sense of dejection that had assailed her the night before, and what better way than to refocus her efforts on finding herself a suitor. A *suitable* suitor.

Unlike Lord Thorwynn. Who was as unsuitable as could be. With a lady clinging to his arm wherever he went. He had left the ball with the turbaned lady, their heads close together, laughing. She had no doubt where they were going.

That was not the kind of husband she needed. Any more than she needed a father who considered her very existence an irritant.

So she went to Montague House, to the British Museum. It was a good place to find herself someone earnest like her, who shared the same interests, whom she could *talk* to, for heaven's sake.

Besides, she had offered to show Amelia the Elgin Marbles.

She met her in the exhibition room. Amelia, gaping with open curiosity, appeared discomfited at the sight of so many naked men.

'I'm so glad you arrived. I felt very strange standing here alone with all these — figures to look at. I asked my maid Hannah to wait outside in the carriage, you see.' She slipped her elbow into Julia's and began to walk around the hall. 'I told Mama I was going to a museum with you. She wasn't very happy about it. I think she's worried that being a bluestocking will rub off on me.' She grinned at her companion. 'She agreed to let me meet you, because she thinks that if you go somewhere, Lord Thorwynn is bound to turn up. She still has high hopes for me with him. As if I'd look at him *twice.*'

Julia raised her eyebrow.

'Well, I wouldn't, and I'm not going to pretend, just because you like him,' she said, incorrigibly.

Julia wondered if she had done the girl a favour by encouraging her outspokenness. But her high spirits amused her, and were a balm at this moment when she needed something to soothe her bruised sensibilities. Amelia would certainly cheer her from her fit of the doldrums.

'Your mother's wrong about Lord Thorwynn. He would certainly never meet me here. I doubt very much he is in the habit of visiting museums,' said Julia.

Amelia clearly had not the slightest interest in Thorwynn's habits. She was examining the marbles surrounding her. 'Mama could *not* have seen the marbles,' giggled Amelia. 'She certainly wouldn't approve of *him*.' She pointed to a nude male figure with nothing like a fig leaf anywhere in sight. 'Is that really what they look like?' she asked. 'Men, I mean?'

The blood rushed up to Julia's face. She had seen the statues and the friezes many times, but had always examined them as one should, as supreme examples of Classical Art. She had never been unladylike enough to stare as Amelia did. 'I wouldn't know,' she said, embarrassed by Amelia's directness.

Amelia tilted her head and inspected her with a directness that was disconcerting. 'I thought perhaps since you were older — and Mama is always going on about how you could corrupt me, and you were kissing Lord Thorwynn in the library . . .'

Julia met that direct gaze with difficulty. 'I

— no, I have not.' She admitted it with embarrassment. It was as if Amelia had discovered something shameful about her. She realized she was not proud of her lack of experience, even if it was only what was expected of her.

Amelia's eyes lit up and she clapped her hands. 'Well, *good.* Because now you can't act as superior as you like to do.' She lowered her voice to a near whisper. 'So we might as well take advantage of the fact that there's no one here, and examine those statues rather *closely,* don't you think? I'd like to know what men actually look like, wouldn't you?'

The expression of mischief on Amelia's face was irresistible. Julia glanced around the gallery carefully to be sure they were completely alone. Then, drawn in by Amelia's little game, she followed the girl, and before she knew it, she was giggling along with her.

They were engaged in viewing a particularly intriguing male torso, consumed with hilarity, when the sound of footsteps caused Julia to jump back and look elsewhere. Amelia, similarly, clasped her hands in front of her and looked cherubic.

The footsteps came closer, accompanied

by the sound of male voices. One of the men was explaining the origin of some of the statues.

As the men came around the corner, Julia stared, her mouth opening in shock. Her whole universe shifted, turning upside down.

'Oh,' said Amelia, in a hoarse whisper. 'He *did* come. Mother was right.'

Julia pulled herself together. She closed her mouth, and her brain raced. She knew both men. The notorious Lord Elgin, his misshapen face looking like one of his broken friezes. And Lionel, who had not yet seen her, but who was engaged in a serious discussion regarding one of the metopes.

For a moment Lionel was too involved in his conversation to notice her. The moment he saw her, however, the serious expression disappeared, replaced quickly by one of cynical amusement. He interrupted Lord Elgin, directing him over to where Julia stood.

'A very pleasant surprise,' he said, bowing to Julia and Amelia in turn. 'May I present Lord Elgin, Miss Swifton, Miss Neville?'

Amelia, who did not seem bothered by Lord Elgin's unfortunate looks, was thrilled to learn she was meeting the very man who had put the collection together. She began showering him with questions, some of them revealing that she knew far more about the marbles than she had let on.

'So, Miss Swifton, do you find the male physique intriguing?' said Lionel, in an undertone.

Julia stiffened. He could not have heard them giggling before their arrival.

'I don't know what you mean,' said Julia, frostily.

Lionel indicated the frieze in front of her. It was of a naked man. Heat rose up to her face. She knew she was turning a very unbecoming shade of purple.

'I — I was examining the minotaur,' she said quickly.

'Ah,' said Lionel, suggestively. If possible, she turned an even darker purple. She knew without looking again that the horse displayed properties that would have made him a good stud.

He grinned, enjoying her discomfort. 'I am sorry to hear you find us poor mortal men lacking. You may perhaps be disappointed, however, if you were hoping for a minotaur to appear in your life.'

She glared at him. How typical of Lionel to *rub it in.*

'It so happens,' she said, stiffly, 'that I am interested in Greek sculpture, and the minotaurs of Phideus are of particular interest to me.'

'Is that so?' said Lionel, his eyes twinkling. 'I beg your pardon for misinterpreting your interest. I thought I heard laughter when I was entering the hall. But perhaps I misheard.'

She ignored him, pointedly changing the conversation. 'How is your mother faring?'

'With the aid of her concoctions, I believe, she is keeping herself alive,' he replied, with a smile. She tried to stay serious, but she could not. In spite of herself, her mouth began to curl. 'I'm certainly glad to hear it,' she said, her eyes dancing in turn.

Lord Elgin excused himself, inviting Amelia and Julia for a personal tour of the marbles, and withdrew.

'If you've finished with your scholarly perusal, ladies,' said Lionel, 'perhaps you would care to accompany me to something less' — he paused, apparently in search of the right word — 'dusty.' He threw Julia a mischievous glance, making it clear he had not meant dusty at all. 'Since the weather is so pleasant, shall we go to Gunter's, for some ices?'

Amelia shot Julia an amused glance. 'Certainly,' she replied, very prettily, 'my mother — I mean — I would be delighted.'

Julia glared back at the girl. She really had to speak to her about watching what she said.

Amelia dismissed her waiting carriage with a message to Lady Medlow that they were going to Gunter's with Lord Thorwynn. She was clearly relishing the situation.

In Berkeley Square they sat inside while Lionel sprang down to stand outside the barouche. Julia watched the waiters scurry to and fro as she always did, marvelling at their ability to carry heavy salvers and trays across the busy road. Today their waiter was a very thin, snake-like man who slithered through the traffic, emerging miraculously intact to take their order.

They ordered a selection of fruit glaces and frozen punches. When the confections arrived, Amelia exclaimed enthusiastically over the perfection of the frozen forms.

'If I didn't know we were at *Gunter's*,' she said, refusing to let anyone touch them, 'I would have thought this was a *real* apricot!' She stared at them so long, Julia protested that they would melt in the sun.

Lionel's manners left nothing to be desired. He was perfectly correct. He ate his ices outside, as was the custom, leaning gracefully against the railings. The three of them exchanged pleasantries and laughed as Amelia tried to salvage a large piece of her confection which slipped out of her reach.

All was well, until Julia asked him playfully about his presence at the museum.

'I did not know you had an interest in classical studies,' she said. 'It seems you have more of an interest in such things than you are willing to admit.'

The shuttered look that was starting to look familiar swept across his face, a curtain keeping her out.

'Lord Elgin was kind enough to offer me a private tour. I could not refuse,' he replied.

Julia wanted to mention that she had overheard one or two of his remarks, and they revealed more than a casual interest, but she held back.

A tension filled the air which had been completely absent only a few heartbeats ago.

Amelia, impervious to the sudden atmosphere, launched into an exuberant account of some of Lord Elgin's revelations to her. Lionel listened with a clear expression of boredom on his face. Julia, wishing more than anything to disprove Lionel's earlier conviction that she knew nothing about the marbles, plied her young friend with questions.

Amelia finally put an end to the conversation. 'La! It's a very good thing Mama isn't here. If she heard this conversation she would be *convinced* I had turned into a bluestocking.'

Lionel, of course, politely refuted that possibility. 'No one could possibly think such a beautiful young lady would carry a thought in her head,' he said, gallantly, but he laughed as he looked up at her in the carriage.

Amelia gave him a corresponding laugh. 'Perhaps I have a *few* thoughts in my head,' said Amelia. 'But it would not do to reveal them, would it?'

Julia could not help but exclaim at her words. 'Perhaps that is true, if you only wish to encourage the most trivial of suitors. But I'm certain it would not drive away any gentleman of integrity and intelligence.' She turned to include Lionel. 'What is your opinion, Lord Thorwynn?'

His eyes met hers. 'I believe any man of intelligence will be delighted to encounter a lady with whom he can have an intelligent conversation,' he said, seriously.

Then, perhaps realizing the conversation had taken too heavy a turn, he shrugged. 'Although there is something to be said for levity. One does not want to be perpetually straining one's thoughts,' he added. 'Which brings us back to this moment, under the sunshine, enjoying Gunter's confections. I would not want to waste such a pleasant circumstance discussing such solemn topics.'

Julia turned away from him, not wanting him to see her disappointment. She had been on the verge of revising her opinion of him. She was beginning to feel there was a different side to him. But instead he seemed intent on avoiding any serious topics, and to steer the conversation towards the trifling.

She did not participate in the light banter between him and Amelia. And when he let the two ladies down at her townhouse a half-hour later, she parted with him with the barest civility.

Amelia maintained a steady stream of cheerful chatter until after the tea was served and they were alone in the parlour.

The next moment the illusion of high spirits disappeared as a teardrop rolled down the girl's cheek. As Julia shot her a searching look, she noticed that shadows marred the corners of the younger girl's eyes, and a couple of small pimples stained her skin. All was not well in the Neville household. She chastised herself for not realizing it earlier.

'You must tell me about it,' she said, gently. 'There's clearly something wrong.'

Amelia did not dissolve into tears, as Julia expected. She held back, and Julia marvelled at how quickly she had learned the ways of Town.

'It's Papa,' she said, her voice distant.

Not the marriage with the old ogre, she hoped. 'Surely he's not forcing you —'

'Oh, no!' said Amelia. 'No, that isn't it.' She stopped, struggling with herself, then decided to take Julia into her confidence.

'Do you remember I told you there was a gentleman who had caught my interest?' Julia nodded, remembering something like that from Amelia's last visit.

'Well, he came to our house, to ask my father's permission to marry me.' She looked almost happy; Julia allowed herself to be happy for her, too.

She looked down at her hands. 'I know we have not known each other long, but I feel a strange affinity with him. As if I had always known him.'

She nodded encouragement.

'It may have been hasty on his part, to speak to my father so soon.' She cast Julia a quick glance, to try and gauge her reaction.

'But at least it shows that his intentions

are honourable,' said Julia.

'That's what I thought. But Papa didn't.'

Here her lips began to tremble. She pressed them close together to control them. Then she gave a little sob and buried her face in her hands. Julia waited until she had recovered enough to continue. 'It was *terrible!* I listened at the keyhole, you see. I know it wasn't the right thing to do,' she said, 'but I was so *excited* and I wanted to know everything.' She paused and shook her head. 'As it turned out, it was a good thing I did listen, because otherwise I wouldn't have known what happened.'

She took out a handkerchief and blew her nose, although she was not really crying.

'Papa was very angry. He told him he would not consider him as a son-in-law for one instant. That he was in the River Tick and would soon be in a debtor's prison. That he had heard other unsavoury gossip about him.' Amelia's voice trembled. Julia patted her awkwardly on the hand. 'Papa was so *cruel,* Julia. I did not think it of him.'

'Did you consider,' said Julia gently, 'that perhaps your young man could be a fortune hunter?'

'He's not really a young man,' said Amelia. 'And no, I don't think he's a fortune hunter *at all.* Why will no one believe that he could *actually* love me for myself? Is there anything wrong with me?'

Julia looked at her perfect little profile and answered honestly. 'Nothing's wrong with you. On the contrary, you're a remarkably beautiful young lady. But there are plenty of merciless fortune hunters out there who would be delighted to have both at their disposal — a beautiful young woman, and a fortune that they can dispose of as they please.'

'Well he's not like that. I know he loves me. The way he looks at me makes it clear.'

There was no point in pursuing that any further.

'Besides, his father is an *earl,* which makes him a very good catch, considering my father is only a baron. And given all the fuss my mother has made over Lord Thorwynn, who's an earl as well, you'd think they'd be happy to have me marry into a title.'

'Perhaps your father's still hoping you'll marry Lord Frugford.'

'Well, I *won't,* and I told him so. I said I would not marry him even if they carried me to him by force, which I didn't think they would, because it would look rather odd, wouldn't it?'

There were many ways to force a young girl to consent. Julia said nothing.

'Anyway, then my father came and jerked the door open and I had to hide quickly under the stairway. I heard footsteps and before I knew it Lord Neave was gone.'

The name startled her into instant awareness.

'Lord Neave?' said Julia, incredulously.

'Oh, I didn't *intend* to tell you, but now that you know I suppose it does not matter.'

'But Amelia! You don't mean Lord Neave is your suitor?'

She stared at Julia as if she had two heads. 'Of course. And I don't see why you're looking so shocked. I told you before that I thought him attractive.'

Julia shrugged. There was little anyone could say to convince Amelia that Lord Neave was far from desirable. She had scarcely listened herself when she had been warned about him. And she was not just turned seventeen, entering Society for the first time.

'I know it will do no good to say so,' she said, 'but I should warn you that Lord Neave is not what he appears.' She was condemned to repeat Lionel's words, with as little effect.

She stood up impatiently. 'Oh, don't tell me now you're siding with Papa! I thought better of you. I thought you are my friend.'

'I *am* your friend,' said Julia. The last thing she wanted to happen was for Amelia to feel abandoned by everyone. She would then fly into his arms, and the situation would be a great deal worse. 'Don't be too hasty, that's all,' she said. 'Give yourself time to get to know him.'

Amelia cheered up. 'Yes. That's what I'll do. And I'll prove to my father and to all of you that he is a good person and worthy of me.'

She nodded. If she knew him long enough, she would know what he was capable of. 'I applaud your resolve,' she said, hoping she did not sound false. 'And I hope you'll continue to confide in me.'

Amelia nodded. 'I will,' she said shyly. 'I'm so glad I fell off the horse at your feet, otherwise I would have never had you as a friend.'

They embraced quickly, and Amelia took her leave, a mix of determination and hope on her face.

Her departure left Julia pacing, pondering how to solve her dilemma. Night came and she still could not find a solution. She could not think of a way to keep Amelia away from Neave without betraying her friend's confidence.

But when she blew out the candle that

night, she did not think of Amelia. Instead, in a state between sleep and darkness, the marbles rose up before her. Great testaments to the male body, sinews and muscles in relief, the best of Greek athletes and fighters. And she marvelled that she had never really seen them before.

CHAPTER 17

'For Heaven's sake, Mama. It's all very well to arrange a picnic on Box Hill, and to invite a handful of houseguests, but I don't mean to attend. My plans are already made.'

'But I *need* you,' said his mama, draped over her favourite seat. 'You can't expect me to oversee such a complicated affair, when you know how fragile my nerves are.'

'You should have thought of it before you issued the invitations,' said Lionel, heartlessly.

'I was counting on your support,' said Lady Thorwynn, eyes plaintive.

'You could have consulted me,' replied Lionel, mildly reproving.

'Well,' she said, stirring in her seat, 'it's no use telling me now I should have consulted you when all the invitations have already been issued. Everything's set up and it cannot be changed.'

'If everything's set up, I fail to see why

you need me,' he said, implacably.

'Oh, stop it, you odious boy! You'll be sending me into nervous spasms.'

That was always her way of ending a conversation which was uncomfortable.

He wanted to go to the picnic. He wanted it very much indeed. He was planning to corner Julia and have that long conversation he had sought for a while. She would not escape him this time.

What he did not want was to spend two whole two nights under Mama's roof, running her errands, and participating in her frenzied preparations.

She knew very well she did not really want him to take charge of the preparations. She simply needed him to prop her up while she worked herself into a state.

On the other hand, the prospect of spending some time under the same roof as Julia had its appeal. In fact, the more he considered it, the more appealing it seemed.

He grinned at his mother. She pined on the sofa and looked hopelessly fragile.

'You know I don't like to be called odious, Mama. And you can keep that fragile act for someone else.'

She sat up, frowning in protest. 'How — ?'

'Hush,' he said, putting a finger to his lips.

'You're as strong as an ox.'

'I hardly think —'

'And you know I know it.'

She smiled and reached out her hand to him. He came and took it, smiling down at her.

'So are you coming?' she said, smiling back.

He wrinkled his nose in mock distaste. 'I suppose I have no choice, do I?'

'You do not,' she said, a satisfied smile on her face.

Once again, Julia entered Lady Thorwynn's residence, though not the same one. It was growing to be a habit. Lady Gragspur was there, having travelled from town earlier with Lady Thorwynn. She indicated the seat closest to her for Lady Bullfinch to join her, and nodded imperiously when Julia curtseyed.

Lady Thorwynn welcomed Julia and her grandmother from her sofa, which resembled the one at her townhouse closely, except for the colour. This one was Pomona green.

'I hope you don't mind if I don't get up to greet you,' she said, waving a wilted hand in the air.

'Of course not,' said Lady Bullfinch. 'You

just stay where you are and rest. No doubt you have exhausted yourself with all the preparations.'

Lady Thorwynn wiped her arm across her face and sighed. 'If only I had more energy,' she murmured, sighing deeply. 'But please, do sit down. The journey must have tired you.'

'Not at all,' said Lady Bullfinch, taking the seat indicated by Lady Gragspur. 'The ride was very enjoyable, in fact. We opened all the windows the moment we left Town. The fresh country air was remarkably invigorating.'

Lady Thorwynn shuddered. 'I'm certainly glad, then, that I came in my own carriage. I dislike draughts above all else,' she said. 'I hope you do not take a chill,' she said, then added ominously, 'People have *died* of colds they contracted riding in draughty carriages.' She rang the bell vigorously. 'I will ask Mary to prepare you both a tonic. It will help ward off a cold.'

'For heaven's sake, Mama, no one here is about to take a chill. Must you force those teas down everyone's throats?'

He stood in the doorway, dressed immaculately. His black hair had that perfect tousled look that can only be achieved with pomade. His neckcloth was elaborately tied in an Oriental, his bottle-green coat draped him like a glove, and his boots gleamed. Julia's eyes followed the sharp outline of his thigh muscles in the tight cream nankeen trousers.

She caught herself staring. Quickly, she averted her eyes, hoping no one had noticed.

'And must you force your vulgar expressions on my guests?' said his mother, but she smiled.

'I do indeed seem to have forgotten my manners,' said Lionel, contritely. He bowed to all the ladies present, then moved to greet them one by one.

'Lady Bullfinch,' he said, bowing over her hand and grinning like a naughty schoolboy. 'Charmed to see you under our roof again.'

'Hrmph,' said Lady Gragspur. 'Don't be taken in by that rascal's charm.'

Lady Bullfinch, however, returned his grin as he took her hand. 'How can you say that, Evelyn? Nothing wrong with charm, in my view. Why, if I was just a few years younger, I would lead him a merry dance.'

'Indeed, Lady Bullfinch, if you put your mind to it, you could lead me a merry dance right now,' said Lionel, gallantly.

She laughed. Lady Gragspur hrumphed again.

He approached Julia. She gave him her

hand. But when he touched it, she almost flinched. The warmth of that contact seemed to spread throughout her body.

'Miss Swifton,' he said. Her name was a caress, his voice velvet. She wanted to close her eyes and . . . swoon. And he still held her hand.

He was holding her hand far too long. Intensely aware of his touch, she let herself ride the sensations that washed over her. She realized suddenly that everyone in the room was waiting for her to say something. Hauling herself back into social interaction took tremendous effort. 'So we meet again, Lord Thorwynn,' she said, the only thing she could think of.

He still held her hand. She tugged at it, as subtly as possible. Yet he did not let go.

The corner of his mouth curled. Of course he found her behaviour amusing. Who wouldn't? Meanwhile, she stared at his mouth, fascinated by the way that small curl created a tiny dimple.

Her hand was still in his. She tugged harder, at the risk of seeming undignified. He let it slide reluctantly out of his reach. *No doubt he uses this method with every woman he seduces.* But it no longer mattered to her. She felt an overwhelming urge to take his hand again and draw it to her mouth, to kiss the tips of his fingers, to lick his palm. . . .

'I'm aware I'm the bane of your existence,' he said. It took Julia a moment to realize he was answering her comment. *What's happening to me?* 'I shall endeavour to stay out of your way, if that is your wish.' But he was smiling, as he stepped away.

The door opened and Lord Benedict walked in. He was such a welcome sight she could not stifle her cry of pleasure. 'Lord Benedict, I did not know that you would be here as well.'

'I would not miss it for the world,' he said, 'when there are so many charming ladies gathered here.'

There were general nods and greetings as he acknowledged everyone and sat down on the chair closest to her.

Thorwynn did not sit. He stood, slouching elegantly against the wall, under an archway of green trellis wallpaper. A trick of light made him look as if he was emerging from some enchanted kingdom beyond, stepping into their world with reluctance. She had never thought of him as particularly Byronic, but in this instant she could see the Corsair in him, dark and arrogant.

Then it was gone.

Certainly his expression was not enchanted. A cynical expression hardened his features as he watched Lord Benedict steer the conversation skilfully to Lady Bullfinch's and Lady Gragspur's favourite topic: the past. Coming to life, they recounted a tale about an acquaintance of theirs, whose escapades were notorious in their days.

'It is difficult for me to believe that girls were so free with their favours in your days. I wonder sometimes if it does not appear so in retrospect,' said Lady Thorwynn. 'Although my mama always said it was so.'

'Your dear mama had much to answer for,' said Lady Bullfinch. 'I can tell you a thing or two about her —'

Fortunately, they never learned about Lady Thorwynn's mother's indiscretions. The door opened and the butler announced Lord Yarfolk.

He came tripping in, looking magnificent in a purple frock coat with a contrasting rich golden waistcoat and a thick border of intricate lace on his sleeves.

'My dear ladies,' he said, bowing elaborately. 'Gentlemen,' he said gravely. He took out his snuff box, flicked the lid open, and inhaled deeply. Then he shut it and stepped forward delicately, seating himself on the edge of a sofa chair next to Lady Bullfinch.

'I hope you are entirely recovered from

your indisposition, Lady Bullfinch,' he said, solicitously.

'Oh, yes, indeed,' she said. 'It was merely a passing weakness.'

'I am glad to hear of it,' said Lord Yarfolk, with concern.

It seemed her grandmother had a new admirer.

How did I turn out to be such a prude? She stared at herself in the mirror, noting the disapproving tightness around her mouth, the faint traces of a frown between her brows. *All the more remarkable since I grew up around Grannie.* She was so far from prudish she would shame the most jaded rake.

Julia had certainly been acutely embarrassed earlier. Lord Yarfolk's appearance had prompted the three older people to launch into a series of reminiscences. These included some ribald tales which left Julia uncertain where to look. The gentlemen, of course, took them in their stride. Eventually, recognizing that Lady Thorwynn shared her embarrassment, Julia moved and sat next to her, and they promptly struck up their own conversation, one that was comfortably proper.

She had never envied her grandmother the

experiences she had. In fact, she had never even comprehended the appeal of such experiences. But for some reason, today she saw her world differently. There was a balance to it, an earthy pursuit of stimulation, whether mental or physical. She did not hesitate. She plunged in.

Their lives could not be more different, as different as water from rock. *I always wanted to be safe.* She preferred solid rock over the uncertainties of a sea voyage fraught with perils and uncertainties. Until today, she was unaware that in her dogged insistence on the rational, she had narrowed her world so completely she had denied herself the opportunity to discover new horizons.

No wonder Amelia sees me as an old maid. Because that is exactly what I have become. I have been so worried that I would repeat the mistakes of my mother that I have never really lived my own life.

She reflected on what she had done so far. She had not been inactive. She had engaged herself in many pursuits. But somehow they rang hollow. When she was her grandmother's age, what stories would she have to tell? How would she remember her past? The fact was, nothing much had happened to her. She could recount tales written by others, but she had none of her own. She viewed her image in the mirror, viewed those calm brown-green eyes, the sedate sweep of her brown hair, the straight line of her nose.

It was not too late to change. She would never live her life as Grannie did, of course. Expectations were different in her time from now. But she could at least do something that she could remember, for herself, many years from now. *I need to know what it is to experience physical pleasure, for once, before I settle into my serene marriage with someone from the museums.*

At the very least she would experience the satisfaction of having stepped off the rock, and allowed herself the chance to flounder.

The day of the picnic dawned bright and clear, with a cloudless sky signalling the heavens' approval. Lionel's spirits soared. The picnic would be a success.

Mama naturally took credit for arranging the picnic on this day. 'I can always tell what the weather will be like. Rheumatism, you know. My knees begin to ache three days before the rain comes. So when my knees did not give me trouble, I knew the weather would be favourable.'

Lionel was in far too good a mood to point out that she had planned the picnic more than three days ago, though he was tempted.

The rest of their group arrived as planned. Lady Talbrook, who had been unable to come the night before due to an engagement, arrived with her son, Lord Talbrook and her daughter, Miranda Flint, a pretty girl of around sixteen who had been away at finishing school, and was planning to come out in the coming year. And they had brought Miss Neville with them.

The preparations were not marred by any mishaps, except when the carriages began to line up.

Lady Bullfinch, stepping out to find the weather was comfortably warm, refused to go by carriage. 'You don't think we're going to be cooped up in carriage on such a fine day, do you? Julia and I will ride.'

'But what if it rains?' wailed Lady Thorwynn.

'If it rains, we will naturally avail ourselves of the carriage,' replied Lady Bullfinch.

This seemed to reassure Lady Thorwynn, for she agreed to the scheme, though reluctantly. She took Lionel aside, however. 'I just hope they don't fall off their horses. With such a steep incline, you know, a fall could be fatal,' she said.

'Mama, I don't think it likely that either

of them will fall. They are excellent horsewomen.'

'Yes, that is true,' she said, brightening considerably. Her voice fell into a conspiratorial whisper. 'I'm certainly glad Amelia is not determined to travel up to Box Hill on horseback,' said Lionel's mama. 'She certainly cannot keep her seat.'

He bit back a remark that a single fall off a frightened steed did not render her a poor rider. But it was useless to argue.

Since the gentlemen would be riding as well, Lionel expected to be able to speak to Julia. However, from the moment she mounted, she rode with Lord Talbrook. They quickly entered into an intimate conversation which excluded everyone else. This left Lionel, as the host, with the task of entertaining Lady Bullfinch.

She would have none of it, however. 'I don't need someone to chatter nonsense to me while I ride,' she said. 'I prefer to enjoy the quiet of the countryside. Go stick with the younger people.'

As a result, he had no choice but to ride with Benny.

They reached the top around one in the afternoon. Lionel dismounted quickly and strode quickly towards Julia.

'Lionel,' said Lady Thorwynn, descending from the carriage, 'you must assist Lady Bullfinch.'

He glanced towards the formidable lady. She had already dismounted, shunning the aid of a groom with a dismissive wave. He strolled towards her, mumbling under his breath.

'I hope the ride didn't tire you,' he said, carefully polite.

She looked him over derisively. 'It was a delightful ride, and well you know it. Your mother may be a fool and wish to think me an invalid, but you have no such scruples, I hope so, at least, or I will think you a bigger fool than she.'

'Um — indeed not, Lady Bullfinch,' he said, grinning. 'I have rarely seen a lady with so much energy.' He said it with feeling.

She grunted, throwing him a piercing look. Then she turned and marched away.

He glanced back to where Julia's horse, Hamlet, stood. He was riderless, of course. Julia was strolling down the slope of the hill, her arm draped over Talbrook's.

He noted how close their shoulders were.

Deuce take it! Why had he promised his mother to help her oversee the picnic arrangements? His presence was completely superfluous. She seemed to have the arrangements very well in hand. Half-a-dozen footmen scurried to and fro from the overloaded wagon, all with a definite sense of purpose. Two of them carried a heavy table and were heading for a small copse.

'Make sure the table is completely in the shade,' said Mama.

'Nonsense,' said Lady Bullfinch. 'A dose of sun is just what you need to improve your complexion. You need a touch of colour in your face.'

'Surely not,' said Lord Yarfolk, shuddering. 'I cannot bear the fierce heat of the sun. Of course, I no longer wear powder, but I still remember those days. All it took was a few minutes of exposure, and the powder would start running.'

'Thank heavens those days are gone,' said Lady Bullfinch. 'Such utter nonsense! Why we should cover ourselves in rice powder, I never understood. I never regretted throwing my powder pot away. It is such a delight to feel the warm sun on one's skin.'

'Oh, but surely, Lady Bullfinch, you can't mean to expose yourself to the sun's rays?' said Lady Thorwynn. 'On a warm day like this I fear you may have a heatstroke.'

Lady Bullfinch opened her mouth to deliver a scathing remark.

It was time to intervene. 'Ladies, gentlemen, I suggest we place the table mostly in the shade, but with a small section exposed to the sun. That way Lady Bullfinch can indulge herself while everyone else will be protected.'

It was clear that the discussion was by no means at an end. But the table was set up, the tablecloth spread. Within a reasonable time Lionel judged that he had asserted his presence long enough. He took his leave and went to join the younger group.

They sat in a circle on a blanket laid on the grassless space under a large beech tree. The bronze leafy cover glittered in the sun, formed mottled shadows as it filtered the sun without eliminating it completely.

Julia's face was partly shaded by a straw bonnet tied down with a lavender ribbon. There was something girlish in her pose, leaning back on her hands with her legs spread straight in front of her.

They were playing spin the bottle. Someone had had the foresight to bring an empty wine bottle with them.

Not wishing to interrupt, he watched as the bottle spun round quickly on a glass salver. It slowed down, then came to a rest, pointing clearly at Julia. There was general laughter as she cried out.

'So, Julia,' said Talbrook, laughing, 'you have to tell us what you dislike most in the world. Say the first thing that comes to your mind.'

'Snakes and rakes,' she replied quickly, laughing.

She did not even look in his direction, but Lionel stiffened. He was on the point of turning to leave when he met Benny's glance. Benny shook his head imperceptibly at him.

He stood there, torn. Julia's remark had wounded him. But he was also the host, and to walk away suddenly would draw more attention than he wanted.

It was Amelia who decided for him. 'Oh, look who's here,' she said, moving aside to make room for him — next to Julia. 'Come and join us. We've decided to do confessions — if the bottle points to you you'll have to answer a question from one of us.'

He smiled, not even glancing at Julia as he sat next to her.

'Spin the bottle,' he said. 'I'm ready.'

Having disposed of a huge spread of cold meats, breads and desserts, the young people determined to go walking.

Lionel acted as a guide, since he had visited Box Hill frequently as a boy. He pointed out features on the landscape, including the sleepy village of Dorking lying in the valley, and the heights of Leith Hill over to the west. He picked wild orchids for each of the ladies, and they all chased blue butterflies that floated lazily in the sunshine.

Somehow, without fully intending it, the group broke up into couples. Benny paired up with Miranda, Talbrook with Amelia, and Julia with him.

'You know Box Hill well,' remarked Julia, 'Was it one of the haunts of your childhood?'

He nodded, remembering. 'Yes. I have many good memories here. I used to come here with three of my friends. We would cross the river on hot summer days and then clamber up the hill.' A look of sadness crossed his face. 'Two of them are dead now. They died in the Peninsular War.'

'I'm sorry,' she said. 'What happened to the third?'

Lionel's face brightened. 'He's happily married, with a brood of children. He lives quite close, actually. I plan to visit him tomorrow.'

They reached a turnstile. Lionel stood to one side, assisting the ladies as they went through.

'Be careful where you stand,' he said, in warning, as he joined the group again. 'You are walking in a cow pasture.'

As if to prove it, a cow came into view, swishing its tail from side to side.

'I grew up in the country, but I've never touched a cow,' said Amelia. 'It's all sheep where I live; sheep bleating everywhere you look. Not a cow to be seen.'

'Allow me, then,' said Talbrook, 'to introduce you to Madam Cow. Madam Cow, Miss Neville.'

The cow looked at Miss Neville without curiosity.

'Do you think I could touch her?'

Opinions differed. Miranda objected strongly to the idea, saying they were dirty creatures, full of flies. Julia encouraged her. Benny laughed and said he'd never heard such a ridiculous notion. Talbrook said there was no harm to it, if Miss Neville wished it. Lionel advised against it.

Amelia's curiosity, however, was too strong for her to be deterred. She moved forward cautiously, her gaze fixed on the cow. Just as Amelia was about to touch her, the cow shifted just out of her reach. She followed. The cow moved again.

'Watch out!' said Benny, but it was too late. Amelia's foot squelched as it landed in a water puddle.

'Urrgh,' she uttered, trying to stay upright

as her foot slipped in the mud. Talbrook sprinted forward and held her arm, steadying her.

She surveyed her muddy boot in dismay, then laughed. 'It is certainly fortunate that I wore walking shoes. And that it wasn't something worse.'

Relieved laughter broke out, as everyone realized she was not going to succumb to a fit of hysteria.

Meanwhile, the guilty cow watched them, chewing indifferently.

'I think, perhaps, with the state of my boots, I need to return to the carriage. I'm glad I brought a change of shoes.'

Talbrook immediately offered to escort her.

It was a signal for the group to break up. Benny tactfully suggested a bench to Miranda to sit on, to wait for Amelia's return. He made a shooing gesture to Lionel, who stood uncertainly on the pathway.

Benny scowled at him, his message very clear.

It said: *Don't ruin it this time.*

CHAPTER 18

She should have gone with the others, but she didn't. She strolled down the pathway, away from everyone, alone with a gentleman, completely unchaperoned, and indifferent to propriety.

They stopped as a vista opened before them. He seemed ill at ease. Oddly enough, his discomfort fed that strange mood surfacing inside her. It was up to her to make him comfortable. She did not want to always rely on others to be charming, to help people relax, to set the scene. She would set it.

Prompted by an evil genie, she settled down on the ground, indifferent to grass stains, and patted the space beside her. He was not prompted by the same genie, and, conscious of his light trousers, he hesitated.

'Come,' she said, challenging him, 'surely you do not wish to remain the only one on this outing with impeccable clothes? I never thought you such a dandy that you would prefer clean clothes over having an enjoyable time.'

She was pushing, of course. He could react with anger, and refuse. She held her breath, watching him.

He gave a quick shrug and, scrutinizing the ground carefully, sat down gingerly on the grass. 'You didn't examine the ground to see if there is any trace of cows,' he said.

She leapt up at that and inspected her clothing. There was a faint wet stain, but no sign of cows. 'Thank heavens!' she said, plonking back down.

He laughed, a deep masculine laugh that sent vibrations running through her. 'It would have served you right if there had been.'

Unruffled, she grinned. 'But there wasn't, so I'm afraid you'll have no chance to moralize to me on the dangers of sitting on the ground.'

He threw her a puzzled glance. 'Is that how you think of me? As moralizing?'

'Well, you've done nothing but tell me what to do and what not to do since I met you.'

He pulled out a blade of grass and looked out over the valley. 'That was simply due to the circumstances.'

She blew out an exasperated breath. 'Let's not talk about the circumstances again. I want this to be a circumstance free afternoon.'

He bowed mockingly. 'As you wish, Miss Swifton. What do you wish to talk about?'

'You,' she said promptly.

'Ah,' he said, with a smirk. 'My favourite topic.' He leaned back on his hands and smiled, waiting. 'You may ask what you wish.'

But the evil genie danced around her. 'I'm glad. Because I want you to explain why you pretend that you don't like poetry.'

He stiffened and sat up. He pulled out several blades of grass, a clump, in fact, and shredded it. He tossed the mangled fragments away and watched them fall. Then he picked the remaining grass specks from his palms, one by one. The moment he had finished, he began the whole process over again, with a new clump.

'Well?' she prompted, making it clear she would not let him evade her.

Giving up on tearing the grass, he drew his knees in towards his chest, hugging himself. He clearly did not want to answer.

'If you would prefer to discuss something more innocuous,' she remarked, 'like the weather, for example, we can do that.'

He turned to face her. His black eyes were opaque, revealing nothing. He still clutched his knees to his chest. 'When I was about seven, I conceived a passion for poetry. I had an aunt who used to visit us often — she died ten years ago — and she always brought me books of poetry. She used to come up to the nursery and read to me. Sonnets by Shakespeare, poems by Goldsmith, Gray, Collins — she was a passionate reader and collector. And though I understood very little of it, I loved the rhymes and the rhythms. So I started trying to write poems of my own.' He paused and put a blade of grass in his mouth, gnawing at it with his front teeth.

'I was a scholarly lad. My tutor was a local vicar who took his teaching seriously. Having discovered in me an aptitude for study, he dedicated himself to training me in good writing, the classics and Greek and Latin.

'Before long, I wanted to spend all my time indoors. I acquired such a passion for reading that I would spend hours in the library, reading anything I could find that could interest a child.' He stared out across the rolling hills below them, and at the valley marked by ragged boundaries dividing up the land.

'My father grew alarmed. He thought the classics a load of fustian nonsense. He and my mother quarrelled about me whenever he graced us with his presence, which, given that he was often away hunting and attending the races, was thankfully not too frequent. But each time he returned, he would turn me outdoors all day, and engage to teach me the manly sports. My tutor was dismissed for months at a time. My father claimed my mother was cosseting me, and would before long turn me into a sickly version of herself.

'He vowed to cure me of this unsavoury habit of reading. He kept the library locked, even in his absence. And if he caught me with a book, he would whip me and send me outdoors for the rest of the day. To make sure I spent time in the fresh air, he said.

'I was glad when I was sent off to school. I expected Eton to be somewhere I could finally indulge myself in my reading habits, without my father's intervention. But it was a grim, gloomy place, and the boys there all seemed younger versions of my father, all contemptuous of learning, and all addicted to physical activity and hunting. There was even a tradition of animal baiting in which we all had to participate.

'It seemed there was no way out. So I

learned to play all the games they played. After all, as Wellington has since said, "The battle of Waterloo was won on the playing fields of Eton".

'But I managed to write poetry. Luckily, I found a sympathetic ear in one of the masters, Dr. Lind, who also interested me in astronomy. And later, I befriended Percy Shelley, even though he was younger than I was, and we used to read and write together, and conduct experiments in natural philosophy.' He smiled at the memory. 'Some of the experiments were rather explosive.'

'One day, on my return home during the holidays, my father came upon me unexpectedly. I was sixteen, and completely engrossed in writing a poem. I didn't even notice him entering my chamber. He tore up a notebook full of poems I had written and threw it in the fire. Then locked me in my room. I resolved to run away from home the next day, but I did not want to leave without first speaking to my mother.

'Well, the next day was too late. I woke to find my father had bought me a commission to fight Napoleon, and that my passage was already arranged.' He bowed his head. 'I didn't even react to that. What upset me was that all the best poems I had written were gone.

'So, you see,' he concluded, 'I never went to Oxford or Cambridge, though I always had hopes of reading the classics there.' He laughed, a bitter, self-mocking laugh. 'I apologize,' he said. 'I've given you a very long story for a very short question.' He rose and put out his hand. 'Shall we continue on our walk?'

She nodded. He had answered her question.

Though the tale he had told was a sad one, she now knew that her instinct had not been wrong. There was much more to him than met the eye. He was not simply a bored rake obsessed by his own pleasures. There was another side to him, one he made every effort to conceal. Knowing that this was the case magnified the curious exhilaration that simmered inside her. Delighted laughter threatened to burst out of her but she contained it, knowing he would not understand. He would think she was laughing at *him*.

A gust of wind rushed up and pulled her hair out of its pins, in spite of the bonnet that anchored it. Long strands blew on to her face, on to her lips, tossed against her cheeks. Now she could laugh at the wind and herself, and she invited him to share in it as she grappled with the hair that lashed at her eyes.

'It's so beautiful up here,' she said, stripping the hair from the corner of her mouth.

'Yes,' he said, surveying the horizon. 'They say you can see over a hundred miles on a clear day.'

'I didn't mean the view,' she said. 'There's an openness, a wildness to it, to the way the wind blows, to the blackberry bushes, to having nothing around as obstruction.'

He threw her a sharp glance, his raven eyes puzzled. 'Hardly wild. We are surrounded by farms, and much of the land is pastureland for the infamous cows.'

She laughed again, thinking of Amelia's dainty foot in the mud. 'Perhaps it is just that we are so high up, at the top of the world. I have never been so far up, you see.'

He nodded. 'Yet this is only a hill, compared to some of the mountains on the Continent.'

A strange longing flowed through her, like the wind blowing around her.

'Someday I want to visit those places. I want to climb one of those mountains and look down at the tiny valleys below. I have seen pictures of the magnificent Alps. I want to go there. I want to stand where Byron's Manfred stood. *"The natural music of the* mountain reed, Mix'd with the sweet bells of the sauntering herd; My soul would drink those echoes". I want this more than anything.'

She had never known she had that longing. But then, she had never been to Box Hill. She watched him, to see what he would say about Byron.

'I hope you do not wish to emulate Byron's Manfred. He intended to throw himself down into the valley.'

'True, but he did not,' she retorted, grinning. He had admitted that he read Byron.

He raised an eyebrow. 'Did I say something amusing?'

She smothered the smile. 'No. I am merely happy.'

Silence reigned for a moment.

'Perhaps you will marry someone who will take you there,' he said, his face closed like a curtain.

Yes. She wanted to marry someone who would take her to the Continent, show her all those places she had read about but never seen. A gust blew up and tossed her bonnet to the ground. She ran after it, caught it just as it was in danger of hurtling down the slope.

'You must help me tie it on again,' she said, the words tumbling out of her mouth.

She had not intended them, but they came out, nevertheless.

She placed the bonnet on her head and held out the ribbons. He stepped forward and took them from her hand. His fingers swept hers and she shivered.

'You're cold,' he said, his eyes fixed on the knot. 'Perhaps we should return to the picnic. There are blankets there.'

'On the contrary,' she said, laughter in her eyes. He was uneasy, she could tell. He did not understand her mood. 'I'm feeling remarkably warm.'

He finished his task and stepped back. He did not glance at her at all.

She enjoyed his unease. She felt flushed with a sense of freedom. Her face burned with the wind and the sun.

She wished now she had not asked him to tie the ribbon. She wanted her hair free, wanted it to float loose, lifted by the breeze.

She was restless. Restless and reckless. Her frame of mind differed from any she had experienced before. She was tired of propriety, giddy with flirting and laughing, and full of frantic energy. She wanted more out of life than just to read and to watch others dally and take their pleasure. The shadows no longer contented her.

She wanted life.

'So tell me,' she said, amazed at her daring, but not wanting to curtail this new self that seemed to have popped out of nowhere. 'Are you considered a good kisser?'

He blinked, stared at her blankly. She laughed. She knew he was wondering if he heard her right.

'You have shapely lips,' she said, 'luscious, even. Very tempting. I'm sure others have told you that.' Even as she said this she quaked at what she was saying. Who was this stranger inside her?

Had she taken leave of her senses?

'You're flirting with me,' he said, astonished.

'I don't know why you're so surprised,' she said. 'I have it on good authority that ladies flirt with rakes.' Her voice had taken on a playful lilt.

There must have been something in the wine, or she would not be talking this way.

He frowned. 'Not young unmarried ladies,' he said, his voice heavy with disapproval.

'But perhaps older unmarried ladies?' she said, laughing at him.

He scowled. 'You hardly qualify as *older*.'

She shrugged. She was tired of being Julia Swifton, Bluestocking. For once she wanted to be wanton, unrestrained. She wanted to

316

be a moth, to come close enough to singe her wings. She no longer wanted to hide in her cocoon while others took flight.

There was a jagged rock between them. She climbed on to it and drew closer to him, close enough to feel his breath on her face. Their faces were level. She raised her hand and trailed her fingers over his cheek. 'I want to learn how to kiss. I want to know how a rake kisses,' she whispered and placed her lips to his.

He stood stock still. He neither pulled away, nor drew closer. She stroked her lips against his, the way he had done with her. His lips spread open, a tiny fluttering movement. She strained forward. She knew nothing about kisses. But she knew she wanted more from the kiss. Her tongue slipped out, taking on a life of its own. She licked him, tasting. She needed more.

But Lionel's hands came to her waist. He picked her up, not gently at all, and swung her down to the ground.

'Rakes have feelings, too,' he said. His voice sounded gruff, and he was breathing hard. He avoided her eyes. 'I think we should return to the picnic, Miss Swifton.'

She was not going to let Lionel's rejection affect her. The same wildness that had led her to kiss him now drove her to prove to him that he did not interest her in the least.

She left him, to flit down the pathway to where Lord Benedict and Miranda had been seated. But they had already returned to the picnic site. She crossed the cow pasture, went back through the turnstile and heard the others, chattering and laughing as if nothing had happened.

Nothing *had* happened.

She went straight to Benedict, who lay on his back on the blanket, staring at the copper leaves and speaking to Amelia. She threw herself down beside them.

'La, it's so windy, I thought I would be blown off the side of the hill,' she said, loudly.

And she kept up a stream of inconsequential chatter until much later, when Lionel reappeared. And until the footmen appeared to gather up everything and take them back to their carriages.

CHAPTER 19

She cringed as they rode in the carriage down from Box Hill. Cringed as she thought of his lack of response. Cringed as she wondered why she believed she could be anything other than Julia Swifton, Bluestocking. Cringed even as she thought how close she had come to giving away everything for a few moments of passion. And how Lionel had the sense — or the experience — to put a stop to her folly.

She had gambled, and lost. And there was the end of it.

She did not know how she would ever be able to look Lord Thorwynn in the face again.

She would have liked to curl up in the corner of the carriage in sheer misery. If at least Lady Bullfinch was riding with her she could have confessed; she could have burst into tears and let Grannie comfort her. But she had chosen to return in another carriage with Lord Yarfolk, Lady Gragspur, and Lady Thorwynn. Their horses followed behind.

If she were more intimate with Amelia, she could have spoken to her. But every instinct recoiled at the suggestion. She could not reveal her idiocy to the younger girl.

So the first part of the journey was spent in silence. Thankfully. Distracted by their own thoughts, neither of the two tried to sustain a social conversation. But then Amelia suddenly began to chatter, and though Julia did not listen, she was obliged to at least pretend to be civil.

'So he asked me to run away with him, can you imagine?'

Amelia's words reached Julia as if from a long distance, but they startled her into awareness. 'Run away with him? Who?' she asked, bewildered.

Amelia looked at Julia scornfully. 'You haven't heard anything I said, have you?'

'Yes, of course I have,' Julia assured her quickly. 'But I just wanted to be certain I had understood you. Eloping with someone is hardly something to be taken lightly.'

She sighed dramatically. 'I suppose you'll tell me that I shouldn't even contemplate it. That I'll be miring myself in scandal and all that faradiddle. But I don't care a hoot about what Society thinks.'

Julia was still in the dark, but she suspected she knew who had suggested such a course of action.

'If you mean that you plan to elope with Neave, well, yes, I don't think you should contemplate it,' said Julia, forcefully.

Amanda's eyes flashed defiance. 'But it's all so *wonderfully* romantic. And if you love someone, you should be prepared to sacrifice *everything* for them.'

Julia shook her head. She had to find a way to convince Amanda that Neave was far from the romantic figure she imagined. 'I think — perhaps — that Lord Neave is not all he seems. He has a rather unsavoury reputation,' she said. 'And why is he in such a hurry to marry you? He could wait for a while at least. You're still very young. Perhaps your parents will relent and accept his suit.'

'My father will *never* relent,' she said, passionately. 'It's *useless* to hope for such a thing.'

'You may be able to convince him. Give it time.'

'I don't *have* time,' she said. 'Warren was very hurt by my father's treatment.' *Warren?* So they were on first-name terms, were they? 'After all, he's not exactly an outcast in Society. He's received by all the hostesses, even the highest sticklers. So I don't see how his reputation can be as you say.' She scowled. 'He is so distraught by my father's rejection, he has fallen into a fit of despondency. In fact, he was ready to give up, saying there's no point in pursuing our relationship when my father is so opposed to the idea.'

'He sounds weak-willed to me,' said Julia.

'Weak-*willed?*' cried Amelia, looking at her as though she had two heads. 'How can you say something like that? When he is *suffering!* Can you imagine the humiliation of being turned out after offering for me, like a common beggar? He's the heir to an *earldom*. And yet my father, who is a baron himself, treats him like a commoner.'

She sputtered into silence, her indignation knowing no bounds. She stared out of the window, anger turning her parchment skin into a mottled pink and beige Comblanchien marble. Julia decided there was no point in remonstrating with her. She was beyond redemption.

Julia turned instead to that pit of misery inside her — that churning whirlpool that sucked everything into its ruthless depths. How had she imagined that, plain as she was, inexperienced, with the social finesse of a mastiff, she could actually seduce someone like Lionel? A rake, a gentleman with the vast advantage of experience, and who no doubt was accustomed to turning away women who pursued him. Her pathetic attempt at a kiss had left him cold. She could have been kissing the chalk escarpment beneath her, for all the reaction it had produced.

So much for her brief — and already dead — aspiration to be a seductive Cyprian. She wouldn't know how to do it if her life depended on it.

Which it did. Not in an immediate sense, of course, but in the sense that it could change her life. Because she wanted Lionel. She wanted him enough that her life was nothing but a hollow ruin without him. She thought of an abbey she had once visited, burned down during the Reformation. The dark gutted ruins stood stark, its blind windows staring at the sky.

That was her life.

She threw a glance toward Amelia, sympathy for her plight surfacing. It was not fair to judge her, simply because the object of her love was unworthy. Who was to say the object of her own love was any more worthy? Just because Julia loved him did not change who he was.

The notion hit her like Sir Isaac Newton's apple, a blow on the head.

She loved him.

Such a simple thing, staring her in the face all this time, and yet she had not known it. Worse, she had allowed it to happen, when all her life she had sworn that she would never love a rake as her mother had.

There was the saying, after all, *like mother, like daughter.* Perhaps it was simply a law of nature, with no escape from it, like death. She was to repeat the mistakes of her mother, to suffer like her, once her husband abandoned her to pursue his own pleasures. Except that she had thrown away even that chance. The opportunity for marriage had come and gone.

The future stretched interminably ahead, a void to which there was no end.

'Why will nobody understand that when you love someone, you want to be with them, *now?*' said Amelia, her voice full of torment. 'You don't want to spend your life waiting endlessly to see if your parents are going to approve or not. And what if they never do?' Amelia's intense eyes bore into Julia's.

She wished Amelia would just go away

and leave her to her own wretched reflections.

But Amelia couldn't. She was waiting for Julia to say something. Julia marshalled her thoughts and tried to answer, if only she had any answers herself. 'I do understand. More than you could possibly know,' she said to her companion. 'But you're still young, and marriage is forever. Once you enter it, only death will relieve you from it.' Julia paused, as she debated whether to tell her something she had never discussed with anyone but her closest relations. 'My mother made that mistake. Of marrying very early. She ran off with my father. He, too, was a man with a long established family, though he was — is — only a baron. They married in Gretna Green, and she was ecstatic, despite the scandal that ensued. Her family welcomed back the young couple openly, and did everything they could to help them.' She sighed. She did not really know her mother's story. She had only heard it second hand. 'My mother was wildly in love with Lord Swifton, you see. So it broke her heart when two months later he was seen at the theatre flaunting his mistress on his arm. Wherever she went, people whispered about it, as if it wasn't already bad enough to have to endure his infidelity.'

Amelia listened, wide eyed.

'This was only the first of many scandals. My mother had a considerable fortune, you see, and it enabled him to live a much more luxurious life than he had lived until then. He used her money to buy extravagant gifts for his light skirts, and he paraded them everywhere.

'In the end, it wasn't the scandals that really hurt her, but the knowledge that all he had married her for was her money. It was fortunate that a large portion was tied up, otherwise he would have left her, and me, penniless.' It was her grandmother who had made sure of that. She had tied up several of her daughter's properties and investments before she had come out, and made them inaccessible to any fortune hunters who night have coveted them.

'Finally, tired even of the pretence of marriage, or annoyed perhaps by her requests for him to be less reckless, he left, never to come back.'

Julia looked down at her hands, examining the uneven lines that ran across them. 'A month after I was born, she fell into a decline from which she never recovered. She scarcely had the energy to take care of me. Even when she was alive, it was always Grannie.' Julia paused to consider this. 'Not long after, she died of some trifling illness.'

'I'm sorry,' said Amelia.

'After my father left my mother, he never set eyes on me again.' Julia looked at her. 'Is that what you want the fate of your child to be?'

Amelia recoiled angrily. 'It's a tragic story,' she said, 'and I'm sorry for your mother. Sorry, too, that you never had a father to care for you, although sometimes I wonder.' The combative look reappeared in her eyes. 'But you *can't* compare Lord Swifton to Warren. Warren loves me. And he will cherish me after we marry. I *know* it.'

Julia had tried. If even Julia's most personal circumstances did nothing to sway her, nothing would. 'If he loves you, then I am glad for you. I wish you well,' she said, resignedly.

'Do you mean it?' she said, shyly. 'I hope you do, because I've made up my mind to do it.'

'Do what?' said Julia.

'To *elope* with him, of course. I already told you I was considering it. But my conversation with you has convinced me.' She rubbed her hands together excitedly. 'In fact, it's all arranged. For Monday night,' said Amelia, lowering her voice. 'After the masquerade ball. I think it's wonderfully exciting, don't you?'

Julia did not answer. She did not think Amelia wanted an answer. She was too busy daydreaming, building for herself a magical castle with Neave as the hero. God help her.

Well, she would have some opposition. Julia would not allow her to throw away her life on someone like Neave.

She threw a quick glance out of the window. The weather was still pleasant, apart from the gusting wind. She knocked on the carriage roof to draw the coachman's attention.

The carriage halted.

Amelia looked at her in surprise.

'I feel rather unwell,' explained Julia, 'Perhaps some fresh air will help me. I think I'll ride the rest of the way.'

'I hope it's nothing serious,' said Amelia, with concern.

Julia shook her head. 'A slight headache. Nothing to worry about.'

The postillion opened the door. 'I believe I need a breath of fresh air,' said Julia 'Is Hamlet saddled?'

'I believe he is, Miss Swifton.'

'Then I will ride.'

Sounds of consternation came from the various carriages as the whole procession of carriages came to a standstill, compelled to wait. The window of Lady Thorwynn's carriage opened and Lady Bullfinch's head appeared.

'What's happening?' she said, casting a disapproving glance on Julia.

'Nothing, Grannie,' Julia replied. 'I just decided I want to ride. It's too hot in the carriage.'

'Then for God's sake get on with it, girl. You're holding us all up.'

Lady Thorwynn's anxious voice reached Julia from inside the carriage. 'Has anything happened, Lady Bullfinch? Has there been an accident?'

'No, no,' she said. 'Just some fool notion my granddaughter has taken into her head.' She slid the window shut. If she could have slammed it, she would have.

Julia wanted to object to her characterization of her. *I do not take fool notions into my head.*

Except for kissing gentlemen who are known to be rakes.

Somehow, she didn't think her grandmother would qualify that as a fool notion. She would probably applaud. Except that she had kissed the wrong person. Lionel had made it abundantly clear that he was not interested.

And now she was going to turn to him for

help. She would be left with her pride in tatters. Like the grass Lionel had torn between his fingers.

She chided herself for thinking that way. In a matter as grave as Neave's abduction of Amelia, she could not afford to let her pride interfere. Whatever his intentions, whether they were indeed an elopement to Gretna Green, or something more nefarious, they could be nothing but disastrous to the young girl. Julia had to set aside her pride and help her.

It was not easy. Her face burned as Lionel rode towards her, and she avoided eye contact with him.

'Anything the matter?' he asked, examining her anxiously, with that grave new look he seemed to have acquired recently.

'The groom is fetching my horse,' she said.

He looked down at her suspiciously. 'Perhaps it would not be wise —'

'This has nothing to do with you,' she snapped, stung by the implication that she was pursuing him.

He raised an eyebrow. 'Then I am intrigued,' he murmured.

The groom approached, leading her horse. He threw her up into the side-saddle, and Julia found herself level with Lionel. She gestured for the carriage holding Amelia to move on. The procession continued on its way.

'I need to talk to you and Lord Benedict,' said Julia. 'It's a matter of urgency.'

She remembered that Lord Talbrook was also riding. It would be awkward to exclude him. But she could not involve him in Amelia's affairs. It was bad enough that Julia was planning to betray her confidence to others.

'I cannot find a way to exclude Lord Talbrook, however, so perhaps you could explain the matter to Lord Benedict afterwards.' Her tone was distant, carefully detached. She did not want Lionel to think she was inventing excuses to be alone with him.

They had reached a bend on the road, and Julia could not help exclaiming at the sharp incline below her feet. This was what an abyss was like. An edge that cannot be stepped over.

She could not bear to glance at Lionel. His assumption that she wished to resume her flirtation smarted, salt in a wound. Did his arrogance have no bounds?

So she came directly to the heart of the problem, without prelude. 'I'm afraid we have another urgent Neave situation,' she said.

'What the devil!' said Lionel sharply, alarming his horse, who tossed his head in protest.

'This time it doesn't involve me,' she said. 'It involves Amelia.'

'I'm aware that I'm betraying her confidence,' she continued, 'but I know that I can't stop this by myself. There's too little time. Especially since we won't be returning to London until tomorrow.' She related what Amelia had told her, drily, and without intonation.

There was a short pause after she had completed her narrative. 'Thank heavens she decided to confide in you,' said Lionel. 'You should not feel guilty, however. You are attempting to save her from ruin.'

Julia did not answer. Instead, having explained the situation, she fell back, joining the other riders. Before long, she was riding alongside her cousin, exchanging reminiscences about one of their childhood companions.

Meanwhile, Lionel and Lord Benedict rode ahead, deep in earnest discussion, no doubt determining how best to deal with Amelia's elopement.

The evening at Lady Thorwynn's country estate was coming to an end. An impromptu dance had followed dinner, in which the younger persons had been reduced to hilarity watching Lady Bullfinch and Lord Yarfolk vigorously hopping a quadrille until perspiration ran down their cheeks. But after a long day out in the outdoors, the general trend seemed to have an early night. Amelia and Miranda had already retired upstairs, and after a rather unsuccessful game of whist in which she partnered Nicholas against Lionel and Lord Benedict, Julia rose and excused herself.

To her surprise, as she reached the bottom of the stairway, she heard her name. It was Lionel.

'We need to talk about our plans,' he said. 'I will need a minute of your time.'

Because she had not expected to speak to him tonight, and because she was still mortified by her actions earlier, she responded coldly. 'Unless you are planning to leave very early,' she said, 'I suggest we postpone this conversation until tomorrow morning. We can hardly talk in the hallway.'

'There is always the library,' he said, grinning.

She stiffened. 'I do not think that is a good idea,' she said, icily. 'Considering the circumstances.'

Lionel ran his hand through his hair. 'You

may wish me to Jericho,' he said, 'but the fact is we have some unfinished business. You cannot simply abandon Amelia to her fate.'

'Of course I won't abandon her,' she said, piqued. 'She has become my friend, and although she will be hurt by this, we must prevent this marriage. If Neave is even planning to marry her.' But she did not want to spend a single moment alone with him. She would not make that mistake again. No doubt he thought her completely devoid of all principles.

'In that case,' said Lionel. 'I will call Benedict on some pretext, and we will adjourn to the library.'

He walked away, leaving her to contemplate how, yet again, she had misunderstood his intent.

CHAPTER 20

'I don't know why you're having such difficulty with Miss Swifton, Thorwynn. I assure you, she's perfectly amiable.'

Lionel and Benny were once more at Brooks's. It seemed they never did anything more interesting these days than dine at Brooks's and attend banal social affairs. And his mother's picnics.

Thorwynn growled. 'She's perfectly amiable to you, you mean.' Benny had the grace to look a bit ashamed, at least. But that did not prevent Lionel from wanting to wring a promise from Benny never to talk to her again.

'She did soften towards you at the picnic. At least for a while. In fact, you and she seemed to be on almost intimate terms. Did you make the best of the opportunity I gave you, by the way?'

Did he make the best of it? He had relived that moment time and again since yesterday.

The way she leaned towards him. The rose-water tinge of her scent. Then her lips. They tantalized, barely connecting with his. A contact as light and elusive as silk. It had been sheer torment to stand still. But he let her explore him, afraid she would draw back if he moved.

His instinct raged at him. He needed to press her body to his. To feel the length of her against him. To demand with his lips. To explore every inch of her. To take advantage before she changed her mind and while she was still willing. Because he knew it would not last. It was an impulse, on her part, and she would regret it.

But he had to let her have her way. Because only then would she learn to trust him. To understand the pleasure he could give her, without being threatened by it.

But he had never struggled so hard for control in his life. That small, shy kiss broke through every barrier in him. Barriers he did not even know he had.

Then she had deepened the kiss, asking for more. He was forced to put her away from him. It was the only way he could resist temptation. One minute longer and his desire would have carried him away like a torrent.

It had taken that gentle kiss to strip away

every illusion he had ever had about himself, leaving him raw inside. He knew then that no other woman had meant anything to him. That she was the only one he had ever cared for.

The only one he had ever loved.

A word he had never thought could mean anything to him beyond an irrational compulsion to bring a woman to his bed. An urge that, once fully satisfied, would begin to fade.

But she had proved him wrong. She had escaped down the path, shamed by his rebuff. She did not know he was saving her from himself.

He had sunk down on to the chalk outcrop she had stood on. The sharp corners bit into his skin. He welcomed the discomfort. It brought him back to his reality, which was that he loved a woman he could not have. A woman who would never seriously consider him for marriage, unless she was forced to. Who saw him as nothing but a dissolute rake. Who thought him so devoid of feeling that she wanted him to give her lessons in the art of kissing. So that she could kiss another man. Probably that toad-faced cousin of hers who seemed to be popping up everywhere.

He sat there on that punishing rock for

what seemed an eternity, gazing out at the mottled green valley before him. The faint scent of blackberry blossoms surrounded him.

After a while, he failed to notice the rock's jagged edges. He had grown numb.

By the time he had followed her back to the picnic, she had withdrawn again. She was chattering warmly with Lord Talbrook, who was more than happy to be on the receiving end of her attention. There was no mistaking the closeness between them.

And to make matters worse, she had flirted with Benny. His best friend. Who had laughed and flirted back.

She did not glance in his direction once.

He even wondered if he had not imagined that little interlude.

Once again, he felt the delicate tickle of her lips as they moved across his. He drank in her scent, mingled with the aroma of flowering blackberry bushes.

He would take her back again to that place on the hill, when the blackberries were ripe. He would watch her as she ate the plump berries, smudging her lips with their dark purple juice. And he would lick it off her. He would —

'If you persist in licking your lips like that in public,' said Benny, 'I'll have to remove myself from your proximity. People may think you're making indecent suggestions to me.'

He plunged down from the heights of Box Hill with its wild berries into the starched world of the gentlemen's club.

He smiled ruefully. 'I need some activity.' He rose. 'Shall we head to the gaming room? I'd like to test my chances.'

He was losing badly. He knew he should withdraw, but he did not want to be alone with his thoughts. The game kept him occupied at least. Even if he did seem to miss a lot of what was happening around the table.

'Your turn,' said Benny. Lionel stared vaguely at his cards.

'Excuse me, sir. This note came for you.' He looked up at the sombre footman, welcoming the intrusion, since he had lost track of the game completely. 'Thank you.'

He glanced at the envelope. He knew the handwriting. He had seen that rushed scrawl before.

He stood up immediately.

'Something wrong?' said Lord Manderton. His voracious eyes met Lionel's, seeking information. Any morsel of gossip would be gnawed to bits by him within the hour.

Lionel's bland mask slipped into place.

'Nothing of interest at all,' he drawled, bored. 'I know the writing. Inside, no doubt, is an exceedingly tedious invitation to dine with a lady undergoing a nervous spasm, namely, my mother. Which saves me from having to lose an even bigger sum of money than I have already lost.'

General laughter followed.

'Good luck,' said Manderton. 'Enjoy the company.'

There were general sympathetic murmurs.

He waited until he was outside the club to open the note. Just as he had thought.

I need to speak to you urgently. Please meet me at 71 South Audley Street as soon as possible.

Like last time, it was unsigned.

It was a Grosvenor Square address, but not among the most fashionable.

He did not make the mistake this time of thinking that it was a seduction. Although when he had first seen the writing his heart had given a little extra beat, a hopeful joyous jump. But of course she would not write this way unless extremely perturbed. Her normal handwriting was elegant and neat.

He called to mind every possible reason she would summon him this way.

All the threads led to Neave. Lionel's hands clenched.

If he had harmed her in any way. . . . If he had touched her. If he had hurt one hair. . . . He would tear him into tiny pieces and drop them one by one in the Thames. He would —

If he had. . . .

He shied away from the very thought, tried to control his towering rage.

He needed to stay calm. To think rationally.

He called a hackney and gave him the address, promising a half-crown if he brought him to the address as quickly as possible.

The jarvey whipped his horses. They tore off through the crowded streets as if driving on a wide open country road. A curricle scraped by, barely an inch to spare. The next instant, the hack swerved abruptly, causing Lionel to slide down in his seat. Through the window Lionel noted with amazed fascination that they managed to avoid collision with a slow cart loaded with vegetables. The owner of the cart shouted and waved his fist at the jarvey, but the hack hurtled onwards, intent on its mission.

Lionel held on tight, expecting any moment they would overturn. The jarvey took a corner tightly, and the hack swayed dangerously, then righted itself. It jerked sideways, no doubt in another near miss, but it did not reduce its speed. As they weaved in and out of the traffic, Lionel lost count of how many times he closed his eyes, thinking an accident inevitable. But their journey continued, the horses' hoofs pounding relentlessly onwards.

By the time they reached their destination, his hands shook from the effort of holding on.

He descended gingerly from the carriage. He paid the jarvey more than he had promised, because he had miraculously brought them there alive. He had never seen a driver so skilled.

The jarvey tipped his hat.

'Shall I wait for you, your lordship?'

Lionel considered him. His clothing was immaculate. Not a hair was out of place. He looked as if he had just gone for a quiet jaunt in the park.

'No, but I'd like to hire you, if you would be willing to abandon your current position. I need someone like you in my stables.' Lionel gave him his card. 'Come and enquire tomorrow. I'll leave word with my butler to expect you.'

The jarvey bowed solemnly. Lionel had no idea if he would accept the job or not. If it were not for the urgency of his summons, he would have stayed to try and convince him.

As it was, he could not spare a moment.

He looked up at the townhouse before him. His heart was pounding. He did not know what he would do if something had befallen her.

A footman opened the door. 'The young lady awaits you in the library,' he said.

The footman led the way at a leisurely pace. Lionel wanted to prod him in the back so he would move faster, but it would not do at all. They finally reached their destination. The footman opened the door and let Lionel in, then closed it behind him.

She was not there.

There was a young girl sitting with her back to him, with gold ringlets that were somehow familiar.

She twisted round, saw him, and turned white.

'Oh, no,' she said, jumping to her feet and putting her hands to her cheeks. 'Not you!'

'Where is she?' he said, his eyes narrowed.

'I suppose you mean Julia,' she said. She was extremely agitated. 'There's no time to explain. You must get away immediately. It's a trap. If they find you in here with me, you'll be compromised, and I'll be forced to marry you.'

He stood frozen in the middle of the room. Somehow, he seemed unable to think.

She ran to him, and gave him a push. 'Hurry! Move, you big oaf! Do you really want to end up marrying me?'

Her frantic actions, especially her jabbing fists, finally penetrated his dull brain. He obeyed. She rushed to the French windows and opened them. 'Go quickly. Get to the street and walk away as fast as you can.' She made shooing motions at him.

The sound of footsteps reached him from outside the library door.

He sprang into motion. He did not walk: he *sprinted.* Out of the windows. Into the garden, and on to the street. There, he slowed down to a quick march, expecting any moment to hear Lady Medlow's nasal voice calling his name. He turned the first corner he reached and bounded down an alley.

He kept going until a stitch in his side brought him up short. Finally, lost in a maze of side roads and alleys, he stopped to take his bearings. He did not think Lady Medlow would hound him now. The stitch pinched at him, a reminder of his stupidity.

He should have known that the handwriting did not belong to Julia. He had never asked her about the first note. He had just assumed that she had summoned him that first time.

In fact, everything pointed to the fact that it was not her handwriting.

He leaned against a wall, catching his breath, and willing the stitch to go away.

In any case, he would not be caught in the same net again. He *always* recognized people's handwriting. Now he knew Lady Medlow's very well.

He leaned against the wall, waiting for the pain to recede. The handwriting was Lady Medlow's. Which meant that Julia was perfectly safe.

His spirits soared as relief flooded into him so quickly he sagged against the wall. She was safe.

The door crashed open. Amelia looked up from her chair and regarded her mama and Lady Telway with apparent bewilderment.

'I thought — I was led to expect that Lord Neave wished to speak to me.'

Mama peered at her with suspicious eyes. 'Where is he?'

'Lord Neave?' she asked. She pouted. 'He hasn't come.'

'Not Lord Neave, you foolish girl,' said Mama, impatiently. 'Lord Thorwynn.'

Amelia put on her stupidest little-girl look. 'But you said it would be Lord Neave who would be offering for me, not Lord Thorwynn.'

The two women were pacing around the room, looking behind the curtains, and, unbelievably, under the large mahogany desk. She stifled a giggle. Did they really think Lord Thorwynn would fit under the desk? He was so *tall.*

'Where is he?' said her mother, advancing on her in frustrated rage.

'Lord Thorwynn, or Lord Neave?' she asked. 'Because if you mean Lord Neave,' she said, putting on a tragic air, 'he never came.'

'We are looking for Lord Thorwynn,' said Lady Telway, bringing the little game to an end. Her icy eyes met hers and Amelia knew she was not fooled for a moment.

Something in Lady Telway's voice communicated itself to Lady Neville. She stopped searching and came to stand next to her friend. 'Yes. Where is he?'

Amelia shrugged. 'I didn't see anybody. I've been waiting here for Lord Neave to call, but nobody came.'

Lady Telway's pale-blue eyes lingered on Amelia's face.

'But we know he came in. The footman

said he'd showed a gentleman in,' said Lady Neville.

Amelia frowned, still maintaining her little girl façade. 'I don't remember seeing anybody. Maybe he showed the gentleman into another room?' she said, uncertainly.

Lady Telway's gaze never faltered.

'He said distinctly that he showed him into the library,' said Lady Neville, her voice growing more high pitched with agitation.

That other woman kept staring.

What business was it of hers, anyway?

Amelia was tired of this game, tired of pretending all the time, tired of having to play the innocent miss and let women like Lady Telway determine her life.

'Very well,' she said, angrily. 'Lord Thorwynn passed through this room. On his way out into the garden.' Her mother gasped and put her hand to her chest. 'I told him not to linger, because I have no interest in him *at all.* I won't marry him in a hundred years, even if *all* the gossip columns in London were filled with delicious bits of scandal about me and Lord Thorwynn. Even if they all whispered about it behind their fans.'

Lady Telway's mouth was rounded with shock. Possibly no one had talked to her like this in her life.

She turned to her mama. 'You will be forced to withdraw me to the countryside in shame, and all the nice clothes you bought me will come to *nothing* because by the time I return to London again they will be so *outmoded* I will not be able to wear a single one, besides, they won't fit any more because I'll be a fat old maid who gorges herself on sweetmeats and cakes. So you might as well get used to it.'

Lady Neville fell back on to the settee, waving her hands and crying for her vinaigrette. 'Please fetch it for me, Amelia,' she said, her voice cracking.

'Fetch it yourself,' Amelia snapped. She shot a glance at Lady Telway. 'Or perhaps your friend can help. She seems more than willing to go out of her way to assist you.'

She walked to the door, pausing to take in the scene. Mama was still waving her hands frantically and gasping for breath, with little cries in between. 'How can she say such things? To her own mother. And to you. After all you've done for her!'

Lady Telway bent over her. 'For heaven's sake, Eustacia,' she said, firmly, 'stop that caterwauling and pull yourself together! We have to sit down and make some plans.'

Amelia left them to each other, and slammed the door shut behind her.

She had taken care of that.

Now she was ready to elope with dearest, *dearest* Warren.

CHAPTER 21

Walking into the masquerade ball was like walking into a pagan festival celebrated in some other area of the world. The flaccid whites and pinks of the debutantes were broken by the lurid colours of the masks. Red, silver, black, green, and gold glimmered and shimmered under the candlelight. The polite masks of Society had disappeared, replaced by grotesque and distorted faces. Julia threaded her way through the fantastical realm, wondering if she was seeing the true selves of the *ton*. Menacing outlaws, growling tigers, tearful clowns. Ladies with hard gold faces and men with glimmering diamonds. Pagan gods and wizards. She had entered a world where all the carefully established rules had lost their meaning.

Lionel had told her he would be in a black and white domino and cloak, but she had already passed a few similarly dressed gentlemen. Nor was it easy to distinguish them under the flowing capes they wore. In the crush, where nothing was in place, she did not know if she could find him. Then someone tapped her on the shoulder. She turned to find Lionel only partly concealed by the black and white domino. She would have recognized him anywhere.

Lionel bowed to Lady Eckles, the agreed upon signal for everyone to make their exit. It was early, but according to the plan, Lord Medlow and Julia had to reach the East India Docks before the fleeing couple arrived.

Julia went to find Lady Bullfinch. She was dancing a waltz with Lord Yarfolk. Julia managed to catch her grandmother's eye. They twirled towards her.

She, of course, knew what was happening. But since Julia could not divulge anything openly, they had agreed on her excuse to leave.

'I have a headache. The Medlows have been good enough to offer their carriage to take me home.'

'Can't it wait a while?' she asked.

Julia raised her hand to her temple and tried to look as if a lancing pain was driving through her head. 'I'm sorry. But the lights, and the crowd . . .'

'Why don't you take Aunt Viola with you?'

'She's in the middle of a card game,' said Julia, 'you know how she hates to be interrupted.'

Lady Bullfinch snorted, sending Julia a piercing glance. 'Very well. Try to get some rest.'

Julia nodded.

As soon as they were safely back on the dance floor, she pressed on through the crowds to the door. By the time she was at the entrance, her toes felt as though they had gone through a clothes press. Her feet had been trodden on more times than she could tell, and the thin silk material of her slippers offered no protection.

She started as a black shadow detached itself from the shadows by the wall and came in her direction. She let out a breath of relief when she realized it was Lionel. He had abandoned his white and black disguise.

'You should be more cautious,' he said. 'What if it was Neave?'

'He's after different prey, don't you think?'

He gripped her suddenly and, drawing her back toward the shadows, crushed his mouth to hers. There was nothing lover-like in the kiss. It pinned her down, a moth caught in the light. She struggled to free herself, but his iron arms held her in place.

Abruptly, the kiss changed. His lips softened and began to move, exploring. She stopped struggling, shocked by the tides of sensation churning through her. Her arms reached up to lock his head down, pulling him closer. She could no longer breathe, but she didn't care. She just wanted the sensations to continue.

He pulled away, gently.

She uttered an incoherent protest. She was tired of being pushed away, just as she was starting to enjoy herself.

'Hush,' he whispered, a silencing finger to her lips. He indicated with his head.

She looked to the right. It was Neave. He had just passed her by, and was now descending the steps. He was wearing a bright red cloak, but had removed his domino. She could tell from his stiff back that he was on the alert, searching for something. Perhaps he had noticed that she had left and come to investigate.

'I'm sorry for my unimaginative attempt to conceal you,' he said, ruefully, running his finger through his hair. 'I couldn't think of anything else on the spur of the moment.'

She was glad it was dark because so much heat rushed to her face, she must have looked like lobster. So he hadn't kissed her in an overwhelming moment of passion, after all. And she, foolish as she was, had practically thrown herself at him, yet again.

'I hope you'll use your imagination next time,' she hissed. 'I could have been completely compromised.'

He grinned. 'It wouldn't have been the first time,' he said. 'Don't worry, I would have offered for you again.'

'I hardly think that's funny.'

He shrugged, still grinning. 'I doubt that many could have known you, with that domino covering your eyes.'

In the confusion of the kiss she had forgotten about the mask.

She ignored him and peered into the street. 'I wonder where Lord Medlow is?'

As if on cue, a carriage drew up. The door opened and Lord Medlow's head emerged. She took a deep breath.

'Well, here goes,' she said. She turned to Lionel, reluctant to leave him. 'I wish you luck.'

He nodded. 'Don't worry. We'll bring her to you safely.'

He handed her into the carriage, his hand lingering on hers. She clung to it, suddenly afraid, wondering if something terrible was about to happen.

By the time she had settled into her seat

enough to look out of the window, he had disappeared once more into the shadows.

The ride through the darkness was uneventful. After a brief attempt at small talk, Lord Neville abandoned any attempt at conversation. She could hardly blame him. His daughter's future was at stake.

He had brought along Amelia's maid, Hannah, to lend some propriety to the situation. Beyond an initial greeting, Hannah said nothing. She seemed subdued. No doubt she had been under a great deal of pressure, even blamed for her mistress' elopement. Julia tried to engage Hannah in conversation, but under Lord Medlow's withering eye the maid faltered so badly that Julia was obliged to give up.

They left the lamplight of London behind and moved into an area where the buildings were large and squat and lights were few and far between. The carriage moved rapidly, unhampered by traffic. A half-hearted moon peered periodically from behind the clouds, giving her a brief glimpse of her surroundings, then disappearing again.

It was essential that they arrive at the inn before the others. The agreement was that they would stop at the inn at the East India Docks, supposedly to arrange for a fresh pair. Amelia's father would open the carriage door when they arrived, intercepting the fleeing couple.

That is, if Neave had not discovered already that his coachman was Lionel. And had not found out that the carriage was heading out to the docks instead of north.

She had never liked that part of the plan. She was sure Neave was bound to look out of the window at some point.

But Lionel had argued that Neave would keep the curtains drawn, not wanting Amelia to be recognized. And that a man intent on an elopement would have no reason to suspect foul play.

Yet even while worry gnawed at her that something would happen to Lionel, she still found herself revisiting that unexpected kiss. She relived the myriad sensations it stirred in her, over and over. It was no longer possible to dismiss the longing in her, the need that had broken open the shell that had enveloped her. She could no more control it than she could control her heartbeat or stop her breathing.

She wanted nothing else but to be held by him, to caress him, to move her lips across his skin, to feel his fingers touching her, his body against hers.

I thought myself immune to the temptations

offered by rakes like Lionel, but I was very mistaken. Even worse, she revelled in it. All sense of perspective was gone. She finally understood what her grandmother called *those carnal urges* that will drive a woman to forget everything. A strange urgency gripped her by the throat and demanded to be satisfied.

She knew he did not love her. That he had no intention of marrying her. *And to think that when Grannie threatened to marry me to Lionel, it had seemed like the worst thing that could happen to me! Even more strange, I actually had the opportunity to marry him, and I tossed it away without a second thought.*

She would no longer deny it. She loved Lionel. And even if it was too late to marry him, even if she had let that chance slip away, she would not deny herself the pleasure she could find in his arms. She would not live her life without at least once experiencing the joys of love.

She knew Grannie would give her blessing. Perhaps that was what she had intended all along. To give Julia a chance to come out from behind her protective wall and enjoy what life had to offer.

Tonight, if they stayed at the inn, which was likely, the stage was set. It would be a simple matter to creep into his room and overcome any reluctance he may have.

But first he would have to return to her safely.

They took refreshments in the private parlour. Lord Medlow behaved as though there was no one in the room. His gaze was distant, and from time to time he ground his teeth, grating them so hard she grew certain they would break.

She wished he would start up some conversation. Any trivial chit chat would do. But his closed face did not invite trivialities, and she dared not intrude on a complete stranger at such a delicate moment. Hannah sat completely still in a corner. She was tempted to engage her in a whispered conversation, but again held back.

The silence in the room stretched onwards, the quiet outside the inn unbroken. The taproom provided the only source of noise, though there were only a few scattered men enjoying a glass of ale and a meal. She found herself straining to overhear their conversation, but they were too far away to make out anything.

She folded her hands one way. Folded them another way. If she had brought a book she could have kept herself occupied.

Anxiety gripped her. Suppose Neave happened to look out of the window? Suppose he had discovered his coachman gone right at the beginning? Suppose Lionel was lying bleeding on some deserted street, blood flowing from a head wound?

She could stand her speculation no longer. She rose and went to the mantel to examine the clock there. Not interesting. She picked it up, looked at it closely, put it down again. She moved slowly to examine a painting of a fox hunt hanging on the wall, then a painting of an Indiaman riding the waves.

Lord Medlow's eyes bore holes into her back.

She returned to her seat, arranged her gown around her very carefully.

At last the clatter of carriage wheels reached her ears. She jumped up.

'Stay out of sight for the moment,' commanded Lord Medlow.

She went to the parlour window and opened it. It overlooked the courtyard where the carriage stood.

Neave opened the door of the carriage.

'What the devil's going on?' he said to the coachman. 'Why have you stopped here? What is this wretched place?'

Lord Medlow stepped forward. 'I believe my daughter is with you.'

Neave's eyes opened wide. Under the pale

light, his face turned ghostly white. He threw a desperate look around him. Lionel stepped forward, bringing his face into the light. Benny did the same.

Neave was surrounded.

A cry came from inside the coach. Amelia appeared in the doorway. Everyone turned towards her. 'Look out!' she said. 'He's armed.'

In the split second during which their attention turned towards her, he had whipped out his pistol.

'Nobody move, or I'll shoot her,' he said, pointing the muzzle at Amelia. He backed up steadily towards the inn.

Lionel, who had started to move stealthily towards him, came to a standstill. The three men stood immobile in the courtyard, dark statues under the grim light.

Neave continued to sidle towards the building. Julia expected him to make a sprint for the alleyway beyond the inn, where a number of warehouses were located. Her mind raced frantically, wondering what she could do to foil his escape.

The static courtyard suddenly sprang into action. Lionel, who was closest to Neave, rashly tried to throw himself at Neave. The pistol went off.

Julia started to run out, to see if Lionel

had been wounded. But she did not have time to see if the shot had found a mark. Now that the pistol was empty, the court-yard turned into a blur of figures converging on Neave.

The window was suddenly wrenched from her hand, and Neave hauled himself inside. Hannah screamed. Remembering his knife on the day he had tried to abduct her, Julia jumped aside quickly just as he reached out to grab her. She knew he would use her as a shield.

Her mind cleared as everything seemed to slow down. She tore off her paisley shawl and threw it at him, making sure to cover his face. She gripped the two ends as hard as she could as he struggled to break free. He pulled at it aggressively. She would not be able to hold him for long.

She signalled to Hannah, who was by the fireplace. The poker was in plain sight. She nodded towards it. She did not want to alert him by speaking.

Hannah looked at the poker uncertainly. Julia gritted her teeth. In a few seconds more, Neave would be free. His strength was superior to hers, and the delicate mate-rial of the shawl was ready to give.

Hannah picked up the poker.

'Hannah! Now!' she shouted, knowing he

was about to get away. Hannah crept closer and raised it. She hesitated.

The edge of the shawl was torn from Julia's hands. She dived for the poker, wrested it out of Hannah's hands, and with a quick movement brought it down on to Neave. He saw it coming and raised his arm. But it slipped through, striking him on the corner of the forehead.

He collapsed to the ground.

Benny crashed through the window, hurling himself at the falling Neave. They fell to the ground together.

Lionel was next. But he came slowly. He placed one leg over the window frame, then the other. As he swung his leg over the sill, a trickle of blood travelled down the wall below the frame.

There was plenty of time for him to observe that Neave was on the ground, with Benny struggling to rise up.

'Thank God, Benny,' said Lionel. 'You got him.'

Lord Medlow appeared in the doorway, completely out of breath. He shut the door behind him. 'You shan't get away, Neave —' He spotted Neave on the floor, with Benny on top of him. 'Well done, Benedict,' he said.

Benny rose and straightened his clothes.

'Actually, I had nothing to do with it at all. It was all Miss Swifton's doing.'

The two men's eyes went to the poker in Julia's hand.

'Good God!' said Lord Medlow. 'I never thought I'd see the day when I would be bested by a female.'

Amelia's head appeared through the window. 'You got him!' she said, beaming at Julia. 'I knew you would do it as soon as I saw him heading for the window. Isn't she wonderful?' she asked the assembled company.

Lionel gave a groan and fell back on to the first armchair he could find. 'Sorry, ladies. I know this is hardly polite —'

Julia flew across the room. 'Someone fetch the doctor,' she said, noticing in some distant part of her mind that she sounded like her grandmother. But she could not just let them stand around while Lionel bled to death. 'And he needs to be bandaged.'

Lord Medlow opened the door and bellowed for the innkeeper. A flurry of movement brought a large, red-faced woman into the room, whom the innkeeper introduced as Mrs Taddle, his wife. She was followed by two maids carrying white sheets and water.

Lionel's face had turned a pasty white,

the colour of porridge. His lips were pressed close together, and Julia knew he was struggling not to cry out in pain. She slipped her fingers into his. 'Hold on,' she whispered, her face close to his. 'You'll be up and about in no time.'

His eyes opened and stared straight into hers. He made a feeble attempt to smile.

'You can't keep your hands away from me, can you?' he murmured.

She smiled back. 'And whose fault is that?' she said, teasingly.

His smile widened, and he closed his eyes again. Mrs Taddle was cleaning the wound, inspecting it with experienced eyes. 'It's nought but a surface scratch,' she said. 'Nothing to worry about. The bullet's not lodged inside. He's just lost a bit of blood. Makes 'em weak.'

She heaved a sigh of relief. 'Are you certain?' she asked.

'As certain as I am my name's Mary,' she said, cheerfully. 'My first husband was a soldier, God rest his soul,' she said. 'I followed the drum with him for three years. I know what a bad wound looks like, and this isn't it.'

She raised her red face from her task to throw her a shrewd glance. 'Don't worry, lass,' she said. 'He'll survive to marry you.'

Heat rushed to her face. She dropped his hand like a hot kettle and moved back. His eyes opened. They were full of laughter.

'You should have told her you have already turned me down,' he remarked.

Julia stepped away quickly. She cast a look around to see if any of the others had heard. Fortunately, no one paid them any attention.

Lord Medlow had left the room.

Benny was busy tying Neave's hands and feet with a piece of cord the innkeeper had given him. A bruise on his chin was turning scarlet and purple.

Amelia sat in an armchair, staring down at Neave. Her neat gold curls were in disarray, and her whole body drooped. A very wilted flower.

Julia's heart went out to her. Nobody had given her a thought. Her father had not even paused to talk to her or to ask her if she had been harmed in any way.

She could only imagine the pain and humiliation Amelia must be going through. All caused by Julia's betrayal. She would never speak to Julia again, once she knew.

Julia brought a chair from the table and placed it next to Amelia's. Amelia smiled up at her, a pale, thin smile. A large red mark stained her left cheek.

'I'm sorry,' said Julia. 'About Neave.' She wasn't quite ready yet to tell Amelia the truth.

She shook her head. 'No,' she said. She coloured and looked down at her hands. 'I'm grateful to you for putting a stop to it. I was unbelievably foolish. I don't know how I'll ever look Papa in the face again.'

'But Neave —'

'Neave?' She examined the prone figure on the ground. 'It didn't take long for me to find out I'd made a mistake.' She settled back in her chair, clearly ready to give Julia an account of the whole ride.

Julia was tired. The events of the evening were beginning to take their toll. She would have preferred to wait until the next day to hear what Amelia had to say. But she had brought the situation upon her friend. Besides, she was curious to know what Neave had done to turn Amelia against him.

'It wasn't at all romantic,' said Amelia, wrinkling her nose in aversion. 'He'd been drinking, and he'd brought a bottle of brandy with him. He kept taking sips of it, which wasn't at all nice. I expected him to be poetic or *something*. But he wasn't. Just sat there drinking.'

She paused, reliving her disillusionment. 'Then he asked me if I'd brought the money. I'd brought everything I could, but I couldn't lay my hands on any more because I didn't want anyone to be suspicious.' She looked towards the doorway from which her father had left. 'I get a quarterly allowance, you know. But I'd spent a lot of it already on ribbons and hats and things. I don't know what he *expected.*' She shook her head. 'He opened my reticule and counted out the money, which took ages because he kept dropping it. When he finished he sort of snarled and tossed it straight at me. There were coins *everywhere.*'

She made a gesture of disgust. 'That's when he changed completely. "You foolish chit," he said. "How do you think we're going to make it to the border?" And then he struck me, hard, against the jaw.' Amelia put her hand to her bruise. 'It *hurt.*' She paused and looked at Julia. 'That had never happened to me. Nobody ever hit me, you know.'

'So what did you do?'

'I scooped the coins up and threw them back at him. I told him he could have what money I had, but I wanted him to let me down. That instant. I didn't want to marry him any more, you see.'

'But he didn't let you down.'

'No, he didn't. Instead, he fell on to his knees. He was *disguised,* you know, and smelled of drink, and I couldn't open the carriage window because I was afraid someone would see me.'

'But why did he kneel?' Julia asked, a little bewildered by this turn of events.

'He said he was sorry for striking me, and he didn't want to, but that he was so nervous with all this elopement business and now it was all for *nothing* because we didn't have the money. Which by that time I was very glad of.'

'Quite rightly so,' said Julia.

'Then he started to cry. He said he didn't want to disappoint me, because he loved me. He'd never loved a woman in his life before. And now he'd made a hash of it, because he had to go and strike me and he was very sorry because he didn't want to be like his father.'

'His father?'

Amelia nodded. 'He said his father beat him and shut him up for days in a cupboard. He made me very sorry for him. But I still didn't want to marry him.' She fingered the bruise again. 'My jaw was hurting, you see.'

Julia did see, very well.

'So I asked him again to let me down, but he said he couldn't. He was sorry, but he couldn't let me go. And besides, he needed the money desperately otherwise he was in dun territory and would be thrown into the Fleet Prison if he didn't marry an heiress quickly. He'd borrowed so much on expectations of his father's death, but his father made a sudden recovery. Of course, when he told me that, it only made matters much worse because I know now that Papa was right about him.'

She looked up at Julia. 'So you see, I was never so glad in my life when I saw Papa open the door. I knew you were behind it, because I'd told no one else and, of course, you were there, standing at the window. I could have *hugged* you right then and there.' She beamed at Julia. 'But then I remembered he had a pistol, because he'd showed it to me, and I wanted to warn everyone. I was *terrified*. Before I knew it, things started to happen. And you knocked him down.'

Neave groaned, and began to stir.

Everyone immediately went on the alert.

He tried to raise himself, only to discover that he was tied up. 'What the devil —' His eyes landed on Amelia, who was closest to him. 'What are they going to do to me?' he asked.

Amelia looked down at him sadly. 'I don't

369

know, Warren.'

'Whatever they may say,' he said, 'I do love you.'

She nodded, 'I know. But it wasn't enough.'

There was a brief flare of something like torment in his eyes. Then his face contorted in anger. He struggled to sit up, hampered by his bonds. Throwing a murderous glance in Julia's direction, he sneered, 'You were behind this, you damned wh—'

Despite his weakened state, Lionel was upon him before he could complete the sentence.

Benny leapt up to hold him back as he was in imminent danger of loosening his bandage.

They collided, landing in a heap on top of Neave.

The door opened and Lord Neville appeared, accompanied by two large tanned men of threatening stance.

'Get him off the floor,' said Lord Medlow, eyeing the skirmish with distaste.

Lionel and Lord Benedict lifted Neave off the floor. Neave struggled. Lionel's bandage began to unravel, and fresh blood spread into a round stain on the linen. Julia stepped forward to say something, but Lionel gave her a warning glance.

'Now here is the situation,' said Lord Medlow. 'The way I see it, you have two choices. These two men here will be more than willing to weigh you down and drop you in the harbour. Left to my own devices, that would be my preference. But Lord Thorwynn and Lord Benedict don't seem to favour that option, unless they're forced to.'

He paused dramatically. Everyone waited.

'The other possibility is that you agree to sign a confession, and we'll put you on the first East Indiaman bound for Calcutta, with the proviso that you will never set foot again in England.' Lord Medlow barely gave him a minute to decide. 'The choice is yours, of course. Which will it be?'

'What do you wish me to confess to?' said Neave, sullenly.

'Obviously we want to keep my daughter out of this. So we will simply have you write a letter to your uncle and your father stating that you were forced to flee England to escape your creditors, and other rather pressing embarrassments which you would rather not divulge, and that you will be seeking your fortune in India. I will need three copies, one of which I will retain, in case for some inexplicable reason your uncle and your father never receive theirs. Do I have your word as a gentleman that if I have you untied you will not attempt to escape or harm anyone?'

'You have it,' said Neave.

Julia wondered if he still qualified as a gentleman in spite of everything. However, Neave himself seemed to think so, as he sat calmly at the table and wrote what Lord Medlow dictated without any problems.

When he finished, the two men took him away.

She very much hoped it would be the last they ever saw of him.

By the time the doctor arrived, it was almost morning. Because of Lionel's injury, they all put up at the inn, with Amelia and Julia sharing a room, and Hannah sleeping in the dressing-room in a truckle bed.

When Julia was sure everyone was asleep, she lit her candle and headed for Lionel's room. She trod carefully, terrified of being discovered, or, what was just as bad, being waylaid by a drunken sailor.

She reached his room uneventfully. She stepped inside and leaned against the door, willing her racing heart to calm down. She approached the bed slowly.

'Lionel,' she said.

There was no answer.

The light of the candle fell on the bed. His face in the candlelight had an unhealthy whiteness to it that alarmed her, and his sleep was restless. All thoughts of sharing his bed disappeared. She felt his head to see if there was a fever, but it felt cool to the touch.

She hovered uncertainly. He could develop a fever during the night. However, at the moment, there was nothing she could do for him. There was, in fact, no point in lingering.

She would return in the morning to make certain nothing had gone wrong. Meanwhile, she needed to slip back into her chamber, before she was discovered.

So much for her second attempt at seduction.

CHAPTER 22

Julia waited for the message. She waited all day. She did not leave the house, in case a message arrived during her absence. She waited all evening. She waited until midnight. But nothing came.

She waited for news of Lionel's recovery.

She should not have left the inn at the East India Docks before making sure Lionel had not contracted a fever. But Lord Medlow had not given her much choice.

It seemed Julia had barely closed her eyes after her trip to Lionel's bedroom, when Hannah was shaking her to inform her that the master needed to leave. When she was able to open her eyes and look at the clock, she discovered it was six o'clock in the morning.

With Hannah's help, she made herself presentable. Amelia, not wanting to offend her father further, no doubt, had already dressed and gone downstairs.

She wanted to reassure herself about Lionel. But she could not visit Lionel's room, and Lord Benedict was still asleep. So she left messages under both Lionel's and Lord Benedict's door requesting them to send a message immediately and tell her that all was well.

When Julia arrived in the private parlour downstairs, she found Lord Medlow and Amelia had already breakfasted.

'No time to eat,' said Lord Medlow, as soon as he saw her, looking pointedly at his watch piece. 'Have to set a spanking pace. Won't do to have my daughter's absence noticed,' he said. 'The sooner we return, the better.' Julia barely had time to grasp a bread roll and hurry after him.

As night fell and she did not receive news, her concern turned to alarm.

She considered calling a hack to take her back to the inn where Lionel was staying. But it would be the height of folly for a lady to go to the East India Docks in the dead of night. Even escorted by servants.

She sent two of her footmen instead, with instructions to enquire after Lord Thorwynn. They returned a little after one o'clock, only to inform her that his lordship had been moved and was no longer at the inn. Mr Taddle, the landlord, had been away from the tap room when they left, and so they could not ask him anything about Lord Thorwynn's condition.

She hesitated on the verge of sending a footman around to Lionel's residence, but thought better of it. Apart from awakening the household, it would generate unnecessary apprehension if his servants discovered his injury. Word of it would inevitably reach Lady Thorwynn, who would fall into a nervous spasm. Besides, there was no guarantee at all that he and Lord Benedict had returned to Mayfair. They might simply have removed to a more comfortable inn. She would send round the next morning, a calm, innocuous enquiry that would not raise anyone's suspicions.

She was to regret her decision. The moment she tried to fall asleep, restless nightmares assailed her. She became Lionel, tossing and turning in bed with fever, his rambling imagination plagued by images of objects crushing him, and pain lancing through his leg.

She would tear herself out from the nightmare. Awake, she would reassure herself that he was well, that Mrs Taddle knew what she was speaking of when she had told Julia the wound was clean. But the moment she drifted back into sleep the nightmares would resume and she would wake up again in alarm.

I don't know what I'd do if I lose him.

She stayed awake for a long time, staring into the darkness, wondering how she would live her life if something happened to Lionel.

Finally, as dawn began to break, completely exhausted, she drifted into a dreamless sleep.

Julia groaned and tried to cover her head with the pillow.

'Not today, Grannie. Why don't you have the Cavalry Charge without me? For once?'

But Lady Bullfinch was ruthless. She pulled off the cover and tossed the pillow on the floor. 'You know the rule. Nothing but sickness can keep us. That's the rule of the Cavalry Charge.'

She groaned again. She knew she would pull her out of bed, if she didn't get up. It had happened in the past, and no doubt would happen again.

Julia swung her legs over the side of the bed and put her bare feet on the carpeted floor.

'I'm awake. No need to hover.'

Lady Bullfinch raised an eyebrow, satisfied herself that Julia would not lie down again, and left.

Before Julia could reach for the bell pull, her maid Bethany appeared.

'Such a lovely day for a ride,' she said, in a painfully cheery voice.

Resigned, Julia submitted to her ministrations, her eyes half closed.

Her aunt was there, as was Miranda. Obliged to be civil, she put on a friendly face, hiding the anxiety eating at her.

Nicholas had also come, but he was not allowed to race with the ladies.

He smiled. 'I'll be your spectator, cheering you on,' he said. 'Though I have not yet decided who I want to win. If I don't support Grannie, she'll slay me with a glance. If I don't support Miranda, she will find all kinds of ways to avenge herself. If I don't support my mother, she will call me an undutiful son. And of course, I want to support you, Cousin Julia, because we're friends.'

Julia smiled. 'Perhaps, in that case, it would be best to cheer everyone. That way you won't lose favour with any of us.'

He laughed and fell back, leaving them to line up.

The horses snorted. Impatient, they strained

to start moving. Poor Hamlet, who had not been given a good run for some time, could hardly wait, his restlessness infecting her. She could not wait to return home to send notes to both Lionel's residence, and Lord Benedict's.

Surely one of them would have written, if he were well? The wound must have festered. With the bandage falling off during his struggle to hold up Neave, something must have gone wrong. Or perhaps the loss of blood had weakened him too much.

Their silence gnawed at her.

She should have refused to leave the inn.

'Gooo forth!' came the command and the horses set off, tearing down the course as if it were a racing track.

Despite Julia's anxiety, the exhilaration of the race caught her, and she was able to set aside her fears, just for a moment, as she began to fly. As the world around her blurred, she put aside her apprehension and allowed herself to enjoy the moment.

Her cousin Miranda was ahead of her now. Julia felt a surge of admiration and pride in the little girl who was growing up into a lovely woman. Certainly Miranda was a superb horsewoman.

But she would not let her win.

She urged Hamlet forward. Always ready

for a challenge, he extended his limbs and shot forward until the two horses were neck to neck.

Suddenly there was a shout.

Julia looked around, startled. She saw Amelia waving at her, saying something.

She waved back, quickly, not wanting Hamlet to slow, but Amelia kept waving, shouting something she couldn't hear. As she drew closer, Julia realized that Amelia was not smiling.

Terror struck at her. Amelia must have heard something about Lionel.

She swerved off the path. Amelia gestured for Julia to follow her, and set out in a gallop. Julia, furious with the young girl for leading her on a chase, followed hard behind her.

'Stop!' she shouted to Amelia, but the girl ignored her.

Grimly, Julia followed. She realized that Amelia was taking her behind a copse of trees. No doubt the news she wished to impart would upset her, and she wanted to grant her some privacy.

But when she reached the copse, Amelia had disappeared. Julia searched the trees, but there was no sign of her.

She slowed down, puzzled.

Then she saw the form. A man lay on the

ground, perfectly still. No doubt Amelia had returned to Rotten Row to find help.

She spurred Hamlet on. As she drew closer, he began to look familiar.

He stirred. Suddenly, very quickly, he sprang up, then fell down on to his knees.

It was Lionel.

Relief at seeing him made her so weak she swayed, almost falling off the horse. She trotted over, slowly, fighting to get her emotions under control.

But he wasn't getting up. Was he hurt? He must have tried to come riding and fallen off his horse, weakened by his wound.

She hurried once again, furious, preparing to scold him for his stupidity in going riding when he had not yet recovered.

But as she approached he smiled up at her, one of those devastatingly charming smiles that made so many women swoon, including her. Especially her.

'Shall I compare thee to a summer day?' he said. *'Thou art more lovely and more temperate, Rough winds do shake the darling buds of May . . .'*

He was feverish.

'Come on, Lionel,' she said gently. 'If you can get yourself up on the horse behind me, I'll take you home.'

But he did not move. He stayed on the

grass, grinning at her.

'You don't like that one? It's Shakespeare, you know. Never mind. I have a better one. Well, not better, but more original, at least:

On a hill above a dale
A certain lady raised a gale . . .'

She frowned and reached out with her hand, urging him softly, as she would a skittish horse. 'Come on, I'll pull you up,' she said.

But he stayed there, kneeling in the grass. 'I see. You weren't impressed with that one. Let me try something else:

When her searching lips touched mine
My soul was filled with love divine
Inflamed with passion . . .'

'Stop!' she said, horrified that someone might hear him.

He grinned. 'Didn't like that, either? Well I have more:

How can I my love declare
When all my love can do is stare?'

She began to laugh. She could not help it. 'Lionel, please get up. You are clearly feverish. And the grass is staining your clothing. And your bandage is getting soaked.'

He shook his head. 'I won't get up until you agree.'

'Agree to what?' she said, exasperated.

'To marry me, of course,' he said.

It had been such an unusual morning, she decided she had heard him wrong. 'Let's talk about it later, somewhere civilized,' she said, stalling, because she was not sure she heard him right, and besides, he could not be held accountable if he was feverish.

'It's no use trying to silence me,' he said, 'because you won't.

Not if the moon should flood with shadows
Not if the sky should fill with pain
Even if my dreams turned gallows
Still supreme my love will reign.'

He was smiling. But there was something else in his eyes. Something more. Something that found an echo deep inside her. A tiny seed of hope grew inside her, bursting open, filling her with strange elation.

But she held back. She could not marry him. He would not be faithful to her.

She regarded him as he kneeled there in the grass. He waited. There was doubt in his eyes, and fear. Fear that she would say

383

no. His smile wavered.

'Please, Julia,' he said softly. 'I love you. Marry me.'

Still she hesitated, though it broke her heart.

'I'll do everything I can to make you happy,' he said.

She slid off the horse and went down on her knees beside him. 'Lionel,' she said, her voice a hoarse whisper. She wanted to believe him. 'What about all those admirers of yours? What will you do with them?'

He grinned. 'They'll just have to find someone else.' Then, seeing the grimness in her face, the laughter faded from his eyes.

'There will never be anyone but you,' he said, roughly. His words carried the weight of an oath. 'There never has been anyone, since I met you.'

She could no longer doubt him. The harsh glimmer in his eyes told her it was the truth.

She threw her arms around him and pressed her lips to his.

A long, dizzying moment later, he pulled her gently away. 'I take it that was a yes,' he said, his voice unsteady.

'Yes,' she said hoarsely.

'About time,' said Lady Bullfinch, emerging from behind a tree. 'That was one of the most drawn out and incoherent proposals I have ever witnessed.'

'You shouldn't be too hard on my boy,' said Lady Thorwynn, affectionately. 'He hasn't had much practice with proposals.'

Startled, Julia sprang to her feet, pulling up Lionel with her.

They were surrounded. Several figures on horseback had emerged from behind the trees. Her aunt Viola. Lady Gragspur, Lord Yarfolk, Nicholas, Miranda, Lord Benedict. And Amelia, who beamed wildly and jumped from her horse to embrace Julia tightly.

'I'm so very glad you are going to marry Lord Thorwynn,' she said, in Julia's ear. 'Now my mother will have to give up trying to marry him to *me*.'

'Where do you want to go for your honeymoon?' he asked, as they sat side by side in Lady Bullfinch's drawing-room. 'To the Continent? I know you once said you would like to see the Alps. Were you serious about it?'

Touched that he remembered her wish, she drew his face to her for a kiss. She brushed her lips against his, savouring briefly the velvet softness of his. But when she started to move away he pulled her against him, so tightly she could hardly breathe. His mouth sought hers and their lips came together with a hunger that she thought would consume her, if it were not for the deep tenderness that rose to transform it. Of their own accord, her hands began their own exploration while his lips moved over her face and down the side of her throat.

She withdrew reluctantly from his grasp. 'We have to stop,' she murmured, her voice completely unsteady, her heart racing like a clock that had gone mad, 'or before we know it, we'll be half undressed on the carpet.'

He smiled lazily, 'I don't see what the objection can be,' he said, his voice husky, his eyes darkened with need.

'But —' She faltered, gesturing with her hand to the door. 'If they walk in on us —'

He slipped his hands under her hair, cradling the back of her head. 'They'll see exactly what they expect.' His lips trailed down her neck, bringing delicious shivers down her spine. 'Why do you think your grandmother left us to our own devices?' She sputtered in laughing agreement, thinking how Grannie had wanted this for her. 'She's probably watching even now,' he added, between kisses, 'and reporting everything we're doing to the others.'

She recoiled in horror, stared fixedly at the keyhole, and edged away from him.

Lionel threw back his head and laughed, a laugh charged with joy and tenderness. 'I'm merely teasing,' he said, drawing her towards him so that she rested her head on his shoulder. 'I can see that I'm going to have to marry you quickly,' he said. 'You seem to be uncommonly afraid of being compromised.' He stood up, took her hand gently in his and drew her up to stand next to him. He straightened out her clothes for her, and smoothed down her hair. 'We're not in a hurry, in any case,' he murmured, planting a feather-light kiss on her lips and looking down at her with love glittering in his eyes. 'We have a lifetime in which to indulge our needs.'

She smiled up at him, laughter bubbling up in her. 'True,' she said. Then she tumbled back down on to the settee and pulled him down on top of her. 'But I'd like to start right now,' she whispered, and threw all caution to the swirling wind.

ABOUT THE AUTHOR

Monica Fairview was born in London, but has lived in many places including the USA. She worked as a university professor, and an acupuncturist. She has written academic reviews and articles for years but her secret desire all along was to write Regency-style romances. She now lives in Cheam, Surrey and loves visiting National Trust properties in the area. When she is not writing, she is busy raising her very energetic six-year-old daughter.

We hope you have enjoyed this Large Print book. Other Thorndike, Wheeler, Kennebec, and Chivers Press Large Print books are available at your library or directly from the publishers.

For information about current and upcoming titles, please call or write, without obligation, to:

Publisher
Thorndike Press
295 Kennedy Memorial Drive
Waterville, ME 04901
Tel. (800) 223-1244

or visit our Web site at:

http://gale.cengage.com/thorndike

OR

Chivers Large Print
published by BBC Audiobooks Ltd
St James House, The Square
Lower Bristol Road
Bath BA2 3SB
England
Tel. +44(0) 800 136919
email: bbcaudiobooks@bbc.co.uk
www.bbcaudiobooks.co.uk

All our Large Print titles are designed for easy reading, and all our books are made to last.